THE NIGHT GUEST

THE NIGHT GUEST
FIONA McFARLANE

SCEPTRE

First published in Australia in 2013 by Hamish Hamilton
An imprint of Penguin Group (Australia)

First published in Great Britain in 2014 by Sceptre
An imprint of Hodder & Stoughton
An Hachette UK company

1

A CIP catalogue record for this title is available from the British Library

Hardback ISBN 9781444776676
Ebook ISBN 9781444776706

Printed and bound by Clays Ltd, St Ives plc

Hodder & Stoughton policy is to use papers that are natural, renewable and recyclable
products and made from wood grown in sustainable forests. The logging and
manufacturing processes are expected to conform to the environmental
regulations of the country of origin.

Hodder & Stoughton Ltd
338 Euston Road
London NW1 3BH

www.sceptrebooks.com

For my parents

I

Ruth woke at four in the morning and her blurry brain said, 'Tiger.' That was natural; she was dreaming. But there were noises in the house, and as she woke she heard them. They came across the hallway from the lounge room. Something large was rubbing against Ruth's couch and television and, she suspected, the wheat-coloured recliner disguised as a wingback chair. Other sounds followed: the panting of a large animal; a vibrancy of breath that suggested enormity and intent; definite mammalian noises, definitely feline, as if her cats had grown in size and were sniffing for food with huge noses. But the sleeping cats were weighing down the sheets at the end of Ruth's bed, and this was something else.

She lay and listened. Sometimes the house was quiet, and then she heard only the silly clamour of her beating blood. At other times she heard a distant low whine followed by exploratory breaths. The cats woke and stretched and stared and finally, when whatever was in the lounge room gave out a sharp huff, flew from the bed and ran, ecstatic with fear, into the hallway, through the kitchen, and out the partially open back door. This sudden activity prompted an odd strangled yowl from the lounge room, and it was this noise, followed by louder sniffing, that confirmed the intruder as a tiger. Ruth had seen one eating at a German zoo, and it sounded just like this: loud and wet, with a low, guttural breathing hum punctuated by little cautionary yelps, as if it might roar at any moment except that it was occupied by food. Yes, it sounded just like that, like a tiger eating some large bloody thing, and yet the noise of it was empty and meatless. A tiger! Ruth, thrilled by this possibility, forgot to be frightened and had to counsel herself back into fear. The tiger sniffed again, a rough sniff, thick with saliva. It turned on its great feet, as if preparing to settle down.

Ruth sent one courageous hand out into the dark to find the phone on her bedside table. She pressed the button that was programmed to summon her son Jeffrey, who would, in his sensible way, be sleeping right now in his house in New Zealand. The telephone rang; Ruth, hearing the creak of Jeffrey's throat as he answered the phone, was unrepentant.

'I hear noises,' she said, her voice low and urgent – the kind of voice she'd rarely used with him before.

'What? Ma?' He was bumping up out of sleep. His wife would

be waking, too; she would be rolling worried in bed and turning on a lamp.

'I can hear a tiger, not roaring, just panting and snorting. It's like he's eating, and also concentrating very hard.' So she knew he was a male tiger, and that was a comfort; a female tiger seemed more threatening.

Now Jeffrey's voice stiffened. 'What time is it?'

'Listen,' said Ruth. She held the phone away from her, into the night, but her arm felt vulnerable, so she brought it back. 'Did you hear that?'

'No,' said Jeffrey. 'Was it the cats?'

'It's much larger than a cat. Than a *cat* cat.'

'You're telling me there's a what, there's a tiger in your house?'

Ruth said nothing. She wasn't telling him there was a tiger in her house; she was telling him she could hear one. That distinction seemed important, now that she was awake and Jeffrey was awake, and his wife, too, and probably at this point the children.

'Oh, Ma. There's no tiger. It's either a cat, or a dream.'

'I know that,' said Ruth. She knew there couldn't be a tiger; but she wasn't sure it was a dream. She was awake, after all. And her back hurt, which it never did in dreams. But now she noticed the noises had stopped. There was only the ordinary outside sound of the breaking sea.

'Would you like to go and investigate?' asked Jeffrey. 'I'll stay on the phone with you.' His voice conveyed a serene weariness; Ruth suspected he was reassuring his wife with an eyes-closed shake of the head that everything was all right, that his mother was just having one of her moments. When he'd visited a few weeks ago, at Easter, Ruth had noticed a new watchful patience in him, and a tendency to purse his lips whenever she said something he considered unusual. So she knew, from the funny mirror of Jeffrey's face, that she had reached the stage where her sons worried about her.

'No, darling, it's all right,' she said. 'So silly! I'm sorry. Go back to sleep.'

'Are you sure?' said Jeffrey, but he sounded foggy; he had already abandoned her.

Jeffrey's dismissal made her brave. Ruth rose from her bed and crossed the room without turning on any lights. She watched the white step of her feet on the carpeted floor until she reached the bedroom door; then she stopped and called, 'Hello?' Nothing answered, but there was, Ruth was sure, a vegetable smell in the long hallway, and an inland feel to the air that didn't suit this seaside house. The clammy night was far too hot for May. Ruth ventured another 'Hello?' and pictured, as she did so, the headlines: 'Australian Woman Eaten by Tiger in Own House'. Or, more likely, 'Tiger Puts Pensioner on the Menu'. This delighted her; and there was another sensation, a new one, to which she attended with greater care: a sense of extravagant consequence. Something important, Ruth felt, was happening to her, and she couldn't be sure what it was: the tiger, or the feeling of importance. They seemed to be related, but the sense of consequence was disproportionate to the actual events of the night, which were, after all, a bad dream, a pointless phone call, and a brief walk to the bedroom door. She felt something coming to meet her – something large, and not a real thing, of course, she wasn't that far gone – but a shape, or anyway a temperature. It produced a funny bubble in her chest. The house was quiet. Ruth pressed at the tenderness of her chest; she closed the bedroom door and followed her own feet back to bed. Her head filled and shifted and blurred again. The tiger must be sleeping now, she thought, so Ruth slept, too, and didn't wake again until late morning.

The lounge room, when Ruth entered it in daylight, was benign. The furniture was all where it should be, civil, neat, and almost anxious for her approval, as if it had crossed her in some way and was now waiting for her forgiveness, dressed in its very best clothes. Ruth was oppressed by this wheedling familiarity. She crossed to the window and opened the lace curtains with a dramatic gesture. The front garden looked exactly as it usually did – the grevillea needed trimming – but Ruth saw a yellow taxi idling at the end of the drive, half hidden by the casuarinas. It looked so solitary, so needlessly bright. The driver must be lost and need directions; that happened from time to time along this apparently empty stretch of coast.

Ruth surveyed the room again. 'Ha!' she said, as if daring it to frighten her. When it failed to, she left it in something like disgust. She went to the kitchen, opened the shutters, and looked out at the sea. It lay waiting below the garden, and although she was unable to walk down to it – the dune was too steep, and her back too unpredictable – she felt soothed by its presence in an indefinable way, just as she imagined a plant might be by Mozart. The tide was full and flat across the beach. The cats came out from the dune grasses; they stopped in the doorway, nuzzling the inside air with their suspicious noses until, in a sudden surfeit of calm, they passed into the house. Ruth poured some dry food into their bowls and watched as they ate without ceasing until the food was gone. Something about the way they ate was biblical, she had decided;

it had the character of a plague.

Now Ruth made tea. She sat in her chair – the one chair her back could endure for any length of time – and ate pumpkin seeds for breakfast. This chair was an enormous wooden object, inherited from her husband's family; it looked like the kind a Victorian vicar might teeter on while writing sermons. But it braced Ruth's back, so she kept it near the dining-room table, by the window that looked over the garden and dune and beach. She sat in her chair and drank tea and examined the new sensation – the extravagance, the consequence – she had experienced in the night, and which remained with her now. Certainly it was dreamlike; it had a dream's diminishing character. She knew that by lunchtime she might have forgotten it entirely. The feeling reminded her of something vital – not of youth, exactly, but of the urgency of youth – and she was reluctant to give it up. For some time now she had hoped that her end might be as extraordinary as her beginning. She also appreciated how unlikely that was. She was a widow and she lived alone.

The pumpkin seeds Ruth ate for breakfast were one of the few items in the pantry. She spread them out on her left hand and lifted them to her mouth, two at a time, with her right. One must go in the left side, at the back of her teeth; the other must go in the right. She was like this about her daily pills, too; they would be more effective if she was careful about how she took them. Through this symmetry – always begin a flight of stairs on her left foot, always end it on her right – she maintained the order of her days. If she had dinner ready in time for the six o'clock news, both of her sons would come home for Christmas. If that taxi driver didn't ring the front doorbell, she would be allowed to stay in her chair for two hours. She looked out at the sea and counted the pattern of the waves: if there were fewer than eight small ones before another big curler, she would sweep the garden path of sand. To sweep the sand from the path was a holy punishment, a limitless task, so Ruth set traps for herself in order to decide the matter. She hated to sweep, hated anything so senseless; she hated to make her bed only to unmake it again in the evening. Long ago she had impressed the importance of these chores upon her sons and believed in them as she did so. Now she thought, If one person walks on the beach in the next ten minutes, there's a tiger in my house at night; if there are two, the tiger won't hurt me; if there are three, the tiger will finish me off. And the possibility of this produced one of those brief, uncontrollable shivers, which Ruth thought of as beginning in the brain and letting themselves out through the soles of the feet.

'It's nearly winter,' she said aloud, looking out at the flattening sea; the tide was going out. 'It's nearly bloody winter.'

Ruth would have liked to know another language in order to revert to it at times of disproportionate frustration. She'd forgotten the Hindi she knew as a child, when she lived in Fiji. Lately, swearing – in which she indulged in a mild, girlish way – was her other language. She counted seven small waves, which meant she had to sweep the path, and so she said, 'Shit,' but didn't stir from her chair. She was capable of watching the sea all day. This morning, an oil tanker waited on the rim of the world, as if long-sufferingly lost, and farther around the bay, near the town, Ruth could make out surfers. They rode waves that from here looked bath-sized, just toy swells. And in every way this was ordinary, except that a large woman was approaching, looking as if she had been blown in from the sea. She toiled up the dune directly behind the house, dragging a suitcase that, after some struggle, she abandoned among the grasses. It slid a little way down the hill. Once she had made her determined way to the top of the dune, the woman moved with steadfast purpose through the garden. She filled up a little more of the sky with every step. Her breadth and the warmth of her skin and the dark sheen of her obviously straightened hair looked Fijian to Ruth, who rose from her chair to meet her guest at the kitchen door. Her back didn't complain when she stood; that, and the woman's nationality, made her optimistic about the encounter. Ruth stepped into the garden and surprised the woman, who seemed stranded without her suitcase, exhausted from her uphill climb, encased in a thin grey coat, with the thin grey sea behind her. Perhaps she had been shipwrecked, or marooned.

'Mrs Field! You're home!' the woman cried, and she advanced on Ruth with a reckless energy that dispelled the impression of shipwreck.

'Here I am,' said Ruth.

'Large as life,' said the woman, and she held out both hands cupped together as if they had just caught a bothersome fly. Ruth must offer her hands in return; she offered; the woman took them into her sure, steady grip, and together they stood in the garden as if this were what the woman had come for. The top of Ruth's head didn't quite reach her visitor's shoulders.

'You'll have to excuse me,' said the woman. 'I'm done in. I was worried about you! I knocked at the front, and when you didn't answer I thought I'd come round the back way. Didn't know what a hill there'd be! Woof,' she said, as if imitating an expressionless dog.

'I didn't hear you knocking.'

'You didn't?' The woman frowned and looked down at her hands as if they had failed her.

'Do I know you?' Ruth asked. She meant this sincerely; possibly she did know her. Possibly this woman had once been a young girl sitting on Ruth's mother's knee. Perhaps this woman's mother had been ill in just the right small way that would bring her to Ruth's father's clinic. There were always children at the clinic; they dallied and clowned, they loved anyone who came their way, and they all left punctually with their families. Maybe this woman came out of those old days with a message or a greeting. But she was probably too young to have been one of those children – Ruth guessed early forties, smooth-faced and careful of her appearance. She wasn't wearing makeup, but she had the heavy kind of eyelids that always look powdered in a soft brown.

'Sorry, sorry.' The woman released Ruth's hands, propped one arm against the house, and said, 'You don't know me from Adam.' Then she adopted a professional tone. 'My name is Frida Young, and I'm here to look after you.'

'Oh, I didn't realise!' cried Ruth, as if she'd invited someone to a social event and then forgotten all about it. She stepped away from the bulky shadow of Frida Young's leaning. In a fluttering, puzzled, almost flirtatious voice, she said, 'Do I need looking after?'

'Couldn't you use a hand round the place? If someone rocked up to my front door – my back door – and offered to look after me, I'd kiss their feet.'

'I don't understand,' said Ruth. 'Did my sons send you?'

'The government sent me,' said Frida, who seemed cheerfully

certain of the results of their chat: she had eased off her shoes –
sandshoes from which the laces had been removed – and was flexing
her toes in the sandy grass. 'You were on our waiting list and a
spot opened up.'

'What for?' The telephone began to ring. 'Do I pay for this?'
asked Ruth, flustered by all the activity.

'No, love! The government pays. What a deal, huh?'

'Excuse me,' said Ruth, moving into the kitchen. Frida followed her.

Ruth picked up the phone and held it to her ear without speaking.

'Ma?' said Jeffrey. 'Ma? Is that you?'

'Of course it's me.'

'I just wanted to check in. Make sure you hadn't been eaten in
the night.' Jeffrey indulged in the tolerant chuckle his father used
to employ at times of loving exasperation.

'That wasn't necessary, darling. I'm absolutely fine,' said Ruth.
Frida began to motion in a way that Ruth interpreted as a request
for a glass of water; she nodded to imply she would see to it soon.
'Listen, dear, there's someone here with me right now.'

Frida clattered about the kitchen, opening cupboards and the
refrigerator.

'Oh! Then I'll let you go.'

'No, Jeff, I wanted to tell you, she's a helper of some kind.' Ruth
turned to Frida. 'Excuse me, but what are you, exactly? A nurse?'

'A nurse?' said Jeffrey.

'A government carer,' said Frida.

Ruth preferred the sound of this. 'She's a government carer,
Jeff, and she says she's here to help me.'

'You're kidding me,' said Jeffrey. 'How did she find you? How does she seem?'

'She's right here.'

'Put her on.'

Ruth handed the phone to Frida, who took it good-naturedly and cradled it against her shoulder. It was an old-fashioned kind of phone, a large heavy crescent, cream-coloured and attached to the wall by a particularly long white cord that meant Ruth could carry it anywhere in the house.

'Jeff,' Frida said, and now Ruth could hear only the faint outlines of her son's voice. Frida said, 'Frida Young.' She said, 'Of course,' and then, 'A state programme. Her name was on file, and a spot opened up.' Ruth disliked hearing herself discussed in the third person. She felt like an eavesdropper. 'An hour a day to start with. It's more of an assessment, just to see what's needed, and we'll take things from there. Yes, yes, I can take care of all that.' Finally, 'Your mother's in good hands, Jeff,' and Frida handed the phone back to Ruth.

'This could be wonderful, Ma,' said Jeffrey. 'This could be just exactly what we need. What a good, actually good use of tax-payers' money.'

'Wait,' said Ruth. The cats, curious, were sniffing at Frida's toes.

'But I want to see the paperwork, all right? Before you sign anything. Do you remember how to use Dad's fax machine?'

'Just a minute,' said Ruth, to both Frida and Jeffrey, and, with bashful urgency, as if she had a pressing need to urinate, she hurried into the lounge room and stood at the window. The yellow of the taxi was still visible at the end of the drive.

'I'm alone now,' she said, her voice lowered and her lips pressed to the phone. 'Now, I'm not sure about this. I'm not doing badly.'

Ruth didn't like talking about this with her son. It offended her and made her shy. She supposed she should feel grateful for his love and care, but it seemed too soon; she wasn't old – not too old, only seventy-five. Her own mother had been past eighty before things really began to unravel. And to have this happen today, when she felt vulnerable about calling Jeffrey in the middle of the night with all that nonsense about a tiger. She wondered if he'd mentioned any of that to Frida.

'You're doing wonderfully,' said Jeffrey, and Ruth winced at this, and her back vibrated a little, so she put out her left hand to hold the windowsill. He had said exactly the same thing on his last visit, when he mentioned retirement villages and in-home carers. 'Frida's only there to assess your situation. She'll probably just take over some of the housework, and you'll relax and enjoy yourself.'

'She's Fijian,' said Ruth, mainly for her own reassurance.

There you are, some familiarity. And if you hate it, if you don't like her, then we'll make other arrangements.'

'Yes,' said Ruth, more doubtfully than she felt; she was heartened by this, even if she knew Jeffrey was patronising her, but she knew the extent of her independence, its precise horizons, and she knew she was neither helpless nor especially brave; she was somewhere in between; but she was still self-governing.

'I'll let Phil know. I'll tell him to call you. And we'll talk more on Sunday,' said Jeffrey. Sunday was the day they usually spoke, at four in the afternoon: half an hour with Jeffrey, fifteen minutes with his wife, two minutes each with the children. They didn't time it deliberately; it just worked out that way. The children would hold the phone too close to their mouths. 'Hello, Nanna,' they would breathe into her ear, and it was clear they had almost forgotten her. She saw them at Christmas and they loved her; the year slid away and she was an anonymous voice, handwriting on a letter, until they arrived at her festive door again; for three or four years this pattern had continued, after the first frenzy of her husband's death. Ruth's younger son, Phillip, was different: he would spend two or three hours on the phone and was capable of making her laugh so hard she snorted. But he called only once every few weeks. He saved all the details of his merry, busy life (he taught English in Hong Kong, had boys of his own, was divorced and remarried, liked windsurfing); he poured them out over her, then vanished for another month.

Jeffrey ended this call with such warmth that for the first time Ruth worried properly for herself. The tenderness was irresistible. Ruth was a little afraid of her sons. She was afraid of being unmasked by their youthful authority. Good-looking families in which every member was vital, attractive and socially skilled had made her nervous as a young woman, and now she was the mother of sons just like that. Their voices had a certain weight.

Ruth followed the phone cord back to the kitchen and found Frida sitting at the dining table drinking a glass of water and reading yesterday's newspaper. She had removed her grey coat and it hung lifelessly, like something shredded, over the back of a chair. Underneath it she wore white trousers and a white blouse; not exactly a nurse's uniform, but not unlike. A handbag, previously concealed by the coat, was slung across her body, and her discarded sandshoes lay by the door. Frida's legs were stretched out beneath the table. She had hooked her bare toes onto the low rung of the opposite chair, and her arms were pressed down over the news-paper. She read with a mobile frown on her broad face. Her eyebrows were plucked so thin they should have given her a look of permanent surprise; instead, they exaggerated each of her expressions with a perfect stroke. And her face was all expression: held still, it might have vanished into its own smooth surface.

'Listen to this,' she said. 'A man in Canada, right? In a wheel-chair. They cut off his electricity one night, it's an accident, they get the wrong house, and he's frozen stiff by morning. Dead from the cold.'

'Oh, dear,' said Ruth, smiling vaguely. She noted that Frida's vowels were broad, but her 't's were crisp. 'That's terrible. You found the water all right?'

Frida looked up in surprise. 'Just from the tap,' she said. 'Who'd live in a place you could freeze overnight? I don't mind heat, but I feel the cold. Though I reckon I've never been really, truly cold. You know' – she leaned back in her chair – 'I've never even seen snow. Have you?'

'Yes. Twice, in England,' said Ruth. Her back trembled but she bent, nevertheless, to reach for a cat. She wasn't sure what else to do. The cat evaded her and jumped into Frida's lap. Frida didn't look at the cat or remark on it, but she stroked it expertly with the knuckles of her right hand. She wasn't wearing any rings.

'He's nice, your son,' said Frida. 'Got any more kids?'

'Just the two boys.'

'Flown the nest.' Frida folded the newspaper to frame the blurry face of the frozen Canadian and shook the cat off her lap.

'Long ago,' said Ruth. 'They have kids of their own.'

'A grandmother!' cried Frida, with bloodless enthusiasm.

'So you see, I'm used to being alone.'

Frida lowered her head over the table and looked up at Ruth so that each brown eye seemed cradled in its respective brow. There was a new gravity to her; she seemed to have absorbed it from the room's more important objects, from the newspaper and the table and the rungs of Ruth's chair. 'Don't think of me as company, Mrs Field,' Frida said. 'I'm not a guest. I come for an hour every morning, same time every day, I do my job, and I'm out of your hair. No surprises. No strangers showing up any time of the day or night. I'm not a stranger, and I'm not a friend – I'm your right arm. I'm the help you're giving yourself. This is you looking after you, this is you mattering. Does that make sense? I get it, Mrs Field, I really do.'

'Oh,' said Ruth, who believed, at that moment, that Frida Young 'got it': that she understood – how could she understand? – the tiger's visit, the smell in the hallway, Fiji of course, that strange, safe place, and the dream of consequence in the silly night.

But Frida broke the spell by standing up. Her bulk arranged itself quite beautifully around her; she suited her size. And her voice was cheerful now; it had lost its thrilling, tented quality. 'Let's leave it at that for today,' she said. 'There's a lot to take in. And I've left my bag outside.'

Ruth followed her into the garden. 'Lovely day,' Frida said, although it was a flat, pale day, and the sea lay dull against the dull sand. Frida paid no attention to the view. She stepped down the dune towards the suitcase with her elbows folded in and her hands up near her shoulders, as if afraid of falling. She was more graceful in descent; her back had so much strength that it made Ruth's ache. Having retrieved the case, Frida paused to check the state of her hair, which was dark and drawn into a no-nonsense knot at the back of her head. The suitcase was heavy and she chatted as she heaved it.

'There's nothing to worry about, Mrs Field,' she said. A rim of sweat shone on her forehead. 'We'll talk duties tomorrow. I cook, clean, make sure you're taking your meds, help with exercise. Bathing? You've got that covered for the time being, is my guess. Whatever's hard on you now, I'm here for. You've got a bad back, am I right? I can see how careful you are with it. Gotta look out for your back. Here we go.' Frida hoisted the suitcase over the lip of the dune, swung it across the garden and into the house, and brought it to rest next to Ruth's chair under the dining-room window.

'What's in there?' asked Ruth.

'Only about three thousand kilos. I've got to get me one of these with wheels.' Frida kicked the suitcase at the same moment a car horn sounded from the front of the house, so that the suitcase appeared to have honked. 'That's my ride,' she said. 'I'll be back tomorrow morning. Nine o'clock suit you?' She seized her coat and hunted for her sandshoes until Ruth pointed out where they lay beside the door. The car horn came again; the cats jumped and flew in giddy circles around Frida's feet. Frida didn't bend to pet them; instead, she looked around the kitchen and dining room as if surveying the goodness of her creation, and walked with confidence down the hallway to the front door.

'You have a nice house,' she said. She opened the door. Ruth, following, saw the rectangle of light from outside, the shape of Frida in the light, and, dimly, the golden flank of a taxi.

'The suitcase?' Ruth asked.

'I'll leave it, if that's all right with you,' said Frida. 'Bye now!' She was closing the door. By the time Ruth reached the lounge-room window, there was no Frida and no taxi. The grass stood high in the winter garden, and there was no sound besides the sea.

2

Ruth's husband, Harry, used to walk, every day, to the nearby town to buy the newspaper. He undertook this exercise on the advice of his father, who retained a spry step well into his eighties and had the blood pressure of a much younger man. It was on one such walk that Harry died, in the second year of his retirement. He proceeded from the front door of his house down a narrow lane (Ruth and Harry called this lane their drive), heading away from the sea. The sea disappeared; the air altered suddenly, became more dense, and smelled of insects rather than seaweed; the laneway was just wide enough for a car, and so Harry, a tall man, could stretch out his arms and touch the high grass and casuarinas on either side of the drive. Behind him was the house, the slope of the dune, the broad beach, and the beginning of the sun. This was six-thirty in the morning no matter the weather. He was in his stride by the time he reached the coastal road, which fell away down the sandy hill on which his own house stood. At the foot of this slope, a bus stop waited in humble circumstances – a torn billboard, a splintered bench – and here Harry leaned against the black-and-yellow sign that read STOP! BUS and felt the strange movement of his active heart. Or so Ruth imagined. Harry sat on the bench with his back to the road. He wore a light blue down vest that was swollen in the back, just a little, as if designed to accommodate a minor hunch. From here he could observe the passage of seagulls over the estuary that separated the road from the beach. He had loved this beach since childhood.

Harry's noticeable height, his excessively straight posture distorted only by the swell of his down vest, the neat white brush of his hair and the startling black of his eyebrows, the soft, dishy ears that sat at a slightly odd angle from his head, and the unusual tremble of his hands in his dignified lap: all of these things attracted the attention of a passing motorist, who drew up alongside the curb. This motorist, a young woman, leaned across the passenger seat of her car, lowered the window, and asked Harry in a loud voice if he was all right. Harry was not all right. His chest moved violently with every heartbeat, and as he turned his body away from the sea and towards the road, he began to throw up onto the sandy concrete. The motorist recalled afterwards that Harry had leaned forwards to avoid soiling his clothes, that his left hand was pressed against his ribs as if in womanly surprise, and that he made an effort to kick sand over the vomit, his head bobbing up and down in a helpless motion of agreement.

The motorist, whose name was Ellen Gibson, described these things to Phillip and Jeffrey the day after their father's death. They quizzed her, and she was forthcoming. There was a phrase Harry liked to say: 'to die like a dog in the gutter'. He said it of men he didn't approve of but was willing to tolerate (certain prime ministers, for example): 'I don't like what he has to say for himself, but I wouldn't leave him to die like a dog in the gutter.' This sentiment formed part of the expansive democracy of his generally approving heart. Jeffrey, with some objections from his younger brother, told Ruth what Ellen had told him, and Ruth loved this Ellen who had made sure Harry didn't die like a dog in the gutter. Ellen held Harry when he began to slip from the bench and onto the ground; she assured him, again and again, that everything would be all right. He was dead when the ambulance arrived.

At Harry's funeral, a group of kindly mourners introduced Ruth to a small, tearless, hesitant woman. They called her 'the young Samaritan'. Until that moment Ellen Gibson had been a principle of humanity and coincidence; now Ruth must acknowledge her as the person who had seen Harry die. Ellen looked as young as a teenager, although she was known to have two small sons. She would not allow Ruth to thank her; Ruth would not allow Ellen to express regret. The women held hands for a long time while the funeral eddied about them, as if hoping to communicate to each other a love that couldn't be justified by the scarcity of their contact.

Now, without Harry for five years, Ruth was prepared to

accommodate the possibility that good strangers could material-
ise and love her for no reason beyond their goodness. Ellen was
proof of that; why shouldn't Frida Young be? Another sort of
woman could have convinced herself that Harry – still present in
some way – had sent Frida to look after his wife; not Ruth, who
was vaguely optimistic about the afterlife, but never fanciful.
She felt similarly about the government and was ready to accept
that it might provide her with Frida after a long, sensible, law-
abiding life. Ruth and Harry had never begrudged paying taxes.
Roads! Libraries! Schools! Government carers! Of course Harry
hadn't sent Frida, but Ruth had a feeling he would approve. Her
sons would approve, and their wives; so would Ellen Gibson, who
dropped in every now and then with a cake or a new book. And
Ruth liked approval. It had shored up her life. It had made her
blessedly ordinary, and now it made her want to swear; but she
still liked it.

With Frida and the taxi gone, Ruth had the day to herself. Oh,
the gentle, bewildering expanse of the day, the filling of all those
more-or-less hours. She inspected Frida's suitcase, which was
taking up audacious space in the dining room: an old-fashioned
cream-coloured case, similar to the one Ruth had carried when she
first sailed to Sydney in 1954. It was heavy, and locked. Ruth worried for a moment that it might contain a bomb, so she nudged
it with a gentle foot and thought she heard the washing of bot-
tled liquid. This reassured her. Obeying her earlier contract with
the number of waves seen from the window, she swept the garden
path of sand. She rested her back and watched the sea. She ate sardines on toast. She took a long shower, sitting on the plastic stool
Jeffrey had bought during his last visit.

As she went about these activities, she thought about the tiger. She thought, too, about other periods of her life when she had felt something approaching this sense of personal consequence. There was her missionary childhood, during which she was told repeatedly that she was part of a chosen people, a royal priesthood, a people belonging to God. She saw it, now, as a strangely urgent life, in which her father must heal the sick and save their souls, and the flowers bloomed in useless profusion, and there was too much of everything: sun, and green, and love. Her parents were fine singers, and every night her mother played hymns on a damp piano. Ruth used to read letters from her cousins back in Sydney and feel sorry for them, with their ordinary lives. Her parents had been called to serve, and she had been called with them. She had been named for a stranger in a strange land. 'How bitter is the path of joy,' she would say to herself; she had read that somewhere. There was never, at that time, a moment to lose. Even as she grew older, and the strong, wet light of Fiji dazzled her less, and the hymns, too, seemed less luminous, Ruth was caught up in consequence. She fell in love – of course she fell in love – with a man named Richard Porter. She was unskilled, and prudish, and baffled by love; she managed it badly. That was dreamlike, too. Every night she endured violent dreams of impossible pleasure. She received her own body, and ate a meek breakfast in the morning.

Then Ruth grew up and left Fiji. She went to Sydney, where her cousins wore the right clothes and knew the right songs; they exchanged friendly jokes about her weird, fervent childhood. And so she made, from then on, a conscious effort to live an ordinary life, like those of the people she saw around her: people who had grown up where they were born, among their own kind, and were making their merry, sad way through a world they understood entirely. For only one period, after coming to Sydney, did Ruth recover her sense of the extraordinary: during a childhood illness of Phillip's, a severe case of pleurisy. For four weeks, Phillip lay in bed with his chest bound. There was fever, pain, and a dry cough like sheaves of papyrus rubbing together. Ruth remembered this period of her life in more detail than any other; the sense of urgency she felt lent significance to the most trivial things. She could still recall, for example, the exact order of the books on the shelf beside Phillip's crib. His laboured breathing reminded her of a toy train ascending a mountain; she thought of it now as she washed herself in the shower, balancing on the plastic stool. She thought of that row of children's books. She could see, in the shower tiles, the faces of animals, and also the man in the moon. By then it was dark, and she had succeeded in passing the day; she had survived it. Before going to bed, Ruth closed the lounge-room door as a precaution.

She woke, just after three, to the possibility of sounds from the lounge room. The cats stirred when she did, but subsided into sleep. She listened for some time, blinking herself awake in the grainy dark, but could hear only an unusual noise of birds and insects, as if it were summer outside, or maybe a jungle. There was a whine or two that might have been a tiger, but might also have been the cats snoring; they produced so much noise for such little sleeping things. Ruth listened for him, her tiger, her consequential visitor, until her eyes drowsed shut. He was a one-off, then, she thought, on the edge of sleep and disappointed.

The following morning, a taxi pulled up in front of the house. Ruth tiptoed into the lounge room to investigate. She was sure it was the same taxi she had seen yesterday: a yellow Holden, an older make with a chariot shine and, painted on its doors, the words YOUNG LIVERY and a telephone number. Its windows were tinted a shade Harry would call illegally dark. Frida emerged from the passenger's side of the car and gave the door a firm but casual slam, as if it required such treatment to close at all. She was wearing the grey coat and, beneath it, white trousers and the same grey-white sandshoes, and her hair fell in loose curls around her face, which made her look younger. Frida walked the few steps to where Harry's car, a silver Mercedes, was parked by the side of the house. She gave the rear wheel an exploratory press with her foot and returned to the taxi; she leaned listening into the driver's open window, laughed, and rapped the dazzling roof. The taxi crept backwards down the drive as if fearful of causing a disturbance.

Ruth went to open the front door. The doorbell rang as she did so: an older doorbell, with a two-note chime that Ruth always thought of as actually saying 'ding-dong'.

'I didn't see the bell yesterday,' said Frida. She was smiling, and not quite as tall as the day before, and had a string bag full of oranges hooked to her elbow; she leaned down to take Ruth's hands, a little as she had when they'd first met, and managed in this gesture to move past Ruth and into the hallway. 'There I was, knocking my little heart out – no wonder you didn't hear me, when you're used to that lovely doorbell. Good morning! Good morning! I've got oranges.'

She swung the bag down the hall and into the kitchen like a priest with a censer.

'You didn't need to bring anything,' protested Ruth.

'I know, I know,' said Frida, pouring the oranges into a bowl she took from an upper cupboard. 'But I've got these beauties coming out of my ears. My brother George knows a bloke who gets 'em free. Don't know how, and I don't ask. That was my brother you saw dropping me off. It's his own taxi – he's an independent. You ever need a taxi, let me know, and I'll call George.'

The oranges made a gorgeous, swollen pile.

'Thank you,' said Ruth. 'I have a car.'

'Well,' said Frida, evidently taken aback by this refusal; her eyes widened in something like disapproval.

'But sometimes you need a taxi, don't you,' said Ruth. 'To be honest, I hate driving.'

Frida, placated, patted Ruth's arm. 'Let's have the grand tour, then.' She hung her grey coat on the hook behind the back door. She wore a different shirt today. It was a brighter white and matched the white trousers. She looked like a beautician.

Frida seemed to lead the tour. She marched into rooms and cupboards and corridors, announcing, 'The bathroom!' and 'The linen press!' as if Ruth were a prospective buyer inspecting the property. No new discovery seemed to surprise her. She was tactful in Ruth's bedroom but pitiless in the guest rooms, going so far as to look under the beds, pulling up wreaths of cat hair from hidden corners and shaking her curly head. Ruth responded with an apologetic smile, at which Frida only tutted; she put her arm around Ruth's shoulders as if to say, 'Don't you worry, things will be different from now on.'

'These were my sons' bedrooms,' explained Ruth, 'when we came here on holidays. This was our holiday house.'

'I see,' said Frida. She ran her left forefinger along a bookshelf and examined it for dust. This was in Phillip's room, and all the books were for bright young boys. 'What happened to your other house?'

'Our Sydney house? We sold it. We moved out here for retirement,' said Ruth.

'We?'

'My husband and I. Harry.'

Frida squeezed Ruth's shoulder again. 'It really doesn't bother you to live out here all alone?'

'Not at all,' said Ruth. 'Why should it?'

Her mother had once warned her: loneliness is off-putting, boredom is unattractive. Ruth was convinced both sensations shone from her face. She was certain she had the odd, unexpected movements of a person used to solitude; when she watched television, for example, she mirrored the facial expressions of the actors. Sometimes she made a game of it. She did once think, while reading a newspaper article about the subject, that she might be depressed, but because Harry hadn't believed in it – 'Happiness is a matter of choice,' he would say – she never mentioned it to her doctor, and certainly not to her sons. She knew quite soon after Harry's death that her grief wouldn't disrupt the public order of her days. She expected, instead, a long and private season.

'Come and have a cuppa and we'll talk things over,' said Frida.

Ruth worried that, if pressed, she would talk too much about Harry; she longed for the chance to and was mortified in advance.

But Frida was all business. 'There's some documents you need to look at,' she said, finding her suitcase in the dining room and hoisting it onto the table with a marvellous grunt. The suitcase looked smaller than Ruth remembered. It only took up the space of a bulky briefcase. Frida searched among its contents, pulled out a plastic sleeve full of papers, and, offering this to Ruth with a look of patient distaste, said, 'Official paperwork.'

But before Ruth could take the sleeve, Frida stepped away towards the window. 'Would you look at that,' she said.

The view from the back of the house often prompted reactions of this kind. There was the dune, sloping away from the garden and down to the beach; there was the wide water and the curve of the bay to the right, with the distant silver of the town and, out on the headland, a white lighthouse. Harry used to stand in the garden with his hands on his hips and say, with satisfaction, 'Nothing between here and South America.' Since his death, it had felt to Ruth that the house was participating in a cosy continental drift, making its leisurely way on an island of its own to the open sea. Ruth liked islands. She had lived all her life on them, and they suited her.

'It's disgusting, is what it is,' said Frida.

'Oh, dear,' said Ruth. She had always been embarrassed by the splendour of the view, as if owning so much beauty was an admission of vanity on her part, and she wondered if Frida was the guest she'd been waiting for, the one who would rebuke her for it.

'Would you just look at this?'

Ruth looked, and saw a group of people on the beach below. There were nine or ten of them, and they were all naked, or almost naked. Some lay on the sand and others played in the water. Ruth felt a cheerful innocence rising from them; it was like standing on a mountain pass and seeing a town down in the snug valley. But Frida was unmistakably affronted, just as Harry would have been, and she loomed out into the garden. Ruth followed. So little happened at this end of the beach during the colder months – lone runners, a few dogs. Once, the old jetty splintered and slumped after a storm tide and over the course of a winter was washed out to sea. Skinny-dippers were a definite event, and Ruth liked the idea of them.

'Think there's no one out here, huh?' said Frida. 'Think you're alone and you can do whatever you want?'

She made her way to a corner of the garden where two abandoned aluminium bins, long ago used for compost, sprang to new life in the martial gravity of Frida's intentions. She took the lids from the bins, gave them a preparatory shake, and turned to Ruth with a look of mirthful cunning. Ruth was startled by this look. Who was this stranger crossing her land and heading for the ocean with the lids of the compost bins in her firm grip? What could justify her warlike march? It was all both splendid and alarming.

Frida stood on the sandy ridge at the edge of the garden and bellowed down at the beach. She brandished the lids and commenced her descent of the dune, giving her war cry; she clashed the lids together above her head. The people on the beach – and Ruth saw now that they were very young, only teenagers – had been laughing but, noticing Frida, they lifted themselves from the sand or scrambled from the sea, their heads dark with water. They looked clumsy and beautiful from this distance. A warp in the clouds flooded sun onto their arms and backs. They jeered at Frida but swept up their possessions in anticipation of her arrival, wrapping themselves in towels and stumbling away over the wet sand.

Frida paused at the dirty line that marked high tide. Holding one lid up over her head, as if shading her eyes to see, she became a ship's captain scanning the horizon; these heroic poses came easily to her and her gallant bulk. She moved slowly towards the sea until she reached the place the children had made camp. Then she threw down the lids and began to kick at the sand so that it rose in wild flurries around her; when she finished, it fell smoothly until there was no sign anyone had ever settled on that spot. She retrieved the lids and made her way back to the house.

Ruth watched Frida's serene face float up the dune. She was hard to recognise as the woman who had laboured up this same slope the day before. It was as if she'd required only that one difficult ascent to become sure-footed; or perhaps the garbage lids were acting as ballast: she did hold them a little way out from her body, like wings.

'That's that, then,' said Frida. By now she was standing beside Ruth and exhaling through her nose with an equine vigour. The incident appeared to have given her a kind of health.

Ruth, unsure of what to say, ventured, 'They shouldn't swim all the way out here without lifeguards. It's not safe.'

'They won't be back.'

'It's just high jinks, I suppose.'

Frida replaced the lids on the compost bins. 'They can have their fun in front of someone else's house, then. Spoil someone else's view.' And with a firm and nursery air she withdrew to the house.

Ruth remained outside long enough to watch the swimmers take the path up to the small parking lot behind the bus stop, where a Norfolk pine had once dropped during a windstorm and crushed a surfer's truck. She had expected the children to move down the beach and set up camp again, but Frida appeared to have scared them off for good. Ruth was sorry to see them go. But a ripe, wet wind was developing, a familiar sea wind which would have driven them away soon enough. Sand and salt flew up and about, into Ruth's hair and over her garden. This end of the beach was empty now. Any car taking the road to town might be full of those banished children. If I see one car in the next ten seconds, she thought, I'll tell her to go away. A white car burst from behind the hill; a dark one followed immediately behind it. Ruth hadn't had time to prepare for two cars.

'Teatime!' called Frida.

Ruth found her bustling in the kitchen among tea bags and mugs.

'How do you take it?' Frida asked. 'Milk and sugar?'

'Lots of milk, one sugar.'

'Milky and sweet,' Frida said. The combination seemed to please her. Her own tea was strong and dark, and she wouldn't sit to drink. She leaned against the kitchen counter.

'So, tell me things,' she said, peering into her steamy tea.

'What things?' Ruth's tongue stammered; she felt something like stage fright.

'I like to get a sense of my clients before we get started. Husband? Job? Family? Childhood? All that stuff.'

'That's a lot of stuff.'

'You can keep it simple,' offered Frida. She was noncommittal; she wouldn't sit, Ruth guessed, because she didn't want this to take all day.

'All right,' said Ruth. 'Harry was a solicitor. He died of a pulmonary embolism five years ago. I told you about my sons. What else? I used to teach elocution lessons. I grew up in Fiji.'

Ruth waited for Frida to react to the mention of Fiji, but she failed to do so. Instead, she narrowed her eyes as if trying to see farther. 'You taught what? Electrocution?'

'Elocution!' said Ruth, delighted. 'Speech.'

'Like speech therapy?'

'No,' said Ruth. 'The art of speaking. Of clear, precise speech. Pronunciation, vocal production —'

'You mean you taught people how to talk posh?' It was difficult to tell if Frida was disgusted or incredulous or both.

'To speak correctly,' said Ruth. 'Which isn't the same thing.'

'And people *paid* you?'

'I taught young people, usually, and their parents paid me.'

Frida was shaking her head as if she'd been told a ludicrous but diverting story. 'Is that why you sound kind of English when you talk?'

'I don't sound English,' protested Ruth, but she'd been accused of this before. Once, it would have been a compliment. There had been a schoolteacher: Mrs Mason. She was of elegant, indeterminate age, had an intriguingly absent husband, and she was English; every rounded vowel that fell from her mouth was delivered like a sweet polished fruit to her students, who were the children of sugar-company executives, engineers, missionaries, and government officials: the children of the Empire. They must be trained to speak correctly, so far from home. Mrs Mason taught them rhymes, tongue twisters and tricky operetta lyrics, and made her students recite the days of the week, over and over, four, five, seven times on the strength of one deep breath. She discouraged the use of pidgin, slang or Hindi; she was vigilant against the lazily dropped 't's of her Australian students; she pounced on the use of *would of* and *should of* and was unfailingly specific about which contractions she would and wouldn't allow. Ruth was her prize pupil.

'You sound pretty English,' said Frida, scooping up Ruth's empty mug. 'You sound a bit like the Queen.'

Ruth had a soft spot for the Queen. 'That's ridiculous,' she said. 'Listen: "How now brown cow." That's how I say it. And this is how the Queen would say it: "How now brown cow." Listen to her diphthongs! Completely different!'

'Dip-thongs?' Frida snorted over the sink. And suddenly it was a funny, stupid, dirty word, and Ruth was laughing, and she loved it, although it hurt her back. Frida laughed, too, and rising from her capacious chest, her laugh seemed a rare and lovely object; it seemed to spread, like wings. Her whole face was transformed: she was warm and pretty, she knocked the mugs together in the sink, and she raised a tea towel to her face to cover her widening smile. Ruth felt buoyant in her spindly chair. She smiled and sighed and thought, Yes, Ruth, silly thing, this could be good, this could be all right.

3

The house took to Frida; it opened up. Ruth sat in her chair and watched it happen. She saw the bookcases breathe easier as Frida dusted and rearranged them; she saw the study expel its years' worth of Harry-hoarded paperwork. She had never seen such perfect oranges as the ones Frida brought in her little string bag. The house and the oranges and Ruth waited every weekday morning for Frida to come in her golden taxi, and when she left they fell into silences of relief and regret. Ruth found herself looking forward to the disruption of her days; she was a little disgusted at herself for succumbing so quickly.

But Frida was fascinating. For one thing, her hair was always different: braided, curled, lacquered, soft. Each morning, just before nine, Ruth opened the lounge-room door she had been so careful to close the night before and went to the window to watch Frida's emergence from the taxi. Frida's hair might be piled on her head or straightened to her shoulderblades. It might be a new colour. One day she arrived with hair so blond, so cloudy and insubstantial, that her head seemed an unlikely match for the capable body beneath it. She was a little bleary that morning; she made a cup of tea first thing and sat on the back step drinking it with an air of bleached glamour. The cats took pains to avoid the chemical smell she gave off. The bright blond lasted only a few days before it became brassier, more yellow; then came a softer, whitish colour, more sophisticated and at the same time more childish. After this blond period came red, and burgundy, and a glossy true black, and back to brown, ready for the cycle to start all over again. Frida accepted compliments about her hair with a dignified smile and raised one careful hand to hover near it.

'It's my hobby,' she said. Ruth had never before met anyone who considered her own head a hobby.

Frida's magnificent hair never interfered with her duties. She worked in her first few weeks with a bright disposition, but was never what could be described as cheery. She had a determined efficiency about her, and at the same time a languorous quality, a slow, deliberate giving of herself. Her suitcase turned out to contain enormous bottles of eucalyptus-scented disinfectant; she cleaned the floors with this slick substance every morning, shepherding the mop with graceful movements of her tidy feet. The house at first smelled sweet and forested, and then so astringent the cats took to sleeping in elevated places, away from the scrubbed wood and tile. When Ruth drew attention to this, Frida only stood over the immaculate floors and inhaled deeply, with a nasal echo, to demonstrate the bracing bronchial qualities of her cleaning regime.

'Smell that!' she cried, and made Ruth breathe in until her throat burned. 'Isn't it great? Isn't it better than seaweed and flies?'

Frida made it clear early on that she disliked the smell of the sea.

While she cleaned, Frida carried out her assessment of Ruth's 'situation'. She noted the absence of rails in the bath and a fence around the garden. She quizzed Ruth about her medical conditions, flexibility, hair loss, sleeping patterns, eating habits ('You're wasting away,' she accused, as if she had long familiarity with the shape of Ruth's body), and frequency of social contact. She made Ruth fill out a number of questionnaires – 'How often do you bathe? (a) Daily; (b) Every two to three days; (c) Sporadically; (d) On special occasions' and 'Circle the box appropriate to your income in the last financial year.'

At the end of her assessment, the first thing Frida announced was that Ruth wasn't eligible for public housing. 'People like you usually aren't,' she said with apparent pleasure. When Ruth protested that she had no interest in public housing, Frida sucked in an experienced breath and said, 'Beggars can't be choosers.'

'Beggars should be no choosers,' said Ruth.

'*Beggars can't be* is the phrase,' said crisp, corrective Frida.

'Yes, I know.' Ruth laughed at herself. 'I was saying the original version, it's sixteenth century, the phrase our phrase was born from. Imagine that – already a cliché four hundred years ago.'

Frida's brows elevated her hairline. 'Is that the kind of thing you taught your students?'

'It is, actually,' said Ruth. She was proud of herself for remembering. She felt she could have lifted her arms and recited the days of the week nine or ten times; or perhaps she would only chant, over and over, *Ineligible for public housing*.

Frida, however, was unimpressed; it showed in the delicate angle of her chin. She gave a small sniff. Ruth found it almost sisterly.

'Well, Mrs Field,' Frida said.

Ruth, not for the first time, said, 'Oh, call me Ruth, please.'

'One hour a day isn't going to be enough, all things considered. I'm going to recommend you're increased to three. That's nine until twelve, and if you like, I'll stay another half an hour to make you lunch. That's if you can bring yourself to put up with my clichés.'

Ruth was contrite now. She loved Frida's clichés; she loved the way Frida believed them; she loved how believable they were. I'm a show-off, she thought, but the lift remained in her lungs.

'All right,' she said, and that was Ruth agreeing to three hours, and an extra half an hour for lunch.

'Good,' said Frida. She seemed to have been made shy by something. Then she said, 'I like that name. Ruth.'

Frida relaxed over lunch. She made Ruth a ham sandwich and, at Ruth's insistence, boiled herself an egg and ate it from a Mickey Mouse eggcup over which Phillip and Jeffrey used to fight. As she ate, she explained the requirements of her strict diet, which was the result of her having been much heavier than she was now.

'My whole family's big,' she said. 'Big-boned.' She sipped at the spoon with which she scooped the egg. 'Mum and Dad are gone, and my sister Shelley, too – all big, though, and when Shell died I said to myself, "Frida, it's time to make a change." That's when I lived in Perth. I did my training out there, in Perth. And I said, "Frida, it's now or never."'

These lunchtime revelations were almost boastful: Frida was like an evangelist describing her conversion from the pulpit of her born-again body. 'I wrote a letter to food, telling it all the wrong it'd done me,' she said. 'Then I demanded a divorce. I had a certificate made up – a friend of mine, a girl I worked with, did it on the computer. Then I signed it, and that was that.'

'Goodness,' said Ruth.

'And look at me now!' said Frida, presenting her sizeable self with a flourish of her palms.

'But you do eat?'

'Of course. You don't leave a marriage with nothing, do you? I took some things with me – healthy stuff. Everything else I was divorced from, so I just had to forget about it. There's that thing when you break up with someone and you hate him like poison but sometimes you just want to touch his shoulder, you know? Or hold his hand.'

Ruth tried to imagine Frida holding someone's hand; she could just about manage it.

'But even if you want to, you can't. That's divorce,' said Frida. It's death, too, thought Ruth. 'And then you forget. There are things I couldn't even tell you how they taste. Ask me how something tastes.'

'I don't know. Lettuce,' said Ruth.

'I'm allowed lettuce. I took lettuce. Ask me something else. Ask me about ice cream.'

'All right. How does ice cream taste?'

'I don't remember!' said Frida. 'That's divorce.'

Ruth was enchanted by Frida's divorce; she wanted to tele-phone everyone she knew and tell them all about it. But who was there to call? Phillip was never home, or she hadn't calculated the time difference properly; she could tell Jeffrey, but he had never quite approved of what he referred to as her 'wicked sense of humour', by which he clearly meant 'streak of cruelty'; he hated to hear people made fun of. So if she said to him, 'This woman, Frida, divorced food,' he would probably make Ruth explain the whole thing and then say, 'Good for her.' He was already inclined to approve of Frida. Ruth had sent him the paperwork, as promised; he also, according to Frida, sent regular emails with instructions on how to care for his mother, a field Frida was trained in, thank you very much, but, as you soon learn, the hardest part of this job is usually the families. Oh, the families.

Frida ate the last of her egg. 'You're naturally thin, aren't you,' she said, with a trace of pity in her voice.

'I've got a bit of a belly these days,' said Ruth, but Frida wasn't listening. She tapped the top of her empty egg until it fell inwards.

'It's good, though, to be a big girl in this job. That's what I've noticed. I've met nurses, though, tiny girls, with the strength of ten men. Never underestimate a nurse.'

'I know something about nurses,' said Ruth, and Frida looked at her in what seemed liked surprise. 'My mother was a nurse.'

'She took you to work with her, did she?' Frida asked, a lit-tle prickly, as if she had a tender bundle of children she had been instructed to leave at home.

Ruth laughed. 'She had to, really. My parents were missionaries.

She was a nurse, and he was a doctor. They ran a clinic together, attached to a hospital. In Fiji.'

This was the first time Ruth had mentioned Fiji in the weeks since Frida's arrival. Frida didn't respond. She seemed to be engulfed in an obscure displeasure.

'I saw how hard my mother worked, and how exhausted she always was,' said Ruth, nervous now, in a bright, chatty tone. 'And I suppose she was never really what you would call appreciated, though she was very loved. My father's work was appreciated, and my mother's sacrifice. That's how people put it.'

'What people?' asked Frida, as if she were questioning the existence of any people, ever.

'Oh, you know,' said Ruth, waving a vague hand. 'Church people, hospital people, family. I've always thought of nursing as a very undervalued profession.'

Frida snorted. 'I wouldn't call *this* nursing,' she said. Then she stood; she seemed to call on the security of her height. She raised her eggcup from the table like a chalice, passed into the kitchen, and pushed open the screen door with one hip, still with the eggcup lifted high.

'For the snails,' she said, and threw the crushed eggshell into the garden.

The taxi called for her soon afterwards, and she left the house in an excellent mood.

4

Ruth often woke with a sense that something important had happened in the night. She might have dreamt a tiger again. She might have dreamt, as she used to, of Richard Porter in her bed – although surely a dream like that should be of Harry. She did think of Richard more now that Frida was in the house, as if to have daily company reminded her of the existence of other people. Between Richard and Frida and this sense of curious importance, the weeks were crowded; they were also thick, Ruth noticed, with a strange hothouse heat. She shed blankets from her bed and wore light clothing – summer dresses, or cotton shorts with the small, soft

T-shirts her sons had worn as boys. The cats lost their winter fur in springtime clumps, and Ruth continued to hear bird and insect sounds at night. But little actually happened: Frida installed bath rails and taught Ruth how to lie down and sit up with the least strain on her back; she mopped and swept; she introduced pills recommended by a naturopath friend of George's, which were supposed to help with memory and brain function and, being made of an ordinary orange kitchen spice, turned Ruth's urine bright yellow; Jeffrey and Phillip telephoned. These things filled the time, but were not extraordinary.

There was, however, the matter of the car. Ruth disliked driving and was frightened of Harry's car; she peered at it through the kitchen windows; she worried over it at night. She began to live off Frida's gifts of fruit and bulk canned goods, all sourced from some inexplicable friends of George's, so that it was no longer necessary to drive or even take the bus into town. She lost weight. She ate the last of the pumpkin seeds, and they went straight through her. Once a week, under Jeffrey's orders, she went out to sit in the car and run the engine; doing so, she experienced a busy, practical sense of renewal followed by the disquieting feeling she was about to drive herself to her own funeral.

One day, while Ruth sat in the driver's seat, Frida's head loomed at the window like a sudden policeman's. Ruth's heart jumped but she kept her hands on the wheel; she was proud of this, as if it indicated that, counter to her own belief, she was a good driver.

'You never drive this thing,' said Frida. 'You should sell it.'

Ruth was afraid of the car, but she didn't want to sell it. That seemed so irrevocable. 'I couldn't,' she said.

A week later, Frida raised the matter again. 'I can think of three or four people who'd buy that car off you tomorrow,' she said.

'Driving means independence,' said Ruth, quoting Harry, who used to make her drive at least once a week. He called this 'keeping your hand in'.

Frida shook her head. 'Not if you don't actually drive.' She promised that her brother's taxi would always be at Ruth's disposal, free of charge. 'After all, you're family now,' she said, with unusual gaiety.

She also offered to take over Ruth's shopping, to buy stamps and mail letters, to pay bills, and to arrange house calls from the doctor if necessary.

'You can't eat tinned sardines every night,' said Frida. 'If the government's paying me to do your shopping, you may as well let me do your shopping. That's what I'm here for.'

Frida liked this last phrase, if using it regularly indicated a preference. It seemed so adequately to sum up the melancholy importance of her willingness to serve. Still Ruth resisted the idea of selling the car. What if, alone at night, she heard an intruder and needed to get away? Or had some kind of medical emergency and the phones weren't working?

'How would you drive in a medical emergency?' asked Frida.

'It might just be a burst eardrum. Or maybe there's a problem with the cats and I need to drive them somewhere. You can't call an ambulance for a cat, can you. Can you?'

What actually worried her, she was surprised to realise, was the tiger. Which was ridiculous, of course. But what if he came back some night on which she'd forgotten to close the lounge-room door? She would hear him coming down the hallway to her bedroom, intent on his agile paws, and her only escape would be

the window. Ruth pictured climbing into the garden and crouch-
ing in the bushes, waiting for the tiger's superior nose to smell her
out. As if, with her back, she could still climb and crouch! Or there
might be a short moonlit dash over the beach with the tiger's hot
breath on her heels, the car meanwhile slumbering in the comfortable driveway of a more fortunate stranger.

'I won't sell it,' she said, and turned the key to kill the engine,
which was the wrong gesture if her intention was to prove her
resolve. The car shuddered and wheezed before falling silent, the
way a much older car might.

'Suit yourself,' said Frida, shrugging her round shoulders. 'I'm
only trying to help.'

After this discussion, Frida's hair entered a dormant period of
brittle French rolls. She spent more time with the floors and her
eucalypt mop, and she made noises as she moved: sighs, soft grunts
and groans; everything required some effort, some complaint,
or, alternatively, an aggressively cheerful energy. She muttered in
passing about aged drivers and overdue registration checks; she
referred, more than once, to the difficulty of helping people who
won't help themselves. Frida stirred the house with these perceptible struggles and satisfactions, and Ruth found it easier to stay
out of her way. She withdrew to her chair. She counted ships and
pretended to read the newspaper. Jeffrey called with the idea of
inviting a friend from Sydney to stay for the weekend; he suggested an unmarried woman who, Ruth knew, was a discreet and
grateful guest and a diligent spy for the worried children of her
elderly friends. Ruth nodded and smiled into the phone. Frida
mopped, and the car waited.

The following week, Ruth sat in the driver's seat facing the sea, which was level and green except in the path of the morning sun; there, it was ribbed with silver. She felt the familiar dread as she turned the ignition key, but today there was an additional terror: the car seemed to press in on her, as if it were being compacted with her inside. It felt small and heavy enough to sink at any moment into the dune, leaving her buried in a sandy hole.

'You hate this car,' Ruth said aloud, and lifted her hands to those places on the steering wheel that Harry had smoothed by touching so often. He believed in buying expensive European cars that would last a long time; this car vindicated him. It was sheathed in indestructibility.

'You hate this car,' said Ruth again, because she did hate it and was afraid, not just of driving it but of the expensive machinery of its European heart. Frida was right, as usual. She was probably right about everything.

But it annoyed Ruth that Frida was right, so she put the car in reverse and backed it down the long driveway with the surety that comes only from bravado. Frida came to the lounge-room window; Ruth could see hands shifting the lace of the curtains. But it was too late – Ruth was on her way down the drive. Out on the road, she turned right, away from town. To her left were the hills; to her right was the sea. A low wing of cloud rolled away as she drove. It was July – the middle of the mild winter. The road was bright and grey, and the car so fast under her heated hands; the word she thought of was *quicksilver*, and that was an important word, a word for a pirate or a tomcat; her own cats had silly athletes' names, human names she disapproved of and declined to use; how focused her mind felt, she thought, even with all of this in it, pirates and tomcats; she was moving towards a definite point and would be delighted to discover what it was. She would find it, and go home again. But her return would have to be perfect: a gesture of both surrender and magnificence. It would have to indicate that Ruth, although prepared to sell the car, was not entirely ruled by Frida's will.

Ruth followed the broad leftward curve of a hillside until she was a little dizzy, and there as the road straightened stood a road-side fruit stand with space for a few cars to park beside it. She had often wondered who stopped at fruit stands like this. Harry always refused. Now she turned off the road, bumped up the grassy verge, and sat for a moment in the stilled car. When she stepped out, the air felt newly polished. It both buoyed and stung.

A teenage boy, dark-skinned and light-haired from too much sun, manned the stall. His blinking face was scrubbed clean by boredom, and the surfboard propped beside him explained his look of marine longing. His stock was almost entirely made up of avo-cados, but a glorious pineapple caught Ruth's eye. It shouldn't have been there: a pineapple, this far south, in July! She approached and laid one hand on its corrugated hide.

'Busy today?' Ruth asked. She had emptied the car's ashtray of coins, and now they weighed down her pockets.

'Nope,' said the boy, and he shrugged and sighed and looked towards the swelling sea. 'I could of been out there for hours.'

'Could *have*,' said Ruth. She produced her coins. 'I don't know how much this amounts to, but I want to spend all of it.'

He was a fast counter. 'Nineteen dollars and forty-five cents,' he said. Harry would have tutted at her for not clearing out the coins before now.

'What will that buy?'

The boy looked at the sea and then at Ruth. 'Everything.'

It took ten minutes to load the car with everything. The boy's chest seemed to expand with every carton; he began to chat about the weather and a shifting sandbar in the bay and finally allowed himself a luxurious scratch of his barely stubbled chin. The back-seat was full of avocados, but the pineapple sat by itself in the front; Ruth was tempted to strap it in. The liberated boy waved as she drove away. The pineapple rolled a little into the coastal curves, and something about it – its swollen movement, its heavy, golden smell, and the absurdity of its spiked green haircut – made Ruth feel like taking a holiday. It made her feel like driving forever and never coming back. But, she wondered, how do you take a holiday from a holiday? And by the time she wondered this, she was home.

Ruth hoped Frida might be waiting in front of the house, or at least hovering behind the front door. She wasn't, so Ruth parked the car in its usual spot. The crushing sensation was gone; the car and the ground both felt solid. She thought of a time when she was young, with young sons, and only ever looked severe while driving: she set her lips thin, her elbows strained at ballet angles from the wheel, and her face took on an expression that used to frighten her children. It couldn't be a mistake to put all that behind her.

Ruth called for Frida from the garden and the front hall; she went back and opened the car's rear doors, looked at the avocado trays, and thought about lifting them. Only then did Frida come out of the house, drying her hands on the hem of her white shirt.

'Avocados? In winter?'

'A present,' said Ruth.

'Not much of a present when I have to carry them myself,' said

Frida, but Ruth saw that she was pleased. The quantity was what impressed her; Frida was a natural friend to bulk. She ferried and puffed until the fruit was inside, and then Ruth went to lock the car. There was the pineapple in the front seat. She lifted it out with special care: for her back, but also for the pineapple.

When Ruth re-entered the house, Frida was in the dining room. She stood at the window making strange sounds in her throat: a low throaty coo that might have been a bird noise. Ruth looked, and there were magpies in the garden. Frida watched them and made her gentle throbbing calls; she stopped when Ruth said, 'I've decided to sell the car.'

Then Frida turned and smiled. 'Yes,' she said. She was lovely when she smiled, with her plump, pretty face. She held out her arms and accepted the pineapple as if she had expected it all along; had placed an order for it. Ruth put the car keys on the table. Her hands, now empty, smelled of coins.

'It's really for my own peace of mind,' she said.

'George can get you a good price,' said Frida, and the next day she introduced a man named Bob, who looked over the car – he insisted on calling it 'the vehicle' – and was prepared to buy it for thirteen thousand dollars.

The idea of freedom from the car delighted Ruth; so did the idea of selling it without consulting her sons. This satisfaction increased when Bob presented her with a cheque. Ruth noted in passing that along with his other misfortunes – Frida mentioned a traitorous wife and kidney stones – Bob bore the unusual surname of Fretweed. He returned that afternoon with a skinny assistant who manoeuvered the vehicle down the drive. The specific sound of the car seemed to her more significant than almost any other noise – even more than the sound of Harry's voice. But the car was disappearing, taking its sound with it; Harry, too, went down the drive for the last time. Frida seemed sensitive to this in the quiet of the house. There was a sense of relief and exhaustion at the end of their little battle, and it manifested in small tender things: tea made, quiet maintained, and no competition over the affection of the cats. The grass beneath the car had yellowed to the colour of cereal. Frida pinned the cheque to the fridge with a magnet and told Ruth she would bank it first thing on Monday.

5

Frida took charge of Ruth's banking. She presented Ruth with statements and letters from the bank, and Ruth waved a regal arm above each one, as if in dismissal. Frida treated Ruth's bankbook like a sacred object, always requesting permission to use it and returning it with a public flourish to its proper place at the back of Harry's filing cabinet. Jeffrey had explained the function of key-cards, but Ruth liked the efficient cosiness of the book; she liked how contained it felt, how manual.

Frida had no time for keycards. 'Money isn't plastic,' she said, although, in fact, it was.

Ruth intended to inspect all this paperwork in private, at night. She remembered her mother's lessons about managing staff: never give them any reason to believe you don't trust them. But the house at night was not the place for these daytime plans; it encouraged a different kind of resolution. After dark, the air thickened so that every noise seemed tropical: palms rattled their spears, insects rubbed their wings in the dripping trees, the whole house shuffled and buzzed. The heat made Ruth's head itch. She listened for any hint of the tiger, but it all seemed safely herbivorous. One night she woke to the sound of a dog crying out, and it made her wonder about wild dogs – she thought she remembered a hyena in *The Jungle Book*. Her mother had read her *The Jungle Book* when she was very young, at the age when her bed was moved away from the window because of nightmares; the view from her pillow was of a chest of drawers, painted green, with a glass night-light that threw pinkish shadows on a framed picture of Sydney Harbour (apparently, she was born in a place called Sydney). So she must have been six or seven.

Now she lay awake listening to the hyena, which was undoubtedly a dog on the beach. The cats fidgeted at her side, but slept again. Her sense of the extraordinary was particularly strong. She might have been seven, waiting to hear her father come home from a late night at the clinic. She might have been nineteen, waiting for Richard's voice in the hall; he came home even later than her father and stepped so carefully past her throbbing door she could easily have missed him. The consequence rose up out of the sounds she heard and those she only remembered; it met somewhere between them, and finding space there, it grew. Ruth lay and listened for it; then she grew tired of waiting. I'm too old, she thought, to be a girl waiting for important noise. Why not go out to meet it, why not prepare? She rose from her bed to run a bath, and as the greenish water filled the noisy tub, she looked in Harry's study for her old address book. If I find it before the bath runs over, she thought, Richard's address will be in there. She found the book before the bath was half full; she opened it, and there under P for Porter was Richard's address. Just reading it felt like a summons.

Ruth lowered herself into the water with the help of Frida's railing. The water amplified the white of her legs, but it smoothed and dazzled all the folds of her skin, so that half of her body was old and actual and the other half was marine and young.

Ruth was happy and clumsy after her bath. She dressed in a new nightgown. It was sleeveless and pale and, although short, felt bridal. Frida had chosen it and dismayed Ruth with its matronly florals; now, in the night, it shone. The heat of the house made a canopy over the hallway, where the moon came in through the fanned glass in the front door. The moonlight lay on the wooden floor like a deck of cards, and Ruth could see that the hall was straight and long and empty of tigers and birds and palm trees. She crossed it with her arms held out because she was afraid of falling (Harry's mother had fallen, in her old age, after a lifetime of robust health, and had never been the same again), and when she opened the door to the lounge room, the light from the windows seemed to jump at her all at once. This room felt comparatively cool and quiet, but it contained an echo of heated noise all the same. It was this noise she was looking for.

Ruth found nothing in the lounge room but the stillness of her furniture, which was either in shadow or patterned by the lace curtains that fell between it and the moon. The moon seemed to be big and full whenever Ruth looked at it, and tonight it was emphatic, as if it had blown itself to a ball in order to assure her that there was nothing unusual in her lounge room. The moon was full on the space in front of the house, but beyond that it was eaten up by the grassy drive. Anything might be lurking in that drive: a tiger, or a taxi. Ruth walked through to the dining room and looked at the garden. Everything on the sea side of the house was blasted white by the moon. All this emptiness had a carved quality that made Ruth want to swear. She loved the crowded bluster of swearing, the sense of an audience; it was so human-ising. She stood at the half-open back door and said, 'Fuck,' and wished for the comforting hot ticking singing jungle she had dis-turbed by getting out of bed. It didn't really sound like Fiji – at night in Fiji she heard cars on the road, her parents moving about, the telephone ringing in the hallway and her father leaving to see a patient, crepe myrtles rubbing at her windows, and the sound of hot water in the pipes when her mother ran a bath – but it sounded different enough to remind her of Fiji; it was enough to make her think of the room with the night-light and the picture of Sydney Harbour. The sound of the jungle was full, and every-thing here was empty.

Ruth went back to the lounge room and listened for some time. Every noise she heard was ordinary, and the cool room was stiff and airless. She lay on the sofa, turned her back from the lace of the windows, and waited. It seemed important that something might touch her, and crucial that she not open her eyes to look for whatever that thing might be. A tiger would be perfect, but anything would do; a bird, maybe, but it needn't be a bird. Just a fly. Just a frond of something, stirring in a yellow wind. Lying on the couch with her eyes closed, Ruth might feel her jungle; there might be yellow light, there might be a tiger to bump its broad nose against her back. The water, at least, might hammer in the pipes. Frida woke her the next morning by turning her on the sofa, peering into her face, and saying, 'I nearly wet my pants, you idiot. I thought you were dead.'

6

Frida gave the floors a thorough mopping that morning and, a-swim in the alluvial muck, with her bare feet depositing grey tracks no matter how long she left the floors to dry, worked herself into a black mood. She persisted with her mop, and eventually the floors were smooth and softly lit. Then she became generous and hearty. She sat at the dining-room table, gazed magnanimously out to sea, and ate dried apricots. Her hair was coiled in a complicated triple braid, and the floors were, briefly, perfect.

Ruth joined her at the table and said, 'Jeffrey thinks I should invite a friend to visit.'

Frida chewed her apricots.

'What he wants,' said Ruth, 'is Helen Simmonds, who's a sensible woman he's known forever who'll ring him up and tell him everything.'

Frida clicked at the roof of her mouth with her cheerful tongue.

'So I thought I'd invite a man instead.'

Frida hooted. Her whole face shone with suggestive delight. 'Well, well,' she said. 'Just when I thought I had you figured out.'

Ruth, pleased by this innuendo, nevertheless dismissed it with an airy hand.

'Who is he, then?' said Frida. 'Your boyfriend?'

'I haven't seen him in fifty years.'

'Ex-boyfriend?'

'No. Sort of.'

'Ha!' cried Frida, triumphant. 'It's always the quiet ones who're up to no good.'

'Oh, Frida, it was the fifties! Nobody was up to no good. Nobody I knew. It was the fifties, and in Fiji it may as well have been 1912.'

Frida snorted as if there had never been a 1912.

'I mean Fiji in the fifties, is all I mean,' Ruth corrected. 'I don't mean Fiji is a *backward* country.'

'I could care less if Fiji is a *backward* country,' said Frida. Each apricot disappeared inside her benevolent mouth. Ruth began to worry for Frida's digestive system, but counselled herself not to; Frida was the kind of woman her mother would have referred to, with approval, as having the constitution of an ox. As a child, Ruth was frightened of oxen, which rolled their eyes and ate the tops of sugarcane and were glossy-flanked in the sun, but she knew now that her mother had never had those real oxen in mind when she complimented anyone's constitution.

'His name was Richard Porter,' said Ruth.

'Oh, yes,' said Frida, lifting one groomed eyebrow as if she'd been anticipating Richard all along. But this was Frida's way: it was impossible to surprise her. She would rather starve than be caught off guard; she had said so on more than one occasion. It was also unnecessary to ask if Frida wanted to hear about Richard, because she would only shrug or sigh or, at best, say, 'Suit yourself.' Much better just to begin.

'He was a doctor who came to help my father at the clinic,' said Ruth. 'I was nineteen. He was older.'

Frida seemed to smirk at this, as if she were hearing a smutty story. But it was hard to tell what she was thinking. She sat, almost tranquillised, with her feet lifted from the floor, and looked out across the bay, where an insistent wind cleared the haze and lifted the flags over the surf club.

Richard, Ruth explained, was in Fiji as a medical humanitarian rather than a missionary, although he'd agreed to profess certain beliefs in order to fill the post at the clinic – it was so difficult to find trained men after the war that Ruth's father was willing to accept this compromise. Ruth's parents referred to Richard, before his arrival, as 'that gifted but misguided young man' and busied themselves preparing the house, since he would be staying with them until he found accommodation of his own. He was Australian, too; Ruth's parents prayed in thankfulness to God for this provision, and Ruth prayed along with them. She was most interested in how handsome he was. He arrived during a rainstorm; Ruth stood on the verandah at the side of the house to watch him run from a taxi through the downpour. She felt a strong sense of destiny because she was nineteen and because he seemed so providential: young, Australian, a doctor, and now coming from rain into her own house. So she rounded the corner, mindful of her own effect – because she had been pretty at nineteen, a lovely pale blonde – and ready, so consciously ready, for her life to make some plausible beginning. But he was sodden and there was some concern about his bags, which the driver was carrying in through the rain. Richard seemed to want to help and was being forcibly restrained from doing so by Ruth's father, who had prepared a welcome speech and was delivering it while holding Richard in a paternal embrace. Ruth was forgotten in the confusion and then only hurriedly introduced; she went to her bedroom and moped over an impression of dark hair and a thin frame.

Later that evening, dry, Richard's hair was light and his body seemed less scarce. *Handsome* was not the right word for him; he was good-looking, but in a neat, shining, narrow way, with his combed hair and his straight nose and a paleness about the lips. It was as if his beauty had been tucked away – politely, resolutely – so that he might get on with the rest of his life, but it made itself known, just the same, in the shine of his hair and the fineness of his face. The faint lines on his forehead indicated seriousness. Ruth liked all this; she approved. Sometimes she tied up her hair too tightly to be flattering because, let loose, it was a long white-gold line, a distraction, and had nothing to do with the work of God.

They all sat together at the dinner table – Ruth, her parents, and Richard – and Ruth saw the dining room as he must have: how long and narrow it was, how dingily white, with the chipped sideboard holding family silver (a tureen, a pepperpot, a punch bowl with six glass cups, each carried lovingly from Sydney, out of the past, and rarely used; isn't it funny, thought Ruth, how some objects are destined to survive certain things, like sea voyages and war). A fan revolved in the upper air. Ruth's mother didn't believe in lamps, only in bright, antiseptic light, and the dining table was laid out, the equator in that longitudinal room, as if emergency surgery might be performed there at any moment. There were no shadows; everything blazed as if under the midday sun. Watercolour landscapes flanked a photograph of the King. When Richard bent his head for her father to say grace, Ruth saw the pale canal of white scalp where he parted his hair. The tops of his ears were red and his forehead was brown and damp. He kept his eyes open and his face still, but he mouthed *Amen*. Perhaps he could be converted. She looked at him too long, and he saw her.

They all ate with that furious attention which comes of social unease and willed good feeling. Or Ruth did, and her mother, and Richard; but her father was relaxed and happy, expanding into male, medical company with obvious pleasure, as if he'd been many months at conversational sea. Ruth supposed he had. Her father dominated Richard, and she barely spoke. She hoped instead to burn with an inner intensity that would communicate itself to him secretly. Richard answered her father's questions with a politeness that suggested he was keeping his true feelings to himself. Ruth recognised and appreciated that kind of reserve. She decided, He's a moral man, and considerate. He's kind. Probably – as she admitted to herself later – he could have been utterly without principles or sensitivity and she would still have found something to admire. She was that determined to love him.

After dinner, they all sat on the verandah (which Ruth referred to, privately, as the terrace) and drank tea. The tea was never hot enough. It was like drinking the air, which pressed close around them, as if the earlier rain had finally just refused to fall any farther and remained suspended. Bats swam overhead. Richard lit a cigarette and Ruth imagined the smoke passing in and out of his lungs. Everything was a vapour – the tea, the damp air, the smoke – but Richard sat distinctly inside all of it. She rarely looked at him or spoke, but she tried to be especially graceful as she fanned her head to keep mosquitoes away; they didn't bite her, but they fussed at her face. Finally her mother grew tired and said, 'I'm sure the young people have a lot to talk about,' and Ruth saw her father look astonished, as if the thought that Richard and Ruth might have anything in common – even the proximity of their ages – had never occurred to him. Then the withdrawal: her mother indulgent, and her father flustered. He'd been caught mid-monologue. They achieved their exit with the utmost awkwardness, and Ruth, mortified, nearly fled.

Richard sat and smoked. There was an atmosphere around him: exhaustion, relief, forced courtesy. All this just in the way he sat and smoked. Ruth liked that he held his wrist rigid. Some men, in her opinion, smoked like women; she liked that he didn't. He wore a wedding band, but not on the correct finger, and she learned much later that it belonged to his father, who was dead. Ruth, afraid of a moment's silence, asked questions. He'd come to Fiji, he said, with the hope of opening a dispensary for the treatment of Indian women.

'For the treatment of – what?' Ruth asked, surprised, because she thought he meant that Indian women suffered from some special malady, unknown to Australians and Fijians and the

English, and although she suspected it might be embarrassing, she wanted to know what it was.

'Of Indian women,' he repeated. Did he think she didn't know Indian women existed? It was a bad beginning.

'Oh,' said Ruth. 'I thought you were here to help us. In our clinic.'

'Your clinic?' he asked.

Ruth considered this rude of him, and enjoyed her resulting indignation. But she was also ashamed: everything she looked at seemed so shabby, so obvious. There was the sound of the house-boy washing dishes in the kitchen, and no real order in the riotous garden, and they were at once too privileged (they were not Indian women, with their mysterious afflictions) and not privileged enough (surely, entertaining a young man on the terrace, she shouldn't have been able to hear dishes being washed in the kitchen). So she corrected herself by saying, '*The* clinic.'

He smiled at her then, and she felt herself smiling back, unable to help it. 'What I really want to do,' he said – and she leaned forward to where his smoke began; she could have dipped her head in it – 'is run my own clinic, once a month to start with, more often if there's interest and resources. There's a man named Carson – do you know him?'

'Yes,' said Ruth with regret. Andrew Carson was a youngish man who worked for the South Pacific Commission. He was suspected, in a genial way, of being a Communist, mainly because he didn't attend church. He approved of Ruth's father because he could have been making money in Sydney as a doctor – 'serious money', he called it, as if there were any other kind – but was here instead, curing Fijians. Ruth's father disliked this secular sort of approval. The thought of Richard and Andrew Carson becoming friends – allies – made Ruth disconsolate.

'He thinks he's found some funds for me. I want to get out to the villages. I want to buy a truck.'

'A truck,' said Ruth, with a solemnity in keeping with Richard's plans.

'And in the meantime, yes, I'm here to help in your clinic.'

'I'm glad,' she said, 'about both things – that you're here to help my father, and Indian women.' This was the most deliberate statement she had ever made to a man she wasn't related to, and she felt as if her ears were burning red.

Richard rewarded her with another smile. The smoke stood beside him without seeming to rise or fall. 'Your father likes to talk, doesn't he?'

Ruth was sensitive to criticism of her father, in that tenuous and personal way in which children are anxious for the dignity of their parents. She worried a great deal for him out in the world.

'Not usually,' she said. 'He's happy to have you to talk to.'

'I like him very much,' said Richard. 'I've read everything he's written on whooping cough.' She waited for him to say, 'But I'm sure you're not interested in all that.' He didn't. His cigarette burnt right down to his fingers, and he shook them as he flicked it away. 'I always smoke them down to the very end. It's a bad habit. Army days.'

'Where were you?'

'Mainly New Guinea, and then for a while in Tokyo.' He was obviously contemplating another cigarette; she saw him decide against it. 'Is it the holidays for you? Do you go back to Sydney for school?'

Ruth stood. 'You must be exhausted.'

'You know, I really am,' he said, standing too. 'You've made me feel very welcome. Thank you.'

He didn't offer his hand. He stood, holding his cigarettes, and his tea was only half finished; he had no idea of the cost of good tea in Suva. The square of the kitchen window went catastrophically dark.

'I hope you'll be happy here,' said Ruth. She was moving inside, too quickly. 'I've finished school. I'm nineteen. Good night.'

She ran up the stairs, thinking, Idiot, idiot.

Now she said to Frida, 'I fell in love with him the very first night. What a goose. I didn't even know him.'

'Usually better not to,' said Frida.

'In some cases, maybe. But Richard was quite a special man.'

'And you didn't marry him.'

'No,' said Ruth.

'Silly bugger.'

'It wasn't up to me.'

'I meant him,' said Frida.

'Oh, he did all right. He got married before I did. We sailed back to Sydney together in 1954, and I hoped something might happen. Something definite, I mean. But it turned out he was engaged all that time. Never mentioned it, not even to my father. I went to his wedding and never saw him again.'

'Really? Never again?'

'Never.' Ruth liked the dramatic finality of *never*, but was compelled to admit there had been Christmas cards.

'If you ask my opinion,' said Frida, who rarely waited for the solicitation of her opinion, 'you're better off. What kind of bloke doesn't tell anyone he's engaged?'

'The girl he was marrying was Japanese. He met her in Japan.' Ruth, defensive, saw Frida dismiss this as a reason for secrecy. 'It wasn't all that long after the war. It was a sensitive subject.'

Frida sent out one blind hand for an apricot. She was thought-ful; she understood sensitive subjects. She chewed her apricot before asking, 'And what happened in the end?'

As if a life is a period during which things happen. I suppose it is, thought Ruth, and they do, and then at my age, at Richard's age, they've finished happening, and you can ask.

'His wife died about a year or two before Harry. She was older than him – older than Richard.'

Now Frida held a hand to her dark hair and produced a sigh so bitter, so exhausted, and at the same time so sweet, that Ruth was tempted to reach out and comfort her. Frida stood up from the table.

'You really want to see him again?' Her mood was shifting; she was already giving a far-sighted frown.

'I think I do. Yes,' said Ruth. 'I do.'

'It'd be a lot of work,' Frida said, and she sighed and stretched as if that work were already upon her. 'I hate to say it, Ruth, but I'm not sure you're up to it. And how old is this Richard now? Eighty? Ninety?' She said 'Eighty? Ninety?' as if there were a neg-ligible difference between those two ages.

'He must be over eighty,' said Ruth. Richard, over eighty! That seemed so unlikely.

'You might call it irresponsible, asking a man like that to travel. Expecting to be able to look after him, at his age.' Frida looked at Ruth in a way that added, 'At *your* age,' and swept the package of apricots up from the table.

'In last year's Christmas card he said he was in the best of health.'

'The best of health for *eighty*,' said Frida with a snort.

Frida believed she had a secret, Ruth saw, and it was this: that Ruth and Richard were innocents, that they were old, older than old, and that while they might still be capable of a sweet, funny romance, any physical possibility was extinguished for them both. Well, probably it was. Ruth wondered. She permitted herself to hope, and at the same time not define the thing she hoped for.

'Jeffrey would agree with you,' said Ruth with a carefully blameless face, and she saw Frida consider this distasteful possibility before proceeding to the kitchen. Ruth sat still with the idea of Richard. She was surprised by how much she wanted to see him, and also by the pleasure of wanting. He would be an arrival – one that she had asked for, that she had planned.

'You know what?' called Frida from the kitchen. She often delivered good news – gave of the bounty of herself – from another room, at high volume, so she needn't be troubled by gratitude. 'I could help out. You know, come over while Richard's here. Not for free, mind.' Now she appeared, briefly, in the archway between the rooms. 'But for a reasonable price, you know, I could cook and keep an eye on things.'

'Would you really?'

Frida made a clatter in the kitchen which meant 'Yes, but don't you dare start thanking me.'

Frida seemed to think it was decided: Ruth would ask Richard to come, and Frida would keep an eye on things. She prepared an uncharacteristically festive meal: a curryish dish, with pieces of pineapple and indecipherable meat. It tasted like the distant cousin of something Fijian.

'What do you call this?' Ruth asked as Frida fastened her grey coat and made for the front door.

'Dinner,' said Frida.

Later, lying in bed with the doubtful meat in her stomach, Ruth fretted about Richard. She wanted to think only of how fine he was, of how every girl had loved him, and of how he liked her best; how she would be walking with friends and his shabby truck would roll by, his mobile dispensary, lifting dust and rattling at the seams, and he would honk his horn or stop to talk and sometimes drive her home, or take them all in the truck to the beach, and when they swam, he stayed close to her, lay beside her in the sun, gossiped about Andrew Carson, poured sand on her feet, asked her advice about some faux pas he had made with the Methodist minister's wife, told her she reminded him of a milkmaid on a biscuit tin, and finally, when the Queen visited Fiji and a ball was held in her honour at the Grand Pacific Hotel, invited Ruth to come with him – although he disapproved of queens – because he knew she wanted to go. And everyone waited for Ruth and Richard – their names were said together so often – to become an item. Even when Richard began to disgrace himself by caring too much about the health of Indian women, by befriending the wrong Fijians ('agitators', Ruth's father called them), by staying at Ruth's parents' house too long ('Saving money for the dispensary,' he said; 'Staying for me,' prayed Ruth), and by refusing church without even being a Communist, the women of Suva hoped to see happiness for Ruth with this 'gifted but misguided' young man. She had given up the hope of converting him. She was no longer much sure of God herself. He came home late at night, and she listened for his soft walk past her door, and he never stopped. Not true: he stopped once. Her door was open. He came in to apologise; he had kissed her the night before at the Queen's ball and would never do it again. People began to wonder if he was quite normal. They wondered about Indian women and Andrew Carson; they never suspected a Japanese fiancée.

And how Ruth had defended him to everyone! Because she was his favourite, his milkmaid on the biscuit tin. But that was exhausting, too. For example, he would lend her difficult books without her having asked for them and want to know her opinion; when the ocean liners docked in Suva carrying orchestras or theatre companies, he took her to see them perform. And if he didn't like what he saw or read or heard, he would call it 'a bad play', 'a bad book'. *Bad* in his mouth was the strongest of adjectives. He always had a definite view of the play or the symphony, and he would presage it with this declamatory staccato, as if helpfully summarising his opinion before expanding upon it: 'It was bad,' he would say, or 'uniformly bad' if he considered it irretrievable. Or, if approved of, things were either 'important' or 'excellent' or 'very fine'. Most of the events he took her to bored her even when she enjoyed them, and she felt Richard notice her exclusion from this whole world of his – by her own choice, it seemed. She saw him observe, mournfully, her over-enthusiastic applause when the thing was finally over.

He was courteous; he always withheld his opinion until it was asked for. He would wait for her to say, 'What did you think?' And then he would say, 'Very bad' or 'Excellent,' and there would be some minutes of talk about why, during which Ruth wondered how he thought of all these things to say. It astonished her that he could have such inexhaustible opinions, and that he was capable of articulating them. He's smarter than I am, she concluded, and he cares more than I do. But part of her was also suspicious of his ability to translate feeling so readily into words. She came away from music with a sense of its shape, and from plays with a suggestion of pulled threads; she had no idea how to describe shapes and threads. Richard would talk, and then he would say, 'What did you think?' And she might say, 'I agree' or 'I liked it.' She didn't have opinions, if what he had were opinions, only preferences, and these were often vague. She knew that her opinions existed – that she responded with true pleasure to the things she enjoyed – but she never found it necessary to scrutinise them. Whenever she was pressed to reveal her tastes in books or art or music, she sounded to herself as if she were discussing her favourite colours. But she shared her pleasures easily with Harry, whose delights were similarly blurry: they both loved Handel's *Messiah*, for example, but felt no need to investigate the particular sensations it aroused in them. Books were different; they were private. No one could read them along with her, reacting and looking for her reaction. Richard had tried to draw her out, and she was afraid to disappoint him with the little he found there. In comparison, the ease of Harry was a relief.

Ruth had expected her character to become more sharply defined with age, until eventually she found that it no longer mattered to her; she left off worrying about it, like a blessedly abandoned hobby. But now Richard might come with his bad books and his excellent symphonies and fill her with doubt all over again. She lay in bed with her hands on her meaty stomach and worried until the cats, from their bedposts, began to perk and stare. They were listening to something, and so she listened, but heard nothing unusual. Her heart was stiff but strong. Not now, she thought, addressing the tiger. Not with Richard coming – which meant she did want him to come. One of the cats gave a low, funny growl, or produced, at least, a growl-shaped noise. When Ruth went to comfort him, he snapped at her fingers, which always made her sad and shy. She moved in the bed, unhappy, and the cats jumped and ran.

'Fine!' she called after them. She would write to Richard. Things could still happen to her. She lifted her back from the bed, went to her dressing table, and found paper and a pen.

'My dear,' she wrote, 'this will be a bolt from the blue, but if you can spare the time and make the journey, this old lady would like to see you again. I live by the sea, I have a very good view (there are whales), and I also have a wonderful woman called Frida whose brother George has a taxi and will collect you from the station and bring you here. We can talk Fiji and fond memories, or just snooze in the sun. Come as soon as you'd like to. The whales are migrating. Come as soon as you can.'

Ruth wrote the letter, didn't reread it, sealed it in an envelope, and sent it out with Frida the following morning. There might have been spelling mistakes, and she worried afterwards about having signed off 'all my love', but the important thing was that the letter existed and had been sent. Five days later there was a reply from Richard. His handwriting was lean as winter twigs. He was delighted to hear from her. He had been thinking about her lately, would you believe; and if she was old, then he was older. His next month was busy, but he would come on a Friday in four weeks' time.

7

Ruth telephoned Jeffrey a few days before Richard's arrival.

'What's wrong?' he asked when she announced herself. His midweek voice was poised for action.

'Nothing,' she said. 'I'm going to be busy this weekend, that's all, so I thought I'd ring you now.'

'Busy doing what?'

'I've invited a friend to stay,' said Ruth.

'Good on you, Ma! Anyone I know? Helen Simmonds? Gail? Barb?'

'No.'

'Who, then?'

'An old friend.'

'If you're going to be deliberately mysterious, I won't keep asking you about it,' said Jeffrey. So like Harry it was unearthly, but Ruth supposed this happened all the time with widows and their sons, and it would be maddening to mention. She'd worked hard to maintain her belief in the distinct differences between herself and her own parents.

'I'm not being mysterious,' she protested. 'This is an old friend from Fiji, a man called Richard Porter.'

There was that same feeling as when she'd told her schoolfriends, 'I'm taking the boat to Sydney with Richard Porter.' Then, in 1954, the girls nodded and smiled at one another. Ruth blossomed in the midst of all that gentle insinuation. Her fond heart filled. Now Jeffrey said, 'That's nice.'

'Do you remember – we used to get Christmas cards from him? And his wife.'

'Not really.'

'He knew me when I was a girl. He knew your grandparents. He was quite an extraordinary man. I suppose a sort of activist, you'd call it now.'

'Find out if he's got any old photos,' said Jeffrey.

'I'm sure he will. I remember he had a camera when the Queen visited.'

Ruth knew that Jeffrey mistook her use of the word *girl* to mean child; he would be imagining this Richard as a considerably older man, avuncular, and he talked about him that way. He claimed to be pleased she would have company, although she should really ask Helen Simmonds up one of these days; he also worried about the extra work a visitor (who wasn't Helen Simmonds) would generate. Ruth explained that Frida was helping, for a low fee – he asked how much and approved of the answer – and she expected they would do nothing but watch whales and drink tea, which would create so little 'extra work' she was almost ashamed of herself. Frida was washing the dining-room windows as Ruth spoke on the phone; she made a small noise of disgust at this talk of her fee.

Jeffrey, who was always interested in the transport arrangements of other people and spent a great deal of time planning his own, asked, 'How's this Richard getting to your place?'

Ruth's answer was insufficiently detailed. The conversation persisted, and Ruth thought, What can I say that means he won't go? But when can I go? She always listened for hints that Jeffrey might be ready to finish a call, and when she identified them, she finished it for him, abruptly, as if there weren't a moment to lose. He didn't seem at all scandalised that his mother was planning to entertain a male guest, which was a relief and also, thought Ruth, something of a shame. Not that she set out to scandalise her sons. She'd never liked that obvious kind of woman.

'I hope you'll have a lovely time,' said Jeffrey.

Ruth made a face into the phone. A lovely time! I carried you under my ribs for nine months, she thought. I fed you with my body. I'm God. The phrase that occurred to her was *son of a bitch*. But then she would be the bitch.

The phone produced a small chime as Ruth replaced it, as if coughing slightly to clear Jeffrey from its throat. She considered the pre-programmed button that was supposed to conjure Phillip.

'What time is it in Hong Kong?'

Frida, with knitted brow, consulted her watch and began to count out the hours on her fingers. 'It's too early to call,' she sighed, as if she regretted the result of her calculations but would bear it bravely. It was always too late or too early to call Hong Kong; Ruth had begun to doubt if daytime existed in that distant place. In the last four weeks, waiting for Richard to come, she had begun to doubt the existence of any place other than this one; it seemed so unlikely that Richard might be somewhere right at this moment, living, and waiting to see her.

Returning to her windows, Frida said, 'Jeff's happy with my salary, is he.' It wasn't a question. The flesh of her arms shook as she rubbed at the windowpanes; the windowpanes shook, too. She had become such a part of the house that this mutual trembling seemed to Ruth a kind of conversation.

Now that she had told Jeffrey, Richard was definitely coming. Ruth inspected her heart: there was a leaping out, and also a drawing back. Difficulties presented themselves. The house was so hot, and there were possibly birds in the night, and almost certainly unseasonal insects. The cats threw up on the floor and the beds, and their fur seemed to sprout from the corners. For the first time in months, Ruth noticed the state of the garden: it seemed to be shrinking around the house. Harry had spent so many hours tending this garden against the sand and salt, climbing ladders and kneeling in the grass wearing soft green kneepads which gave him the look of an aged rollerskater. He would be horrified to see it now. His shrubs and hedges had worn away in patches; they reminded Ruth of an abandoned colouring book. The hydrangeas looked as if enormous caterpillars had chewed them to rags; snapped frangipani branches lay across the grass; and the worn turf gave the impression of faded velvet. The soil there had failed under the brittle grass – had simply blown away. Now there was sand; there was more sand than lawn. The few trees stood embattled against the sea, and the only flourishing plants were the tall native grasses that surrounded the house on three sides.

'He'll take it as he finds it,' said Frida, who saw the dismay with which Ruth surveyed the garden through the dining room's soapy windows.

'Yes,' said Ruth.

'And inside will be pure gold.'

Frida seemed very sensible of the honour of the house; it reflected her own honour, after all, and so she set about cleaning every corner in preparation for Richard's arrival. Ruth had never observed quite this level of zeal in her before. She wouldn't accept any help, but confined Ruth to the dining room, where she would be 'less likely to cause trouble'.

As Frida cleaned, Ruth told her more about Richard; talking about him made her less nervous. She may have told each story more than once. There was the green sari he'd given her for her birthday, and how embarrassed he'd been when she tried it on. There was the first time he ate a kumquat and chased her through the house trying to make her eat one, too. There was the Christmas he made her a puppet theatre out of a tea chest because she was a teaching assistant at the Girls' Grammar School. There was the royal ball.

'I had a dress made up in pale blue Chinese silk,' she said airily, as if she had been in the habit of ordering silken dresses. Ruth didn't mention that Richard had kissed her at the ball and that, ever since, Ruth had felt an unshakeable gratitude towards the

Queen, whose dark royal head had been visible, now and then, among the people in the ballroom. She was newly crowned and not much older than Ruth. The Queen! And Richard! All in the same night. The blue silk lit Ruth's yellow hair. Richard danced with her and asked if she was tired and guided her through the crowd with his hand in the small of her back without telling her why; he led her to a corridor and kissed her there among the potted palms until Andrew Carson came and flushed them out. Andrew Carson, the maybe-Communist, the kiss-killer! It was no chaste kiss, either. Ruth had saved the dress for the daughters she might have and had no idea where it was now.

Frida encouraged these reminiscences by not objecting to them; otherwise she gave no sign that they interested her. She stayed late that Thursday, cleaning and cooking, and for the first time they ate their dinner together. Frida made a slim stir-fry, piled Ruth's plate with rice, and picked at her own vegetables.

'Still dieting?' Ruth asked.

Frida nodded, serene. 'Maybe you haven't noticed,' she said, 'but I've lost an inch off my waist.'

It was strange to have Frida at the dinner table, fiddling with her food. She ate a little and a little more, and stood to clear the table.

'No hurry,' she said, gathering plates, so Ruth pushed her rice away.

'I'm too nervous to eat, anyway.'

'What on earth are you nervous for?' asked Frida, who was already wetting dishes in the sink. The water surged among the saucepans and plates and Frida's hands.

'There's something I'm worried about,' said Ruth.

'What thing?'

'I wouldn't be so worried except that we have guests coming.'

'We have one guest coming.'

'Is it normal for my head to be so itchy?' Ruth held her hand to her hair but wouldn't scratch in front of Frida. 'It's driving me mad.'

Frida shook the suds from her fingers and said, 'How long since you last washed your hair?'

Ruth began to cry. This was unprecedented; it was terrible. But while Ruth knew this to be terrible, she let herself cry, in part because she was so horrified at forgetting to wash her hair and allowing the itch to continue. She'd worried in the night that she had lice or some other parasite, or that she was imagining the itch and going insane. She woke greasily from sleep with these fears and pulled at her hair in an effort not to scratch, and now Frida was reminding her that this was simply the way hair felt when it hadn't been washed. Frida observed Ruth's tears with evident disapproval. But this mode of disapproval was usually the prelude to an act of helpful sacrifice on Frida's part, and Ruth was comforted by the thought of this assistance.

'You want me to wash your hair for you?' asked Frida, and Ruth said, gulping, 'I wash every night.'

'I know you do.'

'I'm very particular about it.'

'I'd know if you didn't, love. You'd smell,' said Frida, so kindly that Ruth pressed a bashful hand to her face. Her scalp raged. It may have been weeks since she last washed it.

Frida pulled the plug from the sink. She wiped her hands with a tea towel, rolled up the sleeves of her shirt, and smoothed her own hair back. 'Don't you worry,' she said. 'We'll get it washed. It'll be nice. Like going to a hairdresser.'

'Oh, dear,' said Ruth, feeling herself settle into a helplessness that was pleasant now, for being a little artificial. She looked forward to surrendering to the complete attention of beneficent hands. 'It's a lot to ask, isn't it?'

'That's what I'm here for.'

At first Frida planned to wash Ruth's hair in the bathroom basin. Ruth liked this idea. She explained that this was how her hair had been washed as a girl. She described the bathroom of the house in Fiji, with its narrow, shallow bath (her father could only squat in it, pouring a small bucket of water over his back). Her mother had hung green gauze at the windows, for privacy and also because she, like the other women she knew, considered green a cooling colour.

'Blue is the coolest colour,' said Frida. And blue, when Frida said it, was the coolest colour; it simply was.

But when Ruth tried to rise from her chair to go into the bathroom, her back objected. Frida – sceptical, impatient Frida, whose reliable spine usually prevented any sympathy for Ruth's lumbar condition – decided the basin would be too much. Instead, she directed Ruth to the wingback recliner in the lounge room: a 'subtle recliner', Ruth had once called it, because she didn't entirely approve of recliners, which she supposed was a very Protestant way to think about a chair. Frida filled a large bowl with water and spread towels over the chair, the floor, and Ruth. She cranked the recliner beyond any previous limits, so that Ruth could see, above her small stomach, the tops of her toes.

Frida was good at washing hair, which was the result, Ruth

assumed, of so much practice on her own healthy head. She took great care over each of the steps: the wetting, the shampooing and conditioning and rinsing, even a head massage in the able, indifferent way of trained hairdressers. Her skill wasn't unexpected; what surprised Ruth was the way Frida, washing hair, began to talk. She started by complaining of sleepless nights, nervous headaches, and bowel trouble.

'If you could just feel my neck and shoulders,' said Frida. 'Like concrete.'

The problem, it seemed, was her brother. More specifically, the house he and Frida owned between them. The house had belonged to Frida's mother, who died four years ago and left her property to her three children: George, Frida, and their sister, Shelley. Shelley died not long afterwards, leaving George and Frida in joint possession of the house.

'A crappy little place, really,' said Frida. 'Ex-housing commission. But it's home, and the view's good. The land's worth a pretty penny these days.'

The house was in the nearby town. Frida's mother and Harry had, it turned out, purchased their houses in the same year. At that time, the town was functional and quiet, with an atmosphere of helpless evacuation: the canning industry that once gave it purpose had disappeared a decade before. In those quieter days, Harry and Ruth, holidaying, would drive in with the boys to buy groceries and linger only to eat slightly greasy ice cream on the waterfront. Ruth recalled streets full of neat fibro homes. They could easily have been housing commission: the cannery workers would, after all, have needed somewhere to live.

Frida's mother and Harry had bought their houses in and close to this unassuming town, and within a few years cafés and boutiques began to open among the greengrocers and newsagents of the main street, and in the old cannery buildings; a small hotel was built, and then a larger; the caravan park shrank to a third of its size to accommodate a marina. Frida's mother and Harry had inadvertently made excellent investments. They were both, as Frida put it, 'sitting on a gold mine'. Ruth imagined them congratulating each other. Frida's mother, in this image, was a rosy, stout Fijian woman who embraced tall, patrician Harry; Harry, never more pleased than when discovering himself to have been astute, shook a bottle of champagne over her head.

But now this house of Frida's mother's was causing trouble. George, it seemed, was a gambler.

'Not big league,' said Frida. 'Just the pokies and keno when he's at the club. But I tell you what, that's more than enough.'

Ruth loved poker machines; she enjoyed the small lights and the tinny music, the complicated buttons and the promise of luck. She didn't come across them often, but she insisted on playing whenever she did and referred to this as 'having a flutter', a phrase she always said in a Cockney accent. It had never occurred to her that a person could fall into debt from a love of poker machines, but this is what George had done. She pitied him and knew Harry wouldn't have, because Harry was so sensible, and every now and then a snob. Ruth suspected she was a snob in ways she wasn't even aware of, but felt that her sympathetic, impressionable heart made up for it.

Ruth felt sorry for George, but mostly for Frida. George had taken out two mortgages, the first to bankroll a business importing and packaging car-phone parts, and the second to establish his taxi company when the first failed. By this time he had moved into the house, and Frida joined him there soon afterwards.

'To protect my inheritance,' she said. 'Or he'd let it go to the piss.'

Ruth didn't comment on Frida's sudden bad language. She liked it. She liked the way Frida's swift hands moved over and through her hair to prevent any water from running onto her face. It was a long time since anyone had touched her.

At first George's taxi was a success. He'd purchased two licences from the friend of a friend, and by the time the town took off, he was in a position to franchise. There was a period when nearly every taxi in town bore the words YOUNG LIVERY. But, according to Frida, poor business sense, lack of organisation, a surly manner and a reputation for unreliability – 'an arrogant prick to all and sundry, customers and employees and drivers alike, not to mention his own sister' – ruined things for unlucky George. His gambling intensified as drivers quit, cabs broke down, and insurance payments lagged. Now he was back to just the one cab, which he drove himself. Only last weekend, a lengthy love affair with one of his former telephone operators had ended in a fight with her husband, and George spent the night in hospital as a result.

In short, George was a mess. Frida had tried everything, but he didn't want to be helped. Ruth sympathised with people who 'didn't want to be helped'; she felt that generally she was one of them, despite her current submission. Frida's concern now was her mother's house, which she referred to as 'the house she died in'.

Ruth made supportive noises. She had never been to the house her own mother died in, which was a rectory in country Victoria. Her mother had been visiting friends and died of a stroke in the night. Ruth's father died in hospital. And there was Harry, who hadn't died in a house at all.

Frida took the bowl to the bathroom to exchange dirty water for fresh. Ruth thought Frida moved much faster than usual, but perhaps less efficiently. Soapy water splashed onto her handsome floors.

'I have no idea why I'm telling you all this,' she said on her return, suddenly prim, but she relaxed again as she combed the conditioner through Ruth's hair. She held the hair at the roots so that it wouldn't tug, just as Ruth's mother had done in the green-lit bathroom. Here was the trouble: two mortgages on the house, and payments lagging. Not minding losing the house so much, except that it was 'the house she died in'. Government carers being paid so little these days.

'I don't need to tell *you* that,' said Frida. 'You know how under-appreciated we are.'

And George too proud to ask for help. Both of them too proud, really. Certain family members might lend a hand, for their mother's sake, and for Frida's, but pride prevented her asking.

'Once you've left home, you've left,' said Frida. 'You go back with your head held high, or you don't go back.'

This indicated to Ruth that Frida had severed her ties with Fiji; that her leave-taking had been dramatic and that she expected the rest of her life to live up to it. So Ruth nodded to indicate that she understood, and Frida stilled her head with strong fingers.

'I thought about taking a second job,' said Frida. She paused as they both considered the noble step of taking a second job. 'Then I thought, Excuse me? I barely have time for this one. But it's not like I'm making millions. You know how helpful it is to have this extra work from you, cooking this weekend? It's paying my electricity bill. George leaves every light on. If it wasn't for me, he'd have the whole place lit up like a Christmas tree, all night every night. And the time he spends in the shower!'

'So wasteful,' said Ruth.

'Well, who doesn't like a good long shower?' said snippy Frida. Now she was drying Ruth's hair with a towel. 'How does that feel?'

'So much better.' Ruth pressed experimentally at her scalp, which responded by flaring into itch.

'What else needs doing? We want you all done up for your visitor, don't we.' Ruth listened carefully for any insinuation in this, but found none. 'Let's take a look at your feet.'

Ruth hadn't thought about her feet in some time. She was mildly surprised to find them intact at the end of her legs; she held them out in the air with pointed toes, and Frida, Prince Charmingly, removed her slippers. Her small feet were freckled, and her brittle nails nestled in her long toes. Frida was shocked by the dryness of her heels.

'We can't have this,' Frida said, and bustled to the bathroom. She returned with another bowlful of hot water, and a small grey lump of pumice stone. 'You know,' she said, 'I once heard the best remedy for cracked heels – you won't believe this – nappy-rash cream!' Frida smirked and lowered Ruth's feet into the steaming bowl. She scrubbed with the stone, and the water went a milky white, none of which seemed to revolt her.

Ruth flexed one experimental foot. It felt heavy and boneless in the heat of the water. 'You're too good to me,' she said.

Frida remained quiet. The wet bowl slopped.

'My father used to do this,' said Ruth. 'He used to hold a foot-washing ceremony once a year. He washed all the patients' feet, then the clinic staff, the household staff, and mine, and last of all my mother's.'

'What for?'

'To remind us and himself that he was there to serve us, and not the other way around.'

Frida paused in her scrubbing and closed one dubious eye.

'And because it was nice,' said Ruth. 'It was a nice thing to do.'

Ruth remembered those ceremonies as gold-lit days, brighter than usual, but there was also something uncomfortable about them, a feeling of potential disaster. Her mother prepared everyone: had the patients' feet uncovered and their toenails cut and cleaned, and lined up the staff. The Fijian nurses giggled as they removed the soft white shoes Ruth's father made them wear. The hospital groundskeeper, a thin, cheerful man, rinsed his feet beneath the outdoor tap until he was beaten back from it by the nurses' cries.

'What if he sees you! What if he sees you!' they scolded.

The clinic was for the Suva poor. They came voluntarily with pains and injuries and difficulty breathing and blood in their stools and numb limbs and pregnancies and migraines and fevers, and Ruth's father repaired them or referred them or sent them home. They weren't supposed to stay overnight, but frequently they did, when the Fijian wards in the hospital were full. So on the morning of the foot washing there would be the patients who had stayed and their visiting families, and there would be the new patients, who had arrived that morning, and before seeing to any of them, Ruth's father washed their feet.

The washing took place on Good Friday: that solemn, reposeful day, set apart from the rest of the year (although the patients still needed tending, the floors still had to be swept, and Ruth's mother had to arrange lunch with the help of the houseboy). First there was church, which at that time of year was full of tense expectation. The chosen hymns were grateful and the Bible passages subdued; the entire service was a form of sheepish mourning. Then Ruth's family walked down the road from the church to the clinic. Ruth's father walked in front, his shoulders set in his church suit. He was a man of tireless industry, of easy good cheer, and he was broad over the back the way a bricklayer is broad, or a sportsman; but his head was small, his Adam's apple prominent, and his hair persisted in a boyish cowlick at the back of his crown. He was thick and strong in the trunk, but contradictory in his extremities: his fine ankles and long kangaroo's feet, his surgeon's hands, his neat head and filigree hair. This gave him a slightly flimsy look. New mothers winced to see their bulky babies in his slim hands. When, on the day of the Easter washing, those bony hands passed soapily over the feet of his staff and patients and family, they felt like a woodworker's precise tools. Ruth recalled the pressing of a knuckle against an instep, and the two long hands held together over her foot as if in prayer.

He crawled along the floor before his staff and patients, loose of limb and unwieldy of body; a baby elephant over the tiles, pulling his bucket of water along with him. The palms at the windows distributed the sun in stripes over the brown feet. After every four sets of feet he stood to fetch new water in a small bucket. They all watched him in silence. The nurses, beforehand, worried they would laugh as he washed; they never did. They stood in a bashful line. As he approached, they might hide their smiles, but during the washing, as he knelt in humility before them, their faces were serious and stern, and even the youngest of them murmured and touched his head. Sometimes they wept.

If only, Ruth would think, he could maintain his dignity as he washed: more than once he farted as he stood, and his knees clicked, especially as he grew older. By the time Ruth was a teenager she was embarrassed by the whole thing; was wrung with protective pride and fear and irritation. She began to notice some resistance among the staff or the patients, but couldn't be sure if it signified boredom or reluctance or dissent. He lost face with some. Others were grateful. Ruth felt maternal towards her father on his clumsy, wholesome knees, felt superior to his defined and allegorical world, and in her superiority broke her heart over him, whose head shrank as he grew older.

Richard refused to take part. He wouldn't wash feet, and he wouldn't allow his feet to be washed. The family stirred with this trouble; Ruth's mother was full of sensitive suggestions, and her father was thoughtful and grave. Ruth swam at the edges of this quiet consternation, indignant for her father and conscious of a mild but growing sense of rebellion. She was ashamed of the ceremony. That couldn't be helped, she decided; nevertheless she admired it. It was pure and good-hearted. Perhaps it was misjudged. But it made Richard so angry. When Ruth asked him why, he wouldn't say. There was nobility in that, too. He vacillated, unsure (she suspected) of her loyalties. She promised not to tell her father, and he said, 'It isn't that.'

On the evening of the ceremony they sat together on the terrace. He was quiet, and smoked, which kept the mosquitoes away. No one had seen him all day. Ruth sat beside him, desperately curious and tending towards comprehensive admiration. There wasn't a part of his body that didn't move her: his firm shoulder, the tic of his tapping foot, his calm eye. The smoke rose around their heads. Their arms weren't touching – but Ruth was conscious of them almost touching. There was that atmospheric sympathy. Wasn't he aware of all this: their arms, the moonlight, the smoke? A dog barked. After the foot washing, Ruth and her parents had eaten a lunch of Easter lamb imported from New Zealand. Richard's place at the table was empty, and Ruth, digging her fork among the lamb's sturdy grey fibres, couldn't bring herself to wonder where he was eating. Now she asked him.

'Where did you eat today?'

'At Andrew Carson's,' said Richard.

'Why?'

'They invited me.'

Ruth considered and then spoke. 'Did you complain to them about my father?'

'No. No, I annoyed them all enough without mentioning your father. They all think your father's a saint. He probably is.'

'How did you annoy them?'

'Oh, politics.' Richard waved his hand with the cigarette in it. 'All this repatriation business – get rid of the Indians, get rid of the Chinese. Send them home or give them the Marquesas, just get them out of here. Let them all kill each other somewhere else, and leave Fiji to the Fijians.' He was silent for a moment. 'And the English.'

'You don't agree.' Ruth knew he didn't agree; they had talked this through before. Ruth never cared so much as when she cared with him.

'I'm tired of controversy today,' he said. 'I think I'd better just go to bed.'

'Not yet,' said Ruth. 'Not until you tell me why my father's so wrong.'

Richard looked at her in a patient way, but it was enough to shake her heart. He seemed to be taking her measure. He had not yet kissed her at the ball.

'All right,' he said. 'All right, tell me something: When does he give them a chance to wash *his* feet? Is it that he's the greatest, the noblest servant of them all? This privilege of service! He calls himself a servant and I know he's referring to certain ideas – abasement, humility, sacrifice, the servant Christ, that whole Christian model of service – I know all that, but hasn't he ever stopped to think that he's in a country where people work and live every day as servants, for him? You have a houseboy! He doesn't wash your father's feet in a great public show – he scrubs dishes every night when no one's there to see him. I'm sorry, it infuriates me. No, but I'm not sorry – God!'

And no one spoke this way; no one grew angry. Ruth was astonished, and in her admiration became clumsy and receptive. None of what he said surprised her; she'd begun to think most of these things herself. But she had never heard a respectable man blaspheme, and this made the strongest impression. She would at that moment have ceded the Church, her family and Fiji and fled with him in pilgrim haste to any land of his choosing – if only he would ask her. But he didn't, so she remained loyal and, as a result, defensive; it was the same impulse that made her ashamed of her father's audible knees.

'You haven't been here long enough to understand about servants,' she said, but that sounded feeble (she had heard so many people say it to newcomers before), so she continued, 'and what else should he do? No foot washing at all? Just hope they all know he doesn't think he's above them?'

Ruth shifted and touched Richard's arm with her elbow, which produced no sensation. But she wanted him to put his hand on hers and agree with her.

'This morning,' he said, 'I drove that bloody truck over those bloody roads because somebody told somebody else who told me that a pregnant woman collapsed at Nasavu – and they wouldn't let me near her, they said the problem was caused by walking on uneven land and she'd go to the temple and be fine, and meanwhile I'd blown a tire, I rode back to Suva with a bloody monarchist, Fijians are all monarchists, and the truck's still out there, I'll have to get myself back tomorrow, and I told you I should go to bed. I really should go to bed.'

And he stood and kissed her on the top of her head, which was nothing at all; she was at her most chaste when she was angry with him, or embarrassed, or particularly in love, and at this moment she was all three. Also, she felt very young.

'Can we talk about this tomorrow?' he said. And then, because he was kind: 'You're absolutely right, about everything, probably, but I couldn't be fair to you tonight. I'm far too sad.'

This astonished her. What was there for Richard to feel sad about?

There had been another moment like this, Ruth remembered, without mentioning it to Frida: on the boat to Sydney. Richard was returning to take up a position with the World Health Organization; Ruth was 'going home', as her parents called it, to find work. She spent the trip in terror that nothing would happen with Richard; that nothing would happen with her whole life. She knew, foolishly, that she had counted on being her parents' daughter forever, even while she contemplated such things as university or teaching or nursing (could she be a nurse, like her mother? Would she really go back to Fiji as a teacher? She vacillated on this point daily). And the trip passed, and on a September morning she stood next to Richard on the deck where schoolgirls played paddle tennis. She looked out at the Heads of Sydney Harbour and said, 'Apparently I'm going to have to *be* something.'

'It's terrible, isn't it,' said Richard, 'this having to be something.'

And Ruth was astonished that a man so obviously *something* – a doctor, a soldier, the saviour of Indian women – could sound so sad about it. But he had held her hand twice on the boat, once to steady her in a rough sea and once for three minutes because she'd been stupid enough to cry a little about leaving Fiji. He had sought her out with drinks and, as the weather grew colder the farther they sailed from the equator, brought rugs for her knees. They were sitting on the sundeck, and because she wore gloves, which might hide a ring, a man had smiled at them and assumed – Ruth was sure – they were married. And Richard had kissed her at the ball for the Queen, although she wondered sometimes if she had imagined that. None of it was enough, but it was a beginning – the passage over, and Sydney waiting, this city Ruth belonged in without knowing anything about it. Richard would show her Sydney, and she would love him, and he would love her back.

The boat entered the Harbour. The wide, bright city crowded

up against the water, but drew back from its very edge; Ruth saw green parklands full of trees with white flocks of parrots bursting out of them. The parrots surprised Ruth, who had expected Sydney to be much more like England than Fiji. And then Richard leaned forward against the railing of the deck and spoke so that she couldn't see his face, but the wind still carried every word he said, and what he said was that he was engaged to be married.

'To whom?' asked Ruth, and Richard had to turn and ask her to repeat herself.

'Her name is Kioko,' he said, which sounded to Ruth like *Coco*, and she pictured a bright blond girl with the kind of brilliant, beautiful face that produces its own light (Ruth's own face only reflected light, like the moon), and she was more surprised – at first – that Richard could love a girl called Coco than she was by the fact that Richard loved anyone at all. There was a strong gagging pulse in her throat.

'Congratulations,' she said, with a stiff smile; she didn't trust herself to ask questions. They were surrounded now by the schoolgirls, waving landwards with their paddles; Ruth felt much older than all of them.

The wind was making Richard's nose run. 'I met Kioko in Japan,' he said. 'She's a widow. She's Japanese.'

'That's nice,' said Ruth, tight-lipped but dignified, she thought, which mattered most. She thought.

'She's Japanese,' he said, 'which is why I didn't talk about it. I wasn't sure – well – what you'd think. All of you.'

Ruth pretended not to have heard him. She shook against the railing but had no intention of crying. The main thing was to extricate herself without revealing the extent of her agony.

Now Richard turned to look at her – to properly look. He cleared his throat and squinted. 'I'm sorry,' he said.

'Oh, whatever for?' cried Ruth, smiling too much and taking a step away from him because she thought he was going to touch her arm. 'Maybe I should go and —' She couldn't think what she should go and do; she had told him a number of times how much she was looking forward to the passage through the Harbour.

'She's going to meet the boat,' said Richard. 'I'd like to introduce you.'

So he and Kioko had exchanged letters with plans and arrangements: I'll be on this boat, I can't wait to see you, there'll be a child with me, a silly girl who hates opera, I'm afraid you'll have to meet her. Ruth saw the soft, admiring faces of all those girls to whom she had boasted about sailing to Sydney with Richard Porter. At that moment, those faces seemed worse than Richard's. The green and grey city tilted at the end of the boat.

'That would be lovely,' lied Ruth.

She felt like stepping off the boat and walking back to Suva across the bottom of the sea. But she planned to be kind and unshakeable, an emissary from her parents, a testament to the marvellous work Richard had done among the Indian women of Fiji; she wouldn't have him think she disapproved of his marrying a Japanese widow, or that she cared about his kissing her at the ball when all the time he was engaged. Perhaps it might be possible, however, in the crowded rush to leave the boat, to meet her flustered uncle and collect her luggage; surely it might be possible to lose Richard, to look only half-heartedly for him – where *could* he have got to? – and not to meet Kioko after all.

And that turned out to be true. Richard was almost too easy to lose, as if he dreaded the meeting himself. Ruth stumbled among her luggage and in the arms of her sentimental aunt, and she was almost sure she didn't see Kioko. There *was* a dark-haired woman waiting in a yellow dress, but she didn't look definitely Japanese. Ruth went home with her relatives to a street lined with heavy mauve jacarandas, to a borrowed bedroom warming in the mild sun, and cried into a pillow that smelled of someone else's hair.

That was a painful hour, and in the midst of it she was self-possessed enough to hope it had taught her humility. Really her heart had been broken in the most inconspicuous way. She had never risked it (she knew this later and had moments of regret). That no one knew she was suffering was both her triumph and, in part, the cause of her torment. After a terrible week or two, it was a very governed torment. In some ways, she passed with relief from the shadow of Richard's opinions, his disapproval and his industry. She was never quite sure how he had made her a less interesting person. Was it nerves? Or did he bore her? She attended his wedding four months later with a tight heart. His imminent wife had dark hair arranged around an oblong forehead. How would it feel to walk down the aisle towards his opening face? She refused all his subsequent attempts to see her, citing busyness; and she was busy, working as a secretary for her parents' missionary society, moving into a flat with some other girls, making resolutions to be like them, to wear the shoes they did and read their magazines, to be just like every other girl in wide, clean, temperate Sydney. She suspected, at times, that Richard would disapprove, and so she made an effort to think about him less, until eventually it was no effort at all. Ruth used to overhear her mother counselling the brokenhearted nurses. 'There are plenty of fish in the sea,' she would say, and from her biblical mouth it sounded like wisdom literature. Now Ruth said fondly to herself, 'There are bigger fish in the sea than me.'

For six months she wore the right shoes and read the right magazines and went out with the right men. Then she met Harry during a work event at which she was guardian of the sandwiches. He had come with his parents, who were missionaries in the Solomons. He seemed to have a great appetite for sandwiches; he ate at least four before asking if he could see her again. And he was kind, and handsome, and effortless. It was as if they had both been raised in the same country – Missionary Childhood – and were now finding their way together in the real world. Harry liked to say, 'Isn't it amazing how *normal* we are?' – which prompted a happy spasm in Ruth's grateful heart. She liked to be reassured. They kissed and courted, and Richard receded; they married, and Richard wasn't invited. Although their parents were missionaries, religion was, for both of them, a private matter; in comparison to their parents' difficult, foreign faith and the vigour with which they had pursued it, their own attempts seemed feeble and best concealed. They fell, together, out of the habit of belief. They liked the same furniture and paintings, the same music, and the same food, and this made for the easeful establishment of their household. When Ruth recalled this early period of her marriage – and she often did – the impression was of an existing happiness that had only been waiting for them to enter into it.

Frida rocked back onto her heels. 'There,' she said, with the same beatific look on her face as when she finished cleaning the floors. She lifted Ruth's feet from the basin and dried them with a thorough towel, and then she rubbed in moisturiser. Her hands were slick and strong. Ruth rested her head against the recliner. She closed her eyes. Frida hummed as she rubbed, and there was only safety in the world, and Richard coming tomorrow, in the best of health for eighty.

8

Ruth, stepping into the garden on the morning of Richard's arrival, was reminded of spring, as if spring were a season that took place distinctly in her part of the world. The air was sweet and dry and green. The house was clean, the cupboards were full of food, and a vase of wattle blossoms stood on the dining-room table. Frida had cut them from a tree at her mother's house; they emitted their own subtle light. Richard was due that evening.

The only flaw in all this beauty was the discovery of a sticky presence on one of the lounge cushions: cat-deposited, which inspired Frida to a brief rant about the cats' gastrointestinal hold over the house (she was convinced their messes were deliberate attacks on her own person). But after all, that was easily solved: Frida sponged the cushion, turned it over, and seemed to forget it had ever happened. She was in an exceptional mood. She was busy and in control without being domineering; she asked Ruth's opinion on everything, fluffed cushions and her currently curly hair, and fussed over Jeffrey's room, where Richard would sleep. She and Ruth made the bed together, using the best, slightly yellowed linen sheets – Frida had ironed them, and spread out and tucked in, they reminded Ruth of well-buttered bread.

The entire house waited expectantly, as if the food and ironed sheets and clean windows were secrets it would be compelled to reveal by delightful means. Frida spent the afternoon cooking, so Ruth swept the garden path clean of sand. She was proud of the smooth sun over her hair and shoulders, the familiar arc of the sea, and the beauty of her house on the hilltop. Her back hurt; she thought about taking an extra pill, but chose not to; she worried the pills made her foggy at times, and she wanted clarity this weekend. She changed into a blue skirt she could belt at her becoming waist and settled to wait in her chair. Waiting was difficult under these circumstances. The sense that something important was going to happen rose in Ruth's chest as if a wind were blowing there.

Richard knocked at the door rather than ringing the bell. Because Ruth didn't hear him knock, it was a moment before she realised that Frida's bustle to the front hallway was in response to his arrival. By the time Ruth reached the front of the house, Frida had taken his bag and coat, and the sound of a car in the lane was George's taxi driving away. Ruth stepped from the door into the front garden, where Richard waited for her. He was older, yes, and he wore glasses, but he was still discernibly Richard, and her heart quickened just as it had when she'd watched him run in from a Fijian rainstorm, except that she was not nervous, or frightened, and she intended to be bold. He held his hands out to hers, and she took them. They kissed on the cheek as if they had always greeted each other this way, and as Frida passed through the door with his luggage, Richard took Ruth's arm to lead her into the house. They spoke together softly and with great happiness: it's so wonderful to see you, it's so good to be here, my goodness, you look marvellous, so do you, just like yesterday, I can't believe it.

'This is exactly how I imagined you to live,' said Richard. He stood without effort in the lounge room of Ruth's house, and Ruth surveyed with him the paintings of pale cattled hillsides, the antique *masi* framed above the fireplace, and the photographs of her children and grandchildren smiling out from among green glassware. She saw evidence of comfort, happiness, and a well-lived life. Richard seemed so inevitable in that room, so welcome, that she hugged him again, and he laughed at her; they laughed together and sat holding hands on the lounge. Frida was making noises in the kitchen.

'Let me look at you properly,' said Richard, and instead of hiding her face in her arm, as she might once have done, Ruth looked back; she held her breath and lengthened her neck while she did so.

His hair had thinned and whitened, but he still had a great deal of it, and perhaps for this reason he'd let it grow longish, so that it stood out from his head in an ectoplasmic cloud. His forehead was high, just as she remembered, and she felt relieved for him that his hairline had barely receded. They'd been young together, and now they were old; because there was nothing in between, this strange telescoping of time gripped Ruth's heart like vertigo. She was touched again by the flattening of his nostrils where they met his cheek, the particular tuck of his smallish chin, and the familiar way he smoothed his trousers out with the palms of his hands. It all reminded her of the night he'd criticised her father for washing feet.

'Do you smoke still?' she asked.

'Not for years.'

'Good,' she said, mindful of his lungs, but she was also disappointed. She wanted to see him smoke again; she had a pretty idea that young Richard would rise up out of those particular gestures – the lift of his wrist and the tap of the ash – and declare himself. Then she remembered his wife had died of lung cancer, and was mortified; she recalled giving Harry this news, and Harry responding by talking about the low incidence of lung cancer among Japanese smokers, so that Kioko Porter's death seemed doubly unlucky, a terrible consequence of having left Japan. Ruth sat, immobilised, while Richard told her about his journey: the traffic in Sydney, the train delayed. Perhaps he and Jeffrey would get on after all. She began to worry that he should never have come.

'Dinner is served,' announced Frida, and Richard stood; Ruth saw his hand go without thinking to button a jacket he hadn't worn for decades.

'Oh, Richard, this is Frida, my dear Frida,' said Ruth. She was gushing, but she pulled herself together. 'Frida Young, Richard Porter.'

Richard extended his hand to Frida, who took it with a solemnity Ruth had become accustomed to; she saw Richard's surprise at it. The two of them, shaking hands, seemed to be agreeing to a matter of national importance on which Frida had forced Richard to compromise. Ruth noticed how trim he still was as he held out his hand and was relieved by the size of her own waist, if not by the plump stomach that swelled underneath it. Richard offered her his arm, and she took it, and they walked that way to the dining table.

At dinnertime, Frida moved between the kitchen and dining room with an efficient, soundless skill. Ruth asked her to join them, but she shook her head and hands in a gracious pantomime. No, her smile said, softer at the corners than Ruth had ever seen, I wouldn't dream of it. Perhaps she was one of these women who behaved differently around men. Had Ruth really never seen Frida with a man? She thought of Bob Fretweed, who seemed too perfunctory to really count as a man; she thought of Frida bending into the taxi window to laugh with George. But George was her brother. Frida dished up beans and poured gravy and retreated to the kitchen, where she hummed as she went about cleaning counters that were already clean. Ruth disapproved of this pointless industry. A triple-cleaned house, in her opinion, looked too much as if it had been licked all over by a cat's antiseptic tongue.

Ruth found it strange to eat a meal with Richard, in a dining room, without her parents present. Because she was determined not to start out with reminiscences – she was afraid of seeming sloppy and sentimental – she was worried there would be nothing to say. Fortunately there were children to discuss. They both seemed to have raised reassuringly ordinary children; there were no drastic prodigies among them. His eldest daughter was a doctor.

'Sometimes she reminds me of you,' said Richard. 'She's so

stubborn, in the best way. I always thought you'd make a good doctor.'

Frida was clearing the plates now, and Richard leaned over the empty table to touch Ruth's hand. His skin hadn't spotted with age, as hers had; it was a clear, folded brown. From behind him, Frida raised inquisitive eyebrows. She shook her head as she went to the kitchen, as if tut-tutting the flagrant ways of the very young.

'What made you think I'd be a good doctor?' asked Ruth.

'I watched you help in the clinic. But it's not just that. You have the right sort of mind: so clear and kind.'

'Not clear anymore.' Ruth shook her head as if to settle a cloudy liquid.

Richard laughed. He said, 'I feel sometimes as if every part of me is different to what it was then. I feel unrecognisable.'

'Oh, no,' said Ruth. 'You're just the same.'

'Really? That's good to know.' He still held her hand, which Ruth found both delightful and embarrassing. She wanted to point out that actually, as a young man, he had never touched her so readily as this. He needed something else from her now, or was more willing to demonstrate that need, or was softer and more sentimental. But he was still Richard. Ruth suggested they move to the lounge room; Richard sat beside her on the couch. Her leg touched his, so she shifted it. It was silly to be shy; she was annoyed at herself, but couldn't seem to help it. She asked questions about Sydney, and he asked questions about her house, and he didn't touch her again.

Frida came in to say goodnight. She stood by the lounge-room door, demure in her grey coat, and Ruth went to her and put a hand against her cheek.

'Thank you for everything, my dear,' Ruth said, and Frida nodded. She seemed bashful. Then she moved out into the hallway and closed the door behind her.

'You're very lucky to have found her,' said Richard.

'It was more the other way around,' said Ruth. 'She found me.'

'Tell me,' said Richard.

Ruth found she didn't want to. She disliked remembering the day of Frida's arrival, without being sure why. 'Oh, you know, the government sent her. Isn't it marvellous? She just showed up. She's basically heaven-sent.'

'A deus ex machina.'

'Yes, yes.' Ruth was annoyed by the flourish with which Richard produced this phrase, a phrase he had once taught her. 'But really, she just came from Fiji.'

'From Fiji? What an amazing coincidence. What was she doing there?'

'She's *from* Fiji,' said Ruth. 'She's Fijian.'

Richard looked towards the door as if Frida might reappear, conveniently, to display her features for him. 'She doesn't look it,' he said.

'You don't think so?'

'I don't know. I suppose if you asked me where she was from, I wouldn't know where to say.'

'I never wanted to be the kind of person who would say, "I couldn't do without her," but I think now that I am.'

'These things creep up on you, don't they,' said Richard.

Ruth wondered who had crept up on him. Her chest tightened – she felt for a minute as she had on the boat in Sydney Harbour, being told about a girl named Coco – and she changed the subject. 'You know, you couldn't have come in a better month,' she said. 'You're here just in time for the whales.'

At this time of the year, southern humpbacks travelled down the coast. They lingered sportively off the headlands and frequently came farther into the bay. When Ruth, younger and subtler of spine, walked down the dune and onto the beach, it had always felt to her that she was going out ceremoniously to meet them. She thought they knew she was paying them court. Phillip came one year and paddled a sea kayak out to get a better look; Harry called to him from the shore in a forlorn monotone, 'Too close! Too close!' The whales' unearthly sounds, urgent and high-pitched, conjured the night cries of wrecked sailors.

It had always been one of Ruth's greatest pleasures to show her guests the whales. She liked to line visitors up on the window seat in the dining room, each of them looking with narrowed eyes out to sea; she passed around pairs of inherited binoculars, all of which had been held to missionary faces in the Pacific; invariably her guests became so agitated that finally, whatever the weather, they rushed outside in an effort to get closer to the water. Everyone shouted when a spout went up, and Ruth felt happily responsible for the communal, mammalian mood on the beach. She looked forward to seeing Richard see the whales, and leaned with relief into his shoulder when they said goodnight in the hallway. He said, 'I'm so glad to be here.' The visit hadn't been a mistake; it would be all right. It would be more than all right. Ruth closed the door to the lounge room. She slept thankfully in her bed.

But in the morning there was rain, and it obscured the view. The sea from the windows was crooked and fogged, with no sign of whales. There were still surfers down at the town beach, and Ruth observed them from the dining room with uncharacteristic bitterness.

'Rain or shine, there they are,' she said, peering out at the blurry sea. She wondered if the boy who had sold her the pineapple was among them. 'Don't they have jobs?' In better weather – in better moods – she approved of their tireless leisure.

Frida cleared the breakfast plates.

'Thanks, Frida,' said Richard. 'It's a long time since I ate such a good big breakfast.'

Frida smiled with pleasure but said nothing.

They stayed in the dining room; Ruth sat in her chair and Richard on the long window seat. The house was peaceful in the rain. The air was comfortable and warm. Frida lit lamps against the dullness of the day, brought tea and shortbread, and worked in the kitchen preparing lunch. She was so far from the Frida of the diet and the floors; her hair was an ordinary brown and she wore it demurely, half up and half down. This placid Frida was efficient as ever, quiet but never invisible. Her presence filled the house with calm, so that Ruth forgot the whales and relaxed into the day with Richard. He was attentive to her and to their shared past, and Ruth took great pleasure in speaking with someone who had known her as part of her family, who had known her parents, and who had seen them all together in Fiji. She could think of no other living person who was capable of remembering her in this way. They talked about her father, about his busy hopes for his clinic and the world, and the quiet, good, regretful way he left both of these places. Ruth reminded Richard about his refusal to participate in the foot washing, and he laughed and said, 'I was such a snob.'

'You were wonderful. At least, I thought so.'

'You were quite wonderful yourself,' he said. 'But very young.'

So, as if she were still young enough to be hurt by being accused of youth, she said, 'You're much older now than my father was then.' Richard gave a good-natured grimace. 'I used to curse you in Hindi, you know,' she said. 'I thought you wouldn't understand me.'

'I understood you,' said Richard. 'And so did your mother. She knew her Hindi from the servants.'

'Oh, dear.'

'We're so transparent when we're young.'

Ruth was horr ified for her young self. He must have known she loved him all along, just by looking – even once – at her devoted face.

'But you stopped when my Hindi improved,' Richard said. 'I remember the day you realised I knew more than you did. You heard me speaking to one of my patients.'

Frida brought them more tea, and the rain still fell over the dim, indistinguishable sea.

'Have you ever been to India?' he asked. Ruth hadn't. 'I have, twice, and when I first arrived, I tried to speak what I remembered of my Fiji Hindi. They only understood every fifth word.'

'I've never even been back to Fiji,' said Ruth. She knew Richard had because he'd sent her a postcard, Fiji-stamped, about five years after her parents retired to Sydney. It was a photograph of the Grand Pacific Hotel, and it said, 'I miss my Fijians – your mother, your dad, and you.' She was a married woman by then, a mother, but still capable of wondering if the hotel postcard was some reference to the kiss at the ball. Overanxious, she hid the card from Harry.

'Why not?'

'At first I couldn't afford it,' Ruth said. 'And then, when I could – when we could – there were so many other places to go.'

'There's some sense in not going back. That way, you preserve it.'

'Maybe you shouldn't have come here.' Ruth laughed. 'You can't preserve me now.'

'Oh, I can,' said Richard. 'I have an excellent memory of you as a teenager, and nothing will change it.'

'What do you remember?'

'Let's see. I remember you reading *Ulysses* faster than anyone in the world has ever read it.'

And then Ruth remembered reading *Ulysses*, which Richard treasured and had brought with him from Sydney. She was determined to read it; she'd never before worked so hard at anything. She remembered, too, that she and Richard had been young people discussing the existence of heaven (she said yes, he said no, but both admitted they had doubts – and that was the first time she realised she doubted). Oh, oh, and she remembered that in her anxiety to appreciate Bach she had found herself in love with Mozart and was ashamed of this for years, simply because Richard didn't love Mozart, until she read somewhere that Abraham Lincoln did. Then she felt herself bloom into the recognition of her own opinion. She'd read about Lincoln and Mozart in a biography of Lincoln that Harry had bought but never read. No, Jeffrey had bought it for Harry (who loved political biographies) as a Christmas present. There was also that particular passage of

Auden's she had loved – Caliban's song in a long poem, she'd forgotten the name of it – and made Richard read aloud for her, and
there was one line that he paused over: 'helplessly in love with
you'. She was overtaken by promise. Surely, surely, she thought
when he paused. And then he continued reading and afterwards
in conversation – just a few days later – Ruth realised he'd forgotten all about it, and she was furious at the way she fell in love with
small things that turned out to be meaningless. Where had all this
been waiting while she worked so effortlessly to forget it? She sat
trembling with gratitude for her brain, that sticky organ.

'You look very happy right now,' said Richard.

She ducked her head but lifted it again to look at him. 'I am
happy,' she said. 'I'm sorry I was in such a mood this morning.
I was disappointed about the weather.'

'The weather is perfect.'

When had she ever heard Richard describe something as perfect? He was looking back at her in a confidential way. If she'd
been told, at nineteen, that it would take over fifty years to have
him look at her like this, she would have been disgusted and heartbroken; now she was only a little sad, and it was both bearable and
lovely. She brushed Richard's arm with her hand.

Frida was quiet in the kitchen, so perhaps she was listening. Richard was talking about the smell of molasses over the
sugar mills, and Ruth told him about the time her mother took
her along to a game of contract bridge with the CSR wives in a
sugar town outside Suva. They sat at little tables while their children ate sausage rolls and scones, and because Ruth's father wasn't
a company officer – wasn't in the company at all, and not even a
government doctor – certain children didn't bother talking to her.

That was the only time her mother played bridge.

'My mother would have loved all that,' said Richard. 'I think she would have managed very well in one of those hierarchical little sugar towns. She would have treated it like some kind of siege.'

'You had to be ruthless.'

'She was. Once my brother was invited to the birthday party of a schoolfriend, but he was too sick to go. I would have been about eight, I think, and he was ten. She made me pretend to be my brother because she wanted to be on good terms with the parents of the birthday boy. She'd been waiting for an invitation to the house, was the thing, and this party was going to be the only way. So we arrived, and the other children knew I wasn't my brother, obviously, but my mother called me James and eventually they did, too.'

'But why?'

'They were well-to-do, well connected, these people. It was an enormous house. I remember being impressed into submission. Invitations of that kind were very important to my mother. She could invite *them* to parties after that.'

This story bothered Ruth; she wanted to swat it away. She didn't like to hear Richard compare his childhood to her own. His childhood was Sydney: liver-coloured brick, ferries on the water, leashed dogs, women pegging out washing on square lines in square gardens.

Richard leaned forward on the window seat. 'It's a relief, isn't it, not to worry about those things anymore. My wife used to complain about the casualness of everything, but I prefer it. Don't you? Kioko ended up getting on very well with my mother.'

Ruth didn't like to hear him criticise his wife either, however gently. She felt that she should respond with a complaint about Harry, and couldn't. How ridiculous, she thought, to be sitting here and worrying about being unfaithful to Harry. But she laid her arm out on the table so that her small white wrist was turned up towards Richard. If he looks at it, she thought – and before she could decide what his looking might mean, he looked.

'I used to throw parties in Sydney,' said Ruth, 'but I was never very good at it. I used to wake up on the morning of the party and think, Damn it, why did I do this again? But Harry loved parties. Then we moved out here and there was no one to throw parties for.'

'How long did you live here together?'

'Just over a year,' said Ruth. Really it was such a little time. 'I always planned to be one of those old women who kept very busy. You know – involved in things, taking classes, cooking elaborate dinners, visiting friends. And I was, in Sydney. I was working – well, *work* isn't the right word – I was helping at a centre for refugees. I taught elocution, did you know? I still had private students, and I taught pronunciation classes at the centre. Then we came out here, because Harry was set on it. He retired so late, which I always knew he would, and what he wanted was to rest by the sea. He'd say, "I'm ready to put my feet up, Ruthie." But of course when we got here, Harry spent all day gardening and walking and fixing things up in the house, and we would drive to this lighthouse or that historic gaol, and the boys came at Christmas and we visited the city. He could just generate busyness for himself. But I'm not like that. Especially not without him. I came out here and just sort of – stopped.'

'That seems a shame,' said Richard. Ruth felt, for a minute, as if he had called her a bad book or a bad play, but he was no longer that man; he was tired, she thought, and it had loosened him. He had been tired by the difficulty of having to be something.

'I don't know,' said Ruth. 'Everyone expected me to go back to Sydney after he died. I mourned so beautifully in every other way, they expected me to be rational about that. Or they thought I should move to be near one of my boys, or that the boys should move back home. But Phil is completely tied up in Hong Kong, and Jeffrey's father-in-law is very ill in New Zealand, and I wouldn't let them. And I turned out to be the one who wanted to rest by the sea.'

The rain stopped in the afternoon. Ruth and Richard stood out on the dune with binoculars, looking for whales. Ruth was in suspense. If we see a whale, she decided, then nothing will happen between us. If we see two, then everything will happen. She was unsure what she meant by *everything*. There were no whales.

Frida had roasted a pork loin and sweet potatoes for dinner. She set it all out on the table and refused to eat, no matter how Ruth and Richard pleaded.

'No! No!' Frida insisted, and laughed as if she were being tickled; she sounded pained and unwilling.

'Then at least leave the dishes,' said Ruth. 'We can sort those out ourselves.'

Frida objected and then acquiesced. Ruth noticed that Frida had trouble looking at Richard. Whenever he spoke to her, she looked to the left of his face and patted her neat hair. She took her coat from the hook in the kitchen, mumbled, *'Bon appétit,'* and went down the hall. The front door opened and closed.

Now Ruth was ready for something to happen. She kept her

hopes vague. Richard was in the best of health. He ate with good appetite and laughed a great deal while telling her about the one and only time his daughter took him to a yoga class. He promised to cook Ruth a Japanese meal. It grew dark on the dune, and Ruth drew the lounge-room curtains while Richard closed the seaward shutters. Neither of them made any attempt to clear the table of dishes. They settled in the lounge room, where Ruth regretted her decision to sit in an armchair and not next to him on the couch. Her nineteen-year-old self would have made the same mistake.

'I was thinking the other day about that ball we went to for the Queen,' she said.

'So was I,' said Richard. He sat on the end of the couch closest to her, and his hands were clenched and unnaturally still on his knees. That's how he quit smoking, thought Ruth, by forcing himself to keep his hands still. That's how he would have done it.

'I still have my menu somewhere. I saved it,' she said, although now that she mentioned it, she was certain Frida had made her dispose of everything of that kind in the spring-cleaning of her early employment.

'What were you thinking, about the ball?' asked Richard.

'I was thinking about you kissing me, of course. How much I liked it.'

'Why were we even there? Why was I even invited?'

'All kinds of people were invited. I remember someone getting upset about it – about your being invited and my parents left out. Do you think they minded? I thought they probably didn't care.'

'And I whisked off their daughter and kissed her.' Richard laughed at himself. 'I thought I was so old and wise and you were so young. I was very ashamed of myself.'

'So you should have been. With your secret fiancée and every-thing.'

'You're teasing me,' said Richard. 'And I think I was drinking. Was I drinking?'

'Everyone was drinking,' said Ruth. 'I never saw a group of people so willing to toast the Queen.' Ruth felt herself lit with the pleasure of laughing with him. It was so good to flirt; it made her think that flirting should never be entrusted to the very young. 'And listen – I told you a moment ago how much I liked you kiss-ing me, and you didn't even say thank you.'

'What I should have said was how much I liked kissing you.' Richard bowed his head at her, courtly. It was ridiculous! And wonderful. Richard in his twenties would never have talked like this. When had he become so much less serious? Even their kiss at the ball had been serious. What we should have done, thought Ruth, was sleep together on the boat back to Sydney and then been done with it, since it would have been a mistake to marry his bad books and good plays. But this, now, was delightful.

'What made you do it?' Ruth asked.

'You were so lovely, of course. Like a milkmaid, remember? And I was thinking – well, I was drinking, but also I was think-ing how sweet and straightforward it would have been to love you. You even looked like a bride, in your white dress.'

'It was pale blue,' said Ruth. 'And why straightforward?'

'Less complicated,' said Richard. He moved his hands; this movement was the first evidence of any nervousness. 'It's all so long ago, it's hard to imagine. Kioko's family disowned her, and the first house we lived in together – well, the neighbours got together and put Australian flags in their windows and refused to speak to us. We expected it, but nothing prepares you. If I'd married someone like you, they would have come to us with cakes and babies.'

'So it wasn't me in particular,' said Ruth. He'd kissed her to see how it felt to be simple and safe; why hadn't she thought of that?

'It was nobody else but you,' he said. The room was quiet. 'I really was ashamed of myself.'

'I was heartbroken,' said Ruth. When she saw his genuine surprise, she smiled and cried, 'Let's have a drink! To toast our reunion. There's still some of Harry's Scotch.'

'All right,' said Richard.

'It's good Scotch.'

'Lawyers always have excellent Scotch.'

'Now where' – Ruth stood up with a small frown and moved towards the liquor cabinet – 'has Frida put the tumblers? She's always moving things around.'

'You seem to manage very well out here,' said Richard.

Ruth was proud to hear this. She poured the drinks and sat down next to him on the couch. Proceedings had a promising air. The Scotch tasted shuttered and old and golden.

'You seem very sufficient to me,' said Richard.

'Self-sufficient?'

'I think you and Frida together are a sufficiency. You're like a little world, a little round globe.'

'That sounds claustrophobic, actually.' Ruth added the cats to the population of this little world. They sat at Richard's feet without touching him. How still they were, how like artificial cats.

'I think it sounds wonderful. I like to think of her looking out for you at any given hour.'

'Not really at any given hour,' said Ruth. 'She goes home at night.'

'Really? I just assumed she lived in.'

'"Lived in"?' It's like we're discussing servants!'

'Isn't it,' said Richard mildly.

'Believe me, Frida's no servant. She's usually only here on weekdays, just for the morning. She leaves after lunch and then her brother, the mythical George, brings her back in the morning in his golden taxi. Young Livery, he calls it. I think it makes him sound like a youthful alcoholic.'

'The driver who brought me here?'

'Yes, of course, you met George! What was he like?'

'He's Frida's brother? Well, *he* certainly looks Fijian. He seemed – I don't know, self-possessed. He didn't talk much. So Frida's just staying over while I'm here, is that it? She seems very settled.'

'She's not staying at all,' said Ruth. 'What gave you that idea?'

'Well, her bedroom.' Ruth lifted her head like a wary cat; Richard paused with his glass at his mouth, as if she could hear an alarm that he, deaf but alert, still listened for. He said, with apology, 'I just assumed it was her bedroom.'

'Which room?'

'At the end of the hall.'

'Phil's room?' asked Ruth, but Richard didn't know the rooms by the names of her sons. He had never met her sons.

He said again, 'At the end of the hall.'

At the end of the hall Ruth found Frida, who earlier in the night had opened the front door in her grey coat and then closed it again behind her. In Phillip's room, Frida lived among her things. The room wasn't cluttered or in any way untidy, but it was distinctly inhabited: the furniture had been rearranged, unfamiliar postcards were stuck to the otherwise denuded walls, and her suitcase was tucked neatly on top of the wardrobe. Frida sat in a chair Ruth didn't recognise, soaking her feet in a basin of water and reading a detective novel. The knowledge that Frida's feet ached and that she enjoyed detective novels was almost as shocking to Ruth as the fact of Frida living – all the evidence suggested it – in her house. Frida laid down her book.

'What's going on?' said Ruth.

The upper half of Frida's body remained still, but she lifted her feet, one at a time, out of the basin of water and set them down on a towel spread on the floor. She had a steadfast quality, as if she had always been in this room and would always remain; it also seemed that she would never speak. In Frida's silence, Ruth heard the sound of Richard in the kitchen, turning on the taps and shuffling dishes.

'What are you doing in here?' asked Ruth, holding tightly to the doorknob.

'What does it look like I'm doing?' said Frida. 'Relaxing at the end of a long day.'

'But why are you *here*?'

'Why wouldn't I be here?'

'I saw you leave,' said Ruth.

'How could you see me leave when I didn't?'

'I *heard* you leave, then. I heard the front door. You came in with your coat and said goodnight.'

'I was taking the bins out,' said Frida. 'It's rubbish night.'

'With your coat?'

'Yep.' Then: 'It's cold out there.'

'I thought you were leaving.'

'You assumed I was leaving, obviously. Who knows why.'

'And why wouldn't I assume you were leaving? It's not as if you live here.'

'Oh, dear.' Frida lifted her feet from the towel, leaving two big damp marks. 'Oh, dear. You knew I was staying over, to help with Richard's visit. Remember?'

'I knew you were coming over the weekend,' said Ruth. 'Not staying.'

'And remember, we talked about George, all my trouble with George? And you said I could stay as long as I needed to. So here I am.' Frida spread out her hands as if her definition of *I* included not only her body, but the objects surrounding it, and in fact the entire room.

'That isn't true, Frida, what you're saying to me now, it's not true. I'd remember.' Ruth was certain, but there was a feeling of unravelling, all the same; an unwound thread. She did recognise the part about trouble with George.

'You know your memory's not what it used to be.'

'I do *not* know that,' said Ruth, but this felt like a confession of ignorance, an admission of something rather than an insistence upon its opposite.

Frida sat on the unfamiliar chair and looked at Ruth, impassive. Her obstinacy had a mineral quality. Ruth felt she could chip away at it with a sharp tool and reveal nothing more than the uniformity of its composition. But her own certainty that Frida was lying had a similar brilliance. Her mind felt sifted and clear; her clear and prismatic mind turned and turned over the fact that

Frida was lying. To know something so definitely was gratifying, and if this was true, what else might be? What other knowledge could Ruth be sure of, with such immaculate confidence? She was hungry, suddenly, for more certainties of this kind. All her life she'd been afraid of believing something untrue. It seemed like a constant threat: the possibility, for example, of believing in error that Christ had died for her sins. She turned with horror from the unlikely thing. It was so improbable that Frida would lie; that Richard could want Ruth after all this time; that the house could really be so hot and full of jungle noises and even, once, a tiger. Who would believe any of it? But it was true.

'You're embarrassing yourself,' said Frida, in a resigned voice. Her face was so still and blank, there seemed to be no Frida in it. Ruth wanted to make the face move again; or she wanted not to have to look at it.

'I want you to go home,' said Ruth. 'I want you to call George and get him to take you home. And then you can come back tomorrow morning and we'll sort it all out.'

'Are you serious?' Frida's eyes, at least, opened a little wider. 'Are you seriously kicking me out of your house in the middle of the night?'

'You heard me.' Ruth was horrified to hear herself say this, with all its false bravado: *You heard me*, as if she were in a movie. As if she hadn't spent her adult years teaching children not to say such empty things.

'Think very carefully,' said Frida. She leaned forward, her forearms on her knees, and Ruth realised that somehow their eyes were at the same level, although Frida was sitting and Ruth was standing. How small had she become? And how large was Frida?

Frida said, 'Think this through very carefully, Your Majesty, because if you make me leave now, I'm never coming back.'

Then she stood. She was enormous. She seemed to have risen up from the ocean, inflated by currents and tides, furious and blue; there was no end to her. Her hair had surrendered to some force of chaos and was now massed, unstyled, around her head. This was another new thing about Frida: her hair was loose and unbrushed. It added to the impression of divine fury. Ruth's fingers were tight on the doorknob.

'I won't put up with ultimatums, Frida,' she said, but she knew how tremulous she sounded, how chiming her voice was, like a small bell rung by the side of a sickbed.

'You're the one telling me to get out or else,' said Frida, leaning in towards Ruth's face. Then she wheeled away and threw her hands in the air; she adopted the mystified posture she always did when appealing to the sympathy of a phantom listener, and her face became itself again. 'You know what? This is one hundred percent typical. You do a good deed for a little old lady – I don't get paid extra for staying over, you know – and the old biddy kicks you out of her precious house in the middle of the night. All so she can cuddle up with her boyfriend. That's the real reason, isn't it?'

'It's not kicking you out if I never asked you to stay,' said Ruth.

'So he *is* your boyfriend.'

'He has nothing to do with this.'

'It's just a coincidence, then, that you're kicking me out when he's here? What's he going to think of that? And who's going to look after him and you tomorrow, huh? You going to cook for him? And for that matter, how exactly do you plan to get me out of here? You going to carry me? You and whose army?'

'You wouldn't dare,' said Ruth.

'Wouldn't dare *what?*'

Ruth didn't know. She pressed against the door. She wished Frida would just go quietly. That's what she hoped to do one day: go quietly.

'What I'm going to say to you right now is – get out of my room,' said Frida. She began to move towards Ruth. 'This isn't over, oh no. Maybe I'll leave tomorrow, maybe I won't. But tonight you're going to get out of my room and we're both going to have a good sleep – if I *can* sleep, after this – and we'll be having words in the morning, believe me.' Frida kept moving towards the door, so that Ruth was forced to step sideways to avoid collision. 'All right? No more orders from you – this is my time off. Right now you're nobody's boss. Got it?'

Frida wasn't threatening, exactly; a funny, frightening smile skewed her face. Then Ruth was in the hall and the door was shut; she was unsure if she had moved into the hall and shut the door, or if Frida had done one or both things for her. She knocked on the door, but not loudly, and Frida didn't answer. Something heavy was pushed against it. Ruth didn't dare knock again, or call out; she couldn't make any more of a fuss with Richard here.

But Richard seemed relaxed in the kitchen, finishing the dishes with his shirtsleeves rolled up to his skinny elbows. He displayed the sort of sweet, studied cheerfulness he might have perfected as the father of teenage daughters. He had rubbed wet hands through his cloudy hair and revealed his architectural ears – when had his ears become so large, like an old man's? If he'd been less helpfully serene, Ruth might have wept, or at least called upon his medical expertise: 'Please, Richard,' she might have said, 'how can I tell if

I'm losing my mind? Are there definite signs? Please, is there some kind of test? What would *you* say to an old woman who heard a tiger in her house at night, who forgot to wash her hair, who didn't notice her government carer had moved in?' But his whole manner was designed to convey to her that he had noticed nothing amiss about Frida and the guestroom; that he valued Ruth's dignity; that he didn't want to get involved. And so she thanked him for washing up, he deflected her thanks, and in a volley of pleasantries they said goodnight and went to their respective bedrooms alone.

The cats were buried under the quilt and twisted in protest when Ruth disturbed it by sitting on her bed. The bed seemed haunted, then, by phantom lumps of Harry: one turning arm, or a twitching foot. It was macabre and awful and stupidly comforting all at once, and just thinking of it embarrassed Ruth, what with Richard in Jeffrey's room. And Frida in Phillip's room. When had her house become so populated? Ruth, the cats, Frida, Richard. It occurred to her that Frida might actually do what she'd threatened: that she might leave. Ruth stretched out her feet – when she was sitting on the bed, they didn't quite touch the ground – and said, 'I've done it now, haven't I.' She saw her head speaking in the dresser mirror, and that was another thing she used to do: pretend to be Harry as he watched her move and speak. She turned her head away; she had no time for herself. Had she really forgotten that Frida was living in her house? But she had forgotten to wash her hair, and it was Frida who fixed it.

So the day was over, and Richard would leave tomorrow afternoon. The weekend was just like the boat to Sydney: days of promise with Richard on which nothing definitive happened. Now she had lost him again, because of Frida. But as she lay in bed and thought this through, and considered Frida reading a detective novel and soaking her feet, and remembered Richard's sad, smug explanation of the difficulties of having a Japanese wife and why that meant he was allowed to kiss whomever he felt like, her anger turned in his direction. Why had he come? And since he'd come, why was he only here for a weekend, when the days of the week didn't matter anymore? They were both old, and outside of time. She lay in bed, pinned by the cats, and fumed. And why had he told her Frida was in the house at night? Now she would lose Frida, thanks to him. She would lose him because of Frida, and Frida because of him; and with that thought, her last before sleep, the whole house emptied out.

9

Ruth woke late the next morning. The day was so clear that when she went into the kitchen she could see the town lighthouse from the dining-room windows. She called for Frida, and Richard answered. He came from the lounge room looking like Spencer Tracy: all that bright hair and good humour, only taller.

'Frida's gone out for the morning,' he said.

'Gone where?'

'She had some shopping to do. Her brother came in his taxi.'

'How did she seem?'

'Fine,' said Richard. He put his hands on her shoulders and

kissed her cheek good morning; she was far too distracted to enjoy
it.

'She's just gone to do some shopping,' said Ruth. Sufficient,
she thought; a little world. 'It was all just a misunderstanding.' She
resisted the temptation to run to Phillip's room – Frida's room – to
see if it was empty of Frida's possessions.

'These things happen,' said Richard.

He made her a cup of tea and sat on the window seat close to
her chair while she drank it. He touched her arm and her hair as
they talked about the weather and the day's activities: Ruth's back
was fine, the weather was fine, and they could walk on the beach
with binoculars and look for whales. They might even make it as
far as the northern headland. George wasn't coming for Richard
until the afternoon: they had hours yet. They talked about these
plans, but made no effort to execute them. Ruth couldn't help
thinking about Frida.

'Just a misunderstanding,' she said again. 'My memory's not
what it used to be.'

'Your memory is fine. Think what you remember about Fiji, all
those years ago.'

'But that's what they say about being old, isn't it? That you'll
remember things from years and years ago, and not what you ate
for breakfast. And sometimes I do – you know – imagine things.'

'You're not old,' said Richard. 'You're a girl in Fiji coming to
meet the new doctor.'

It was a silly and untrue thing to say, but Ruth ignored that;
she inclined her head towards the pleasure of it. He was looking at
her now in exactly the way she'd wanted him to when she was that
girl. Time and age were a great waste laid out before her; they had

also brought her here, so quickly, to Richard. But she was embarrassed by her pleasure, despite herself.

'Look at the birds,' she said, and finally Richard looked away from her and out the window. White and black seabirds gathered in particular places on the bay; they seemed all at once to throw themselves at the water and then rise again. 'The whales are there where the birds are – that's one way to spot them. Can you see anything? A spout? A tail?'

'No,' said Richard. 'But the birds are beautiful.'

'Look at everyone on the beach,' said Ruth. Weekend whale watchers stood motionless on the shore, and every now and then an arm would point, or someone would jump up and down. 'Should we go out?'

'I predict rain,' said Richard. 'Rain, rain, and more rain. Best to stay indoors.'

Ruth gave a small laugh and wouldn't look at him. Instead she watched the people on the beach, and when they turned and pointed in one direction, she looked there, hoping to see a whale, but saw only the slap of travelling waves. It was odd to watch this from the window without going out or using the binoculars. Harry would disapprove. But then Harry wasn't here.

Richard leaned closer and kissed her, on the side of her face at first, and then, when she turned towards him, on her mouth. He was so exact, his hands were so dry, and he gave out such a lonely heat. With the sea and the window and the birds over the water, it was like – but at the same time not at all like – daydreams Ruth had nourished in Fiji; it was as if her youthful tending of those dreams had been so timid that only now could they bear fruit. And of course her body had been through a great deal since then – sex, and childbirth, and the effort of fifty years – and its response to Richard bore little resemblance to that girlish pulse. A dry warmth came up to meet his. And stop thinking these things, she told herself, you are being kissed. Richard is kissing you; isn't this what you invited him for? You are a chaste and vain and sentimental old woman. She faltered and Richard drew away, but she pulled him back again by catching one hand on his shoulder.

'Frida?' he said.

'We'll hear the car.'

So she knew that she meant to do more kiss him. What confidence she had! In him, and in herself. She stood and said, 'Come with me.'

Richard took her hand and it felt as if she had lifted him from the window seat with her strength. They walked to her bedroom. Ruth didn't like seeing their reflections in the mirror, but she scolded herself: she knew it was ridiculous to be shocked by this kind of sensible sex. There was no one to ask, Can I have this? Is this allowed? It felt like swearing: something small and private she could pit against the orthodoxy of her life. But she didn't mean to sound ungrateful. She had refused a little of this, a little of that, until she found there was nothing much left to agree to; now she could agree to this.

They were both prepared to be practical. Ruth arranged the pillows on the bed the way she knew from experience would be best for her back, and Richard drew the curtains. Then, in the false twilight, they approached each other. There was no rush, and as a result no fumbling; she let him unbutton her shirt, but removed her bra herself. It was the sturdy, flesh-coloured kind that left ridges on her shoulders and torso, and her loosened breasts were powdery and white. He ran his hands over the crepe of her skin, as if he had grown old with it and knew every stage of its buckling. Then, still wearing her skirt, Ruth removed his glasses and helped him pull his shirt over his head, where it caught for a moment and submerged his face. She kissed his mouth through the cotton. Richard had a sweet, monkeyish, fluffy chest, and his breasts and stomach were puckered. It seemed important that they both be naked. They finished undressing and Richard stood as if holding his hands in his pockets while Ruth settled herself on the bed. Then he lay over her.

There was no sense of Harry in the room or in the bed; there was no sense of anything besides Ruth and Richard. There were noises, but Ruth didn't speak. Richard was tender and obliging and prudent. He would probably have been the same fifty years ago, but now there was an additional care, a familiarity, and a relief in not loving him except retrospectively. She had observed something similar about sex with Harry as they grew older: that nothing depended on it, not in the way it used to. Richard was so calm, and he was so graceful, although his frame was thin and his breath scraped over her face. He was good-humoured, too, and patient; they both were. They attempted little, so as not to be disappointed, and also because less was required, but Ruth bit the inside of her mouth because she felt more pleasure than she expected to. This made Richard kiss her on the shoulder. Richard! The cats might have been here or anywhere, and Frida might have come down the drive and walked in on them; but she didn't.

Afterwards, Richard helped her dress. They sat on the edge of her bed. He was still shirtless, and she saw moles on his lower back she'd never known were there.

'I wish I could stay,' he said.

'Why don't you?'

Richard pulled on his shirt and laughed, and she shook her head in order to say, Of course not.

'It's my granddaughter's birthday tomorrow,' he said. He held her hand and kissed it. 'I'm not going to ask you to marry me. I think it would be unfair to our children to muddy the whole question of inheritances. I mean, at our age. Do you mind my being practical?'

Ruth said, 'Not at all.' And she didn't.

Then he lay his head in her lap. She brushed back his hair so she could see the upturned dish of his ear.

'How would you feel about coming to live with me?' he asked.

Ruth saw herself sitting by Richard's bed. She watched him dying. Frida had once said of Harry, 'At least he spared you a sickbed,' and Ruth had been appalled. Now the weight of Richard's head in her lap was both heavy and dear. She pressed the hair above his flat ear and might have bent to kiss his forehead, but he sat up and said, apologetic, 'Sorry. I'm rushing things.' Then he was buttoning his shirt, and she saw how thick his fingernails had become, and how his hands shook. 'But you'll think about it?'

'Yes,' said Ruth. She stood up, aware of her calm, her lack of surprise, and her feeling not of great luck or pleasure but of amusement, as if someone had told her a slightly sad joke. None of this seemed urgent. They had waited half a century, so why were they talking like teenagers, as if they couldn't bear to be apart? But she would think about it.

They were both dressed now, and they brushed each other down, laughing, the way their mothers might once have done.

Together they walked through the house discussing possibilities. Ruth could come to Sydney in a few weeks. Richard could visit again. They could talk on the phone and write to each other. There might have been a conquering armada of whales in the bay, and they would never have noticed. In fact they avoided the sea and sat in the lounge room, where the white light of midafternoon flooded through the curtains, and Richard placed his right hand on Ruth's left knee and said, 'Please think about it.' They heard George's taxi in the drive, which surprised them both; he wasn't due for half an hour.

Frida had been gone long enough to do more than shopping, and Ruth was afraid for a moment that George was only here to pick Richard up; that this was his last act of service before he and his sister disappeared from Ruth's life altogether. But there was a bustle in the garden, and then at the front door, of plastic bags and exaggerated breath, and then Frida announcing that George had a fare and would be back for Richard at the appointed time.

'So what's news with you two?' She wore her grey coat and looked unusually jubilant.

Ruth and Richard smiled and shrugged.

Frida, distracted, was giddily confidential among her shopping bags. 'Well, *I* have news. Big news. Shark attack at the beach.'

Richard and Ruth, still dazed, struggled up out of their privacy. Richard managed, 'A shark!'

'Oh, dear,' said Ruth. And she made Frida tell every detail – it was years since the last attack, and the news would be in all the papers. He wasn't a local boy (not the pineapple boy, thought Ruth), but a surfer who came regularly from the city; he wasn't dead, not yet, but things were bad, loss of blood, and a leg that would most likely have to come off.

'He'll either wake up dead or one-legged,' said Frida, with a small grimacing laugh.

So the visit came to an end in the commotion of this disaster. They all went out into the garden and saw a helicopter flying low over the bay.

'They're tracking him,' said Frida.

'The boy?' asked Ruth.

'The shark.'

The knots of whale watchers scanned the sea in frantic sweeps. Frida walked down the dune towards them, and Ruth and Richard followed. Richard, gallant, held Ruth's elbow on the slope.

It seemed natural for the whale watchers to turn to Frida and call out, as she advanced over the sand, 'Is it a shark? A shark?' They gathered about her, and she answered all their questions with a festive confidence. A young girl in a wet bathing suit began to cry, and others took out their mobile phones to take photographs of the empty sea. There were no visible whales. There was instead a continuous scurfy roll of post-storm waves onto the shore. The helicopter produced an insectile buzz that came and went over the water. Richard held Ruth's hand as they watched it, finally, lift away from the bay; then the group on the sand disbanded.

Richard went to help Ruth climb the dune, but Frida took her arm from the other side and almost lifted her away from him. Richard walked behind them; he was like a small boy whose every attention is focused on how inessential he is. So he must make unnecessary noise, and Frida must wilfully ignore him, and Ruth must not notice, must climb the dune in Frida's arms with only the dune on her mind. But all the while she replayed the way he had put his hand on her knee and said, 'Please think about it.'

The taxi was waiting for Richard. Ruth even saw, for the first time, the bulky and unmediated form of mysterious George. His window was rolled down and there he sat, in shade, at the wheel, with one meaty forearm crooked into the pink of the sun. Frida made no move to speak with or introduce him. Richard's small suitcase was standing by the front door. That was the weekend over; it had passed without Ruth's noticing. She kept expecting something more to happen, and she supposed it had, but she was still in a state of anticipation. It was George who spoiled things; George who took people away. His taxi was waiting, so Richard must wheel his suitcase out, and Ruth must stand with Frida on the doorstep and smile.

'It's all right about last night,' said Frida.

'Of course it is,' said Ruth.

'What I mean is that I forgive you.'

Ruth and Frida held up their hands, and Richard waved from the back of the taxi, which reversed down the drive and vanished among the yellow grasses.

I O

Ruth became sick almost as soon as Richard left. She decided
these things were related, because of the timing – she couldn't keep
down the cup of tea Frida made her immediately after Richard's
departure – and because there was nothing specific about her illness. She was heartsick, possibly. It was too much to stir up her old
heart, she thought; in her less sentimental moments, she berated
herself for behaving like a schoolgirl, but remained quietly pleased
at this evidence of her continuing romantic sensitivity. Still, she
spent a few days in bed, always tired and rarely hungry, but never
with a fever or headaches or any particular pain besides her back;

she took her prescriptions and assured Frida that a doctor wasn't necessary and her sons needn't be alerted. Frida thought she had simply over-exerted herself with Richard; Ruth blushed, but Frida paid no attention.

Frida was a good nurse. She made soup and cleaned and checked on her patient in a sensible way, clinical rather than confiding. She exhibited no sympathy, but was never dismissive of Ruth's vague troubles. She kept Ruth's fluids up and, having quizzed Richard on the benefits of fish oil for elderly brains, introduced a large capsule fuzzily full of golden liquid. Ruth's only complaint was that Frida kept the cats from the bedroom. A new atmosphere of calm settled over the house; it was cool and clean, and noiseless in the night. Frida didn't mention George, her money troubles, or the argument about living in Phillip's room. During periods of restless confusion – when she had slept too much, or too little – Ruth would try to talk about Richard, but Frida, so serene and straightforward, only shook her head a little. She wore the plump smile of a Madonna looking over the head of her child, as if deciding what to cook for Joseph's dinner. Ruth, considering the possibility of going to Richard, sometimes said aloud, 'Why shouldn't I? Who could stop me?' and other times argued, 'Anyway, I'm not the kind of woman who would up and leave her whole life for a man.' At still other times, she felt she had an important decision to make, but was pleasantly unsure of what it was. Frida read detective novels and said nothing. The sun came through the window in long lines over the bed, and these lines moved throughout the day, and then it was dark again.

These were comfortable days, although swampy and forgetful. Ruth found it easy to surrender to Frida's care, and so, even when she began to feel better, she composed her face into wan expressions and pretended to sip soup. She was caught out of bed one morning, preparing to smuggle one of the cats through the window, and then there were recriminations.

'This is what I get, is it, for looking after you like a saint?' Frida cried. 'All right, up and out. No more of this lying around with me waiting on you hand and foot.'

Frida behaved as if Ruth were not only better, but in the best of health: youthful, but lazy. She shooed her charge into the garden, where Ruth was expected to sit in the sun and tail beans or polish silver.

'And don't tell me any old family stories about that silver,' Frida warned.

In the garden, in the afternoons, Ruth was supposed to 'take the air' – instead of an indoor nap.

'We'll have you walking on the beach in no time,' said Frida, as if Ruth had been accustomed to daily canters on the sand, and whenever Ruth complained about her back, Frida tapped her temple and said, 'Have you ever stopped to think it might all be in your head? What's the word for that? Jeffrey would know.'

'Psychosomatic,' said Ruth.

'Jeffrey would know.'

One morning, Frida returned from the letterbox with a pale blue envelope. She presented it to Ruth with some ceremony and hovered to see it opened. Ruth didn't hurry. She looked at the return address: Richard Porter, and then the number and street of the house in Sydney she could live in if she wanted to. Frida shuffled and sighed beside her.

'Can you get me the letter opener?' asked Ruth. 'It's on Harry's desk.'

'Just open it.'

'I want to slit it open. I want to keep the address.'

Frida shook her head and bugged her eyes, an uncharacteristically comic face, and went inside. This gave Ruth the opportunity to smell the envelope. She pressed her fingers along the closed flap, feeling the places where Richard's hands – and maybe his tongue – must have touched. Ruth had expected to hear from him sooner, but she wasn't entirely sure how much time had passed since his visit.

Frida returned with a small, sharp knife from the kitchen.

The envelope contained a card, and the card held a sheet of that same thin paper on which Richard had written to accept her invitation to visit. The card had a photograph of a beach on it – not this beach, not Ruth's bay – and the sky in the picture was a ludicrous blue. Ruth found it hard to imagine Richard selecting the card. It said, 'To dear Ruth and Frida, with thanks for a very special weekend.'

Ruth passed the card to Frida, who took it with some care, as if it might be the bearer of exquisite news. Meanwhile, Ruth read the note, which was addressed only to her: 'Dearest Ruth, I hope you're feeling better. I would love to hear your voice and know what you're thinking. My garden is full of day lilies, all of them pink, which I want you to see – my daughter tells me I'll enjoy them for another three weeks or so. She has the family's green thumb – and all our fingers. Please telephone as soon as you're well enough, or write, or else! Or else I'll come back up there and fetch you.'

Ruth wondered if she would enjoy being fetched.

Frida was watching. 'Can I see?' she asked.

'It's private.'

'Oh, *private*.' Frida appeared to find this funny and raised her arms as if she were in a movie and a man in wacky stripes had just told her to stick 'em up.

'How does he know I've been sick?' asked Ruth. 'Has he been calling?'

'He called,' said Frida.

'When?'

'When you were sick.' Frida stuck the card in the waistband of her trousers.

'I don't remember.'

'Do you want me to start writing everything down? I'm not your secretary.' Frida shifted her weight from foot to foot. 'He just wanted to tell us thank you. Like he says in his card. I don't think you missed a big chinwag.'

'If you must know,' said haughty Ruth, 'he wants me to go and live with him.'

Frida's face registered surprise for only a moment; then she mastered it. Ruth had never seen Frida off guard, and there was something alarming about the visible motion of her thought.

'And?' Frida said.

'I haven't decided,' said Ruth. She already regretted telling Frida; she remembered a phrase of Mrs Mason's: 'Trap your tongue if it tattles out of turn.'

But Frida said nothing more. She evidently had further questions, but wouldn't lower herself to asking them. She flicked at the card in her waistband and rolled away into the house.

Jeffrey telephoned that evening. 'I've just had a very interesting call from Frida,' he said. 'She's worried about you.'

Ruth wondered when Frida had found the time; she seemed to have spent the last few hours in the bathroom, dyeing her hair.

'She actually asked me not to mention our chat,' said Jeffrey. 'I don't like that kind of subterfuge, though I'm sure she has her reasons.'

'She usually does.'

'Now, about this Richard. How old is he, exactly?'

'He's about eighty.'

'Oh. He's eighty,' said Jeffrey, so Ruth knew his wife was listening. 'That's different. Frida made him sound like some kind of gold digger.'

'Harry isn't a gold digger!'

'You mean Richard.'

'Yes, Richard. I've known him for fifty years. He isn't after me for my money.'

'But he is after you?' asked Jeffrey.

'I think, yes, he is *after me*. Is that all right with you, darling?'

'What are we talking here? Companion? Boyfriend? Husband?' There was a boyish tremor in his voice, but it seemed to stem from embarrassment rather than anxiety. He mastered it by clearing his throat.

'I think it would be unfair on you boys to drag mud over the question of inheritance, at my age,' said Ruth.

'What?'

'I'm not going to marry him.'

'I know you need companionship. I worry about you out there on your own, I really do.'

'I have Frida.'

'And thank God for Frida,' said Jeffrey.

'Does Richard have your permission, then, to be after me?'

'You don't need my permission, Ma. This is about what you want. But I'd like to meet him before you make any decisions.'

'The lilies only have three weeks or so,' said Ruth.

'What was that?'

'He wants me to see the lilies. They're pink.'

Jeffrey cleared his throat; Ruth thought she might have said something wrong.

'Pink lilies, right, okay. Where does he live?'

'In Sydney, like your father.'

'Are you going to invite him for Christmas?' asked Jeffrey. 'So we can all meet him? Oh – but where would he sleep?' Small, practical details of this nature had always bothered him, even as a young boy; and then he seemed to realise he'd asked a more personal question than he'd intended, and he said, 'I mean, with all of us staying.'

'And Frida already in Phil's room,' said Ruth. 'Or maybe she wouldn't want to stay for Christmas.'

'What do you mean?'

'She'll probably want to spend Christmas with George.'

Frida appeared, without sound, at the door between the kitchen and the hall. Her hair was now a light reddish brown, rounded and shiny, like a polished apple, and her face was terribly blank.

'But why is Frida in Phil's room?' asked Jeffrey.

'Well, she lives there now,' said Ruth, irritated; how many times did she have to say it?

'Is she there? Put her on.'

Already Frida's hand was stretched out. Ruth offered up the receiver like a heifer for Juno. Frida's voice sounded bright when she said, 'Jeff,' into the phone, but her flat eyes remained on Ruth's face.

'Yes, Jeff,' said Frida, with a noble weariness. 'Yes, that's right. I assumed she'd told you.'

Jeff's voice was so small on the other end of the line – just a pitch, really, rather than words – and this made it seem to Ruth as if an argument were already over, and he had lost. As Jeffrey buzzed, Frida flicked her eyes from Ruth's face to her own fingernails, which she held away from the shadow of her body.

'Look, Jeff, this is between you and your mother. Who hasn't been well these last couple of weeks, just FYI. She didn't want to worry you – overdoing things, is all, with Richard and everything. She's no spring chicken. I wanted to be on hand. We talked it through, didn't we, Ruthie?'

Frida didn't look at Ruth, who retreated into the dining room, annoyed at her son for making a fuss. This is my house, she thought. It isn't Phil's room; it's mine. If I want to install one thousand Fridas in Phil's room, one thousand Richards in Jeff's room – in *my* room – then I will. And Jeffrey didn't seem to care one bit about the lilies, which would be long gone by Christmas.

'Just some tiredness, loss of appetite, nothing serious,' said Frida into the phone. 'And we're much better now, aren't we, Ruthie?'

'Yes!' piped Ruth from the dining room.

'You go right ahead and do that, Jeff,' said Frida. 'Look, I didn't see the need. I'm a trained nurse, and the only person whose time I'm willing to waste is my own. All right, first thing in the morning. You're welcome. Not at all. There's no need, Jeff – I'm happy to do it. And she likes the company, the dear. Don't you, Ruthie? All right, now.' Frida turned and carried the handset, on the end of its long white cord, to Ruth, who held it with reluctance to her ear.

'Ma, if you're sick, you've got to tell me. I want you to tell me. All right?' Jeffrey's voice was exasperated, like a boy's, as if tired of these adult games from which he was unjustly excluded.

'Actually,' she said, 'I don't have to tell you anything. What do you think of that?'

And she hung up, or tried to, but she was so far from the wall, with all that cord between them, that she succeeded only in dropping the receiver. It rolled stupidly on the floor until Frida picked it up, looked at it as if she'd never seen its like, and then replaced it in its cradle.

'Thank you,' said Ruth.

The phone began to ring again, but Frida only looked at Ruth with that big, blank face and shook her head as she walked away towards Phil's room. The phone rang and rang, and Ruth didn't answer it until she heard a door slam; then she did. It was Jeffrey, of course, upset.

'Did you hang up on me?' he demanded, and Ruth, until that moment proud of her defiance, repented and said, 'I dropped the phone.'

Then he was warm and fatherly. 'I just feel that one of us should come out there and meet this woman who's living in your house,' he said.

'You'll meet her at Christmas.'

'She calls you Ruthie.'

'No, she doesn't,' said Ruth.

'What are you paying her?'

'I told you, I'm not paying her a cent.'

This wasn't true; they had worked out a small salary in return for Frida's extra services. It wasn't generous, but Frida insisted on the smallness of the amount.

'Christmas is weeks away,' said Jeffrey. 'Would you object to a quick visit before then?'

'Lovely,' said Ruth. Was it lovely? It occurred to her that Jeffrey might be planning a visit in order to stop her from going to Richard. Would Richard come, then, and fetch her, as he threatened?

They spent some time – more than usual – saying goodnight to each other, as if they were sweethearts who couldn't bear to part, until the cats came to Ruth's feet to say, 'Bed! Bed!' She hung up and took them into her bedroom. They rolled and begged and bathed, and finally they slept. Ruth went noisily to the bathroom, washed herself with maximum fuss, and closed the lounge-room door with some force, but there was no sound at all from Frida's part of the house.

II

The tiger came back that night. At least, the noise of him did; or whatever it was that produced his noise. Ruth was lying in bed thinking about Richard and what it might be like to live in the city again. Richard lived in a sunny, hilly part of Sydney, north-west of the Harbour, where the trees tended to lose their leaves in the autumn and the wide evening roads were strung with homewards traffic. The gardens up there were all rhododendrons and azaleas, as if the climate were cooler and wetter than in other parts of the city, and Ruth, who didn't know the area well, associated it with the large, heavy house of one of her elocution students whose parents had invited her to dinner and then argued with each other over the cost of her lessons. Ruth also thought about Jeffrey, how boyish he had sounded on the phone, and the way he'd said, 'This is about what you want.' Could that be true? Since Harry died, she'd rarely thought about wanting anything. Frida was the one who wanted. She wanted clean floors, a smaller waist, and differently coloured hair. Frida filled the world with her desires. And Ruth admired it. Why not be like that?

The cats heard the noises first. Ruth was almost asleep, but they sat up, sphinxlike, their paws folded inward and their eyes slit. They were like little emperors on fabric shipped from China to England in the eighteenth century. Their ears moved and their tails were alert. Ruth, sensing their attention, turned her head on her pillow to listen, and there it was: something moving through the lounge room, shifting the furniture; but its tread was so light, so subtle; there was a louder exhalation, the amplification of a house cat sniffing under an unaccountably closed door, and at this the cats lost their composure and fled.

Now Ruth noticed an unusual smell, which seemed to enter the room as the cats left it. This very particular smell, concentrated and rank, was quite unlike the actual jungle, although it was this childhood scent that Ruth recalled now. The smell reminded her of the warning cries of seagulls in the garden when the cats were in the grass: not a specific panic, just a general alarm. Could a smell be a seagull? Perhaps it was more like a parrot. The tiger shook his head – new breathing accompanied the shake – and padded through the lounge room. It annoyed Ruth to hear him, because there was no point to him now that she had Frida and Richard; the tiger had prepared the way for them and was no longer needed.

She listened for any modulation in the tiger's sounds, and when she heard it, she drew wild conclusions: the tiger is in the hallway, there are two tigers, the insects are eating the furniture, there may also be a wild pig. Lost in these conjectures, she fell asleep. Ruth was fortunate in this way – she always slept, no matter her anxiety, but she suffered through the night with fretful dreams. Waking in the morning, with the cats anchoring the quilt around her feet, she concluded that her ability to sleep despite the danger indicated a lack of belief in the tiger.

'After all,' she said, aloud, 'there is no tiger.'

The cats gave her their quizzical attention and then began to bathe. Ruth dressed. She brushed her hair. There was no tiger, not last night, not ever. Today she would telephone Richard, not to say she would come to him – not yet – just to hear his voice.

But the lounge room, when Ruth entered it, did look dishevelled. An armchair stood in closer than usual proximity to a lamp. One corner of the rug lay folded back. And were the feline hairs she found rubbed into the rug more bristly than usual, more orange? The light fell innocently through the lace curtains. Everything was calm, but each piece of furniture seemed unmoored in the flat, insipid light, as if it had been stranded in its insistence on the ordinary. Ruth had the feeling that her whole house was lying to her. How could it smell of a jungle in the night and now so strongly, so freshly, of eucalyptus? But that was Frida, mopping the floors. Ruth thought, She's hiding the evidence, whether she knows it or not. Does she know it?

'Frida!' she called.

Frida came. She came with all the Valkyrian majesty of Frida in the morning, when her mood had not yet solidified for the day, and any whim might take her: to be kind, to be sullen. Capricious Frida of the milky mornings, who might eat yoghurt or deny herself dairy, who might wash Ruth's hair or kick at the cats (never striking them), and who carried with her a new kind of privacy, which also emanated from what had formerly been Phillip's room so that Ruth knew it was off limits. The floors gleamed with water, and they threw up light so that Frida, moving over them, seemed larger than ever. How was it possible, Ruth wondered, that as Frida shrank (her diet was working), she also seemed to take up more space? It must be a trick of all that light bouncing up from the immaculate floors.

'You're up,' said Frida, good-natured. 'I'll call the doctor.'

'What for?'

'Your son told me to – on the phone last night.'

'I'm not sick anymore.'

'Fine,' said Frida. 'No doctor.' And she turned to leave.

'Frida!' cried Ruth. Frida hated to be stopped when she was busy, and she hated to hear her name called out. Ruth would do it only under special circumstances; twice in one morning was quite remarkable.

'What?' Frida asked, revolving. She seemed placid enough. Her toffee-coloured hair made her sweeter.

'Did you notice a funny smell in here this morning?'

'What d'you mean, funny?'

'I suppose a sort of animal smell.'

'The cats, you mean? They're stinkers. Not much we can do about that.'

'No, no, more than the cats. Stronger than that. Do they really smell so bad? Cats are clean little things, aren't they?'

'If they're clean, then I'm the Queen of Sheba.'

Frida probably was the Queen of Sheba. She stood robed in magisterial light; she had just proceeded with wisdom and splendour from the court of Solomon, where she solved all manner of problems: unnecessary automobiles, impossible tigers, the melancholy of the king. She was a golden opportunity.

'This is a golden opportunity,' said Ruth.

Frida shook her head and began to move back towards the kitchen.

'Frida, wait!' Now there was urgency: when Frida shook her head, it was necessary to tell her things quickly or not at all. 'What would you say if I told you a tiger walked around the house last night?'

'Walked around inside the house, or walked *around* the house?'

'Inside,' Ruth said.

'What kind of tiger?'

'What kind of tigers are there?'

'A big tiger? A boy tiger?'

'Yes.'

'Big or boy?' asked Frida, still reasonable.

'Big boy.'

'A Tasmanian tiger? Or the ordinary kind?'

'Ordinary,' said Ruth.

'And what makes you think we've got a tiger?'

'I thought I heard him.'

'You didn't see him?'

'There's a smell, too. That's why I asked you about the smell.'

Frida sniffed luxuriously and long. She leaned into the sniff, and her nostrils flared, her eyes narrowed; she leaned farther, as if into a fragrant wind. 'A kind've hairy smell, is that it? Like a rug that needs washing?'

'Like a jungle,' said Ruth. And then another possibility occurred to her. 'Or maybe a zoo.'

'So, what you're telling me is, even though I bust my gut daily to get this place spotless – and beach places are the hardest of all to keep clean, believe me, what with the salt and the sand – even though I work myself to the bone to keep this place spotless, you're telling me it smells like a *zoo*?'

'Oh, Frida, no!' cried Ruth. 'I noticed the smell last night, but you already have everything perfect again.'

'Then it's the cats, you mark my words,' said Frida. Problem solved, she swivelled away on one crisp foot.

'Of course it is,' said Ruth, relieved. 'Or it's nothing at all. I'm imagining it. Thank you.'

But Frida turned to face her again. The light that leapt up around her, off the floors and the sea, hid her face.

'And what would a tiger want with you?' she asked; she was baffled, clearly, by the possibility that a tiger might take any interest in Ruth. She propped her mop in a corner, crossed to the recliner, and sat in it. Her face was full of jovial scorn. She settled into the possibility of the tiger; she made herself comfortable.

'You think this tiger's got it in for you? Maybe you killed its mum in that jungle you grew up in, and it's here to hunt you down.'

'I didn't grow up in the jungle,' said Ruth. 'I grew up in a town. And there are no tigers in Fiji.'

'If there's jungle, there's tigers.'

'That's not true. Tigers like cold weather. They live in India and

China. Maybe Russia.'

'There's Indians in Fiji.'

'I thought you didn't know anything about Fiji.'

'Everyone knows that, from the news.'

'Just because there are Indians in Fiji doesn't mean there are Indian tigers. I thought everyone knew *that*.'

'What I do know is, there's no tigers in Australia,' said Frida. 'There's no seaside bloody tigers in the local area. Unless they're on holiday.'

'I know that. It was just funny noises in the night.'

Frida sat on the recliner. Her face was immobile with thought. 'It's the cats, then,' she said.

'Yes, the cats,' said Ruth. The cats were frightened of something; that was undeniable.

'I mean, it's not so surprising, when you think about it. You leave the back door open every night for the cats to come and go. That'll be how this tiger of yours got in. What if Jeff knew that, huh? What if I told Mr Fantastic you left your back door open and a tiger walked in? I wonder what he'd say to that.'

Ruth had always pictured the tiger just appearing in the lounge room, the way a ghost might; he was a haunting and required nothing so practical as a door. Now she saw him coming by road and through the high grasses of the drive; she saw him moving with intemperate speed over the beach and ascending the dune; she saw him in the dark garden, making for the open door. One of the most fanciful things Harry had ever said to her had to do with the quality of moonlight by the sea. It was brighter and bluer, he said, with the sea to reflect it. Now Ruth saw the tiger under the bright blue seaside moon, and she saw her own house high on the dune's horizon; she ran towards it alongside the tiger, and the back door lay open for both of them. But the foolishness of having left her door open at night struck Ruth as too childish to have such terrible consequences.

'Nothing to say to that, have you?' said Frida. She tilted the recliner back and her magisterial stomach arced into the air; all her neat chins folded into place, like a napkin. 'Why don't you just bring the phone over here and I'll call that son of yours? Let him meddle in that.'

'He already knows about the tiger.' That was satisfying to say. Ruth felt as if she'd thought ahead to this moment and called Jeffrey in order to have an answer ready for Frida now. Frida regarded her from the recliner. Her legs in the air were undeniably slim, and she flexed her nimble feet in their unlaced sandshoes.

'He does, does he?' She made a small grunt. 'You told him before you told me?'

'I told him before I even knew you.'

'Wait a minute. I thought you said this tiger just showed up last night.'

Ruth reddened; she felt caught out in an unintentional lie. 'I thought I heard it once before.'

'And you told Jeffrey. Well, how about that. No son of mine would hear I had a tiger and leave me all alone to deal with it.'

'I'm not alone, am I,' said Ruth, but she was alone when the tiger first appeared, and Jeffrey hadn't come. He'd told her to go back to sleep and made jokes about it the next morning.

'Your own son left you alone with a man-eating bloody tiger. A woman-eating tiger. You're lucky you haven't been gobbled up in your bed.'

Ruth gave her nervous laugh. She knew how transparent this laugh was, but it flew out of her regardless. She blushed again. She saw herself in bed with the tiger's hot face over hers.

'It's not a tiger,' she said.

'I saw a TV show once.' Frida tilted her head back against the soft seat of the recliner. 'Yeah, a documentary about man-eating tigers in India. You know what they say, once a tiger gets a taste of human flesh, that's all it wants to eat.'

'That's only the old tigers with broken teeth,' said Ruth, recalling a documentary of her own, possibly the same one. It had been intensely yellow-lit, as if the heat of India were perceptible in the shade of its sunshine. 'And anyway, it's not a real tiger.'

'Oh, a *ghost* tiger, is it?' Frida heaved her body forward to right the recliner. 'Here I was thinking a real tiger was dropping in for social calls. A ghost tiger is totally different. Nothing to worry about, in that case.'

'Well, obviously there's no tiger,' said Ruth. 'You didn't hear it. You said you didn't smell anything.'

'I said I smelled something. Like a rug that needs washing.'

'That's just the rug needing washing.' Ruth prodded it with her foot.

'Don't get your knickers in a twist. I'll wash it today,' said Frida. She dragged herself up from the recliner, which shook in alarm.

'So you see – just a silly old woman.' Ruth laughed with one coy hand at her throat. 'Of course there's no tiger.'

'I don't know, Ruthie.' Frida headed back to the kitchen with her mop. 'Stranger things under the sun.' She shook her head, looking out at the sea as she walked, so that Ruth saw she was taking the possibility of the tiger seriously; that the wide spread of her thoughts was growing wider still. Frida rarely looked at the sea.

Ruth set about scrutinising every corner of the lounge room. The only thing now was to find a tuft of orange fur, one frond of a parrot's tail, or any tangible proof that her house had a habit of turning into a jungle at night. And conversely, in the absence of such evidence, that it didn't. She flipped the rug with her foot, lifted the curtains, and snuck a broom from the kitchen to poke under the sofa. Frida, with a submerged mutter, stayed out of her way. Ruth remembered a period during which she had worried over the existence of God. At that time, when she was aged eleven or so and was reminded everywhere and at every hour of the goodness of God's provision, she developed a horror that she would be visited by an angel and that all of it – all that awful good news – would be proven, absolutely, to be true. How she longed to see that angel, and how terrified she was. She would lie awake at night, afraid to open her eyes and afraid to sleep. It never came.

Besides the slight disarrangement of the furniture, nothing in the lounge room suggested a jungle except the carcass of a spider, cat-killed and crumpled deep under the sofa; Ruth extracted it with the assistance of the broom.

Frida, her mop rinsed and squeezed and left to dry for the day, marched into the room and, without speaking, rolled up the rug and carried it away, corpselike, over her right shoulder. Stripped of the rug, the room appeared defenseless, and much larger. It was a long way, for example, from the window to the door. Ruth swept the dead spider through the expanse of the lounge and dining rooms, to the kitchen and out into the garden. Frida had hung the rug over a long frangipani limb and was beating it with a wooden spoon. She pulled her arm back, holding the spoon as if it were a tennis racquet, and unleashed it with such force that dust and hair rose in grubby clouds above her shaking back.

With Frida out of the house and the lounge room empty of evidence, Ruth called Richard. She carried the receiver, on the end of its long white cord, down the hallway and into her bedroom, listening with pleasure to the ring of his phone in her ear and in his house. Frida was still beating the rug, and the sound of it was like a flag snapping against its pole in a high wind.

Richard's phone rang nine times before somebody answered it.

'Hello?' said a young woman. Her voice sounded harried, and out of it came the absurdity of a house in Sydney that Ruth had never seen, daughters and grandchildren related by blood to Richard and Kioko, a whole life that had never been dismantled and moved to the sea, with no imaginary tigers, no Frida beating a rug over a frangipani branch, and Richard over eighty, herself old; and the voice, more weary this time, as if it would wait forever, firm, polite, and inconvenienced, repeated, 'Hello?' Ruth, sitting on the bed where she had recently lain down and – awkwardly, optimistically, and not without pleasure – slept with a man she hadn't seen for fifty years, listened for another 'Hello?' and then, holding one palm against the receiver so as not to hear anything more, hurried into the kitchen and hung up the phone.

Frida was also in the kitchen, filling a bucket with water. 'Everything all right?' she asked.

Ruth nodded. They went into the garden together, Frida holding the soapy bucket against her leg, and together they washed the rug. Ruth liked the short, rough feel of the bristles under her fingernails. She liked the thin dust that coated the ground under the frangipani tree, and the soapy grey water that ran out of the rug and over the garden. Frida laid the clean rug over the hydrangea bush to dry, and for the rest of the day it fidgeted in the wind as if something trapped underneath were making half-hearted attempts to escape. She swept and polished the lounge-room floor, every now and then taking an exploratory sniff. There was no discernible smell in the room; nothing left of the long, hairy bass note Ruth had suspected of issuing from a tiger. The animal odour had only been the rug, after all. Ruth, dirty, tired, and still hearing that 'Hello? Hello?' in her inmost ear, took a long bath during which she repeatedly bit the inside of her mouth to stave off self-pity. But as she dressed afterwards – not in pyjamas, not before bedtime, that would be sloppy – she remembered that strange feline stain on the lounge right before Richard's visit and wondered about it.

Frida cooked steak for dinner – an extravagance – and when Ruth asked the occasion, she answered, mysteriously, 'Red meat for strength.' After the meal, she brewed a pot of strong tea, made Ruth drink two cups, and suggested they sit together in the lounge room. Frida never sat in the lounge room at night. If she didn't go out – there were nights when George's taxi drew up, pumpkin-coloured, and carried her away – she usually stayed at the dining table, reading the newspaper or detective novels; or she went into her bedroom to soak her feet and try new hairstyles; or she occupied the bathroom for hours, dyeing and washing and drying her hair. But tonight, she said, her arms were sore from beating the rug and she wanted to sit in the lounge room, watch a little TV, and talk. She made more tea and carried it in to Ruth, who was sitting in the recliner and who protested, 'Three cups! I'll be up all night.'

'That's the idea,' said Frida.

'Why?'

'I want to see this tiger of yours.'

Ruth sipped her too-hot tea and gave her girlish laugh, the one she hated the sound of.

'Don't be scared, Ruthie. Between you and me' – Frida flexed a savvy biceps – 'your Frida is a match for any old tiger.'

'Stop it,' said Ruth. 'Turn on the television.'

Frida didn't move. Her face was agile with anticipation. 'We'll be bait. Lure him out, then *kapow*! Though maybe that's not the best idea. Wouldn't want to hand you to him like a meat tray in a raffle.' Ruth began to ease herself out of the recliner. 'Where are you off to?'

'If you're going to be ridiculous, I'm going to bed.'

'Tiger on the loose, chances are it's a man-eater,' said Frida. 'We should check the news for zoo escapes.'

'I don't intend to be laughed at in my own home.'

'I wish you'd told me about this before, Ruthie. For one thing, I might have run into it on the way to the loo one night. Couldn't have it see me without my hair all done.' Frida laughed, and her belly shook.

'Good night, Frida,' said Ruth, and the cats, only just settled on the sofa, followed her to her bedroom, where she took her pills before lying on the bed and remembering the voice at the end of Richard's phone number saying, again and again, 'Hello?'

Frida turned on the television and the sound of it comforted Ruth, like a light under a door. She lay on her bed, still dressed and without even her lamp on: she wanted the dark to cool her burning face. The television continued to buzz until late, and every now and then Frida laughed from the lounge room.

When she woke early the next morning, Ruth couldn't remember falling asleep. More than this, she couldn't remember her own body; it seemed to be missing. Nevertheless, she was able to move. She got out of bed in the slow, deliberate way Frida had taught her: bend your legs, roll onto your side, keep the spine intact, think of it as a steel rod, let gravity do the work, stay relaxed, sit up, don't twist, move the spine as a unit, rest, stretch as tall as you can, bend forward and lift, straighten your legs, and then you're standing, Ruth was standing, without quite knowing how she came to be on her feet. She felt nothing. This might be the true weight of age, she thought, without feeling her thought; it was weightless, everything was, but not in a light way. That might be pleasant. This weightlessness was all absence. Her back should hurt and her legs should be shaking. And she wanted Richard, but her heart didn't ache. Then there was a noise in the room, which finally she recognised as her own voice – she wasn't sure what her voice was saying, but the existence of it, and its definite sound, returned sensation to her back and legs. Her skin was dirtily damp. There she was in the mirror, and the cats had found her and were running in and out of the door pleading for breakfast. It wasn't long past dawn, the sea was outside; it was audible, as were her feet on the floor, so she called to the cats just to hear her voice again. 'Kit! Kit!' she called. Her tongue was sticky in her mouth.

Out in the lounge room, Frida was asleep on the sofa. She woke when Ruth came in, starting up with a hand to her hair and rubbing her bleary face. Ruth couldn't think what to say. Her body had returned to her, but she was still unsure of her control over it.

'Whatsa time?' enquired Frida, but Ruth didn't know. They looked at each other, Frida from the sofa and Ruth standing by the window, and after a moment of this, Frida shook her head and stood up. The ease with which she stood was awe-inspiring. She was like a wave. But strands of her hair were stuck to the sweaty sides of her face.

'It didn't come,' she said, stretching her arms behind her head and walking towards the kitchen. Her hair had flattened in the back. 'The tiger.'

Ruth made a small sound of disgust. It was childish of Frida to persist in teasing. But she saw, without wanting to, evidence of Frida's seriousness: her crushed hair, the displaced sofa cushions, the cups of tea. Now Frida came back into the lounge room with pills and a glass of water; Ruth accepted them; she put the pills in her mouth, swallowed, and felt safer for knowing she was able to do so.

She wanted to telephone Richard while Frida was making breakfast, but it was far too early. So she called him later, while Frida was in the shower, and this time he answered.

'Ruth!' he cried, obviously delighted. 'Ruth, Ruth, Ruth!'

She wanted to hear his dear voice settle down into a slow, happy rhythm, but he talked too much and too quickly: about his garden and the local council, who were sending men to remove a tree that afternoon, an old juniper that was threatening the neighbour's roof but gave Richard such pleasure because of the way the cockatoos ate the berries and rolled around drunk on the grass, and about his great-granddaughter who had just gotten a part in the school play, she would play a pirate with a wooden parrot, and he was in charge of finding an eye patch and a scarf fringed with gold coins, and also, and this was sad news, but Andrew Carson – did she remember him? – his son had died last week, very unexpectedly, a stroke, and Richard would be at the funeral tomorrow; of course, Andrew was long gone himself – this phrase *long gone* dismayed Ruth – but he would pass on Ruth's sympathies to the rest of the family.

Ruth listened and asked questions and made appropriate noises; she was reminded of the old Richard with too much to say after a play or a film, except that now his talk was full of people and events and objects, and not the abstract things that used to frighten her. But she found herself missing them, or missing the man who had waited for her to talk about them with him, because she couldn't contribute to the pirate play, the juniper tree, or even Andrew Carson's son, who had been born not long after the kiss at the ball, and consequently quite soon before Ruth left Fiji. Was it that Richard remembered her as only being capable of this sort of low-level chat? Or was it that she was exhausted and saddened by this evidence of the vitality of Richard's life, which failed to appeal to her? So she ended their chat without saying any of the things she wanted to: that she missed him, for example, and that she thought every day about their morning in her bedroom. It was only as they said goodbye that Richard said, 'I've rattled on, I'm sorry, I get nervous on the phone,' and she was ashamed for him – Richard, nervous! Ruth promised to call him again soon, but thought she would write him a letter instead.

That night, Frida joined Ruth in the lounge room after dinner. She brought two of her detective novels with her and dropped one into Ruth's reclining lap. It was called *The Term of Her Natural Life*.

'I heard you were a big reader,' Frida said, before positioning herself on the cat-abandoned sofa and opening her own novel.

So Ruth read along with Frida. She liked the book: it was set in Australia, which charmed her, as if it had never occurred to her that ingenious crimes might be committed and solved in her own country. The harsh cries of native birds frequently interrupted the musings of the plucky protagonist, and the seasons were all in the right places. Frida didn't speak, but the sound of turning pages and the light of the lamps produced a mood so confidential and snug that Ruth found she wanted her to. She cleared her throat and asked, 'What will you do for Christmas?'

'I'll be gone by Christmas,' said Frida, still reading.

'What do you mean, gone?'

Now Frida raised her head. She kept one finger on her place in the book. 'I'll take a holiday, is what I mean. I'll be out of your hair.'

'I might take a holiday myself,' said Ruth.

'Ah. Richard.'

'Yes.'

'Good for you.' Frida bent her head over her book, then lifted it once more, with a wise expression, as if she couldn't help herself. 'It's best to take these things slow, though, isn't it. I always preach caution – look at poor George. You don't want any nasty surprises.'

Ruth remained quiet. She was unsure of what nasty surprises George might illustrate.

'What's that machine for, for one thing?' asked Frida.

'What machine?'

'The one he sleeps with. The mask over his face.'

Ruth looked back at her book. She had no idea Richard slept with a mask over his face.

'And it's not as if he hasn't surprised you before,' said Frida, with a sympathetic chuckle. 'The Japanese girlfriend! Better make sure he doesn't have another one of those up his sleeve.'

Ruth's chest fell inward and her ribs felt tight against her lungs. She made a show of reading so that Frida would stop talking. But Ruth couldn't turn the page. She read the same sentence again and again: 'Leaning warily into the burnt car, Jaqui swept the fibres into a small transparent bag.' Stiff tears stood in her eyes, and she blinked them back.

'Did you hear that?' asked Frida.

Ruth's jumping heart jumped faster. 'What?'

Frida didn't answer for a few long beats. 'I thought I heard something outside.'

She stood. Her arms were bare and her face was flushed with red; she was in a marvellous mood. It was a cool evening, but the house, Ruth noticed now, was jungle-hot. Here he comes, she thought, without meaning to. She was reminded of a poem she'd made her students recite: 'Here comes the tiger, riding, riding, up to the old inn door.'

'You go to bed,' said Frida, heading into the dining room. She stood tense at the window, baring her equatorial arms, still wearing her whitish uniform.

'I'm not tired,' said Ruth. But she was gathering her things – her teacup and book – and preparing to stand.

Frida was so still. 'Hear that?' she said, cocking her head. 'I'm going out there.'

Ruth listened. 'There's nothing,' she said. But Frida was already outside and had closed the back door; Ruth watched her from the dining-room window. Frida stood on the grass in the window's light, her nose lifted and her head moving from side to side. The beach, empty under the spring moon, had that bare, blanched look of a seashore at night. Frida waved Ruth away from the window, and when Ruth didn't move, she waved again. The cats sniffed and howled at the closed door.

'Quiet,' Ruth ordered; she shepherded them into the bedroom and turned on her bedside lamp. 'She can't scare me,' she said to the cats. She sat on her bed, and among the ordinary stirrings outside she heard Frida stepping through the brush by her window. There were three taps on the glass, and Ruth, unsure of how to respond, turned her lamp off and then on again. Or, because it was a touch lamp – a gift from Jeffrey – she turned it dim, dimmer, off, and back to bright again. Frida moved on. She circled the house for at least the next half-hour and, for the first few rounds, tapped at the window as she went; Ruth responded with her lamp, so that she imagined her window as a lighthouse over the bay: off and on, on and off, signalling both safety and danger. It was like being a girl and singing hymns with her parents; on those nights, it was as if her family had sung together not towards God but against death, which pressed up at the windows but knew better than to expect an invitation. The brighter the light in the house, the safer they were, and the singing doubled and then tripled the light; the house was so luminous with song and with the presence of her parents that it must shine out over the garden, the town, the island, all of Fiji and the entire Pacific. This, she had understood, was how to be a light in the world. Frida stopped tapping, but Ruth continued to operate the light. After this tense half-hour Frida came inside and said, 'Enough with the lamp. Go to sleep.'

'How could I possibly sleep?' protested Ruth. She propped up her pillows and sat unbending in the dark, listening for Frida's footsteps outside her window. The cats curled at the hinges of her arms and legs. She slept and woke and slept again, still listening for Frida. An hour might have passed, or six, when she heard a cry – Frida screaming, was that possible? – and the back door rocking shut. She tapped the lamp and checked to see if the light had disturbed Harry. Of course not. There was no Harry.

'Ruth! Ruthie!' Frida called, and when she swung on the door into Ruth's room, her face was pale and her torso shook. 'Thank God you're all right!'

'What is it? What happened?'

Frida collapsed onto the bed and over Ruth's legs. 'Look at this!' She presented her left forearm, where three long scratches already brimmed with blood.

'What is it?' Ruth felt at that moment more curious than concerned, but she made herself lift her hands, in horror, to her mouth.

'He may have hurt me, but I scared the bejesus out of him.'

'Who?'

'Who do you think?' snapped Frida.

Ruth couldn't think. George? Richard? She gathered blankets into her hands.

'I don't know how he got in,' said Frida, 'but I sure as hell know how he got out. I opened the door and he bolted right through. Knocked me arse up on the sand, as a matter of fact, and I'm lucky I've still got all my parts. But he gave me a good swipe. A parting gift.'

Ruth sat up as best she could and looked at the curtained window. She half expected to hear three taps against it. Frida was crushing Ruth's legs, and Ruth's heart pumped a strong, slow beat. 'There's no tiger,' she said.

'You think I clawed my own arm?'

'He's not real.'

'He's real all right, but he's also gone, and he won't be back in a hurry. Scared him right off.'

'The cats?' Ruth asked in a small voice.

'Don't you want to know how I scared him off?' Frida propped herself up with her uninjured arm and made a terrible face at Ruth: she bared her teeth and gave out a noise somewhere between a growl and a hiss, and her face was so human that Ruth was frightened. 'He ran off with his tail between his legs. Ha! Some tiger.' Frida lay back on the bed and laughed, as if it were typical of Ruth to have been harbouring such a timid tiger. 'But' – Frida raised her wounded arm so that it waved above her like a cautionary stalk – 'that doesn't mean the danger has passed.'

'Let me see your arm,' said Ruth. She tried to shift her legs. Frida was a set stone.

'Don't you worry about my arm. It's seen worse than a few fingernails, believe me. Stop wriggling!'

Ruth stopped. Frida, completely horizontal, shrank in on herself; her belly flattened, and her breasts. Her delicate ankles jutted out over the floor. Her hair looked black, as if she'd chosen this colour specifically for nocturnal camouflage, and was pulled back into a jaunty ponytail. She shook her sandshoes off and fanned her toes like a peacock's tail.

'You actually saw it?' asked Ruth, whose legs were beginning to fall asleep. She could feel her buzzing blood.

Frida didn't answer.

'Frida?'

Frida smiled. She closed her eyes. 'Oh, Ruthie,' she sighed. 'What on earth would you do without me?'

Ruth had no idea.

12

Frida spent the next morning building tiger traps around the house.

'I thought you scared him off,' said Ruth.

'Scared him off *for now*,' said Frida. 'Tigers can be patient. They know all about lying in wait.'

She devoted most of the morning to the largest trap: a hole halfway down the dune, in the middle of the rough grassy path to the beach. When the hole was deep enough to satisfy her, she walked along the shore gathering fallen pine boughs and brought them back to fill it with. Her left forearm was bandaged to cover last night's tiger scratches, and she stretched it out to look at it from time to time, as if inspecting an engagement ring; otherwise, her arms seemed normal, capable, as she carried the branches with the sprightly bustle of a nesting bird.

'Don't walk there,' Frida said, pointing out the pit.

No tiger will fall for that, thought Ruth. Already the dune was subsiding into the hole. Ruth remained inside and wrote her letter to Richard. It was only supposed to be a short note, designed to seem casual and pretty, in which she would suggest a weekend visit to see the lilies. 'At least the lilies,' she wrote, noticing as she did so that her handwriting was not what it once was. It was quite clumsily square now; Mrs Mason would be disappointed.

In the late morning, George's taxi rolled up to the front of the house. Ruth watched from the lounge room as Frida chattered through his open window before hauling a bundle of barbed wire from the boot. George reversed the car expertly down the drive; only then did Ruth go outside.

'Did you say anything about the tiger?'

'What do you take me for, an idiot?' said Frida, but she wasn't angry. She was genially indignant, which was one of her best moods.

'Then what does he think all this is for?' Ruth asked, indicating the wire.

'I told him it was to stop erosion.' Frida smiled, as if the gulling of George were one of life's simple pleasures. She took the wire out onto the dune and wrestled with it in the grasses. Ruth worried about cats caught on hidden barbs, but Frida dismissed her fears.

'Look at them watching every move I make,' she said. 'They know what's going on.'

The cats did sit in watchful poses, very still, which they occasionally animated with the urgent bathing of a paw.

'So the tiger is biding its time, is that it?' Ruth asked.

Frida nodded. She wore thick gardening gloves – Harry's – and they seemed to require a strict rigidity in her arms and shoulders. Only her head could move freely.

'How will we know when the time is up?'

'We won't,' said Frida. 'He'll just show up.'

'Like a thief in the night.'

'Exactly,' said Frida. 'Therefore: traps. I'd love to rig up a whole video system, like I bet they have in zoos.' She explained to Ruth that surveillance was a hobby of George's; she looked philosophically out to sea. 'A cabbie can't be too careful, you realise. Poor Georgie.' Ruth felt a shiver of jealousy at this affectionate name. 'He's no green thumb when it comes to growing money.'

Frida was finished with her traps by early afternoon. The sky had clouded over.

'That's good,' said Ruth, looking out at the garden from the dining room. 'Clouds mean a warmer night.'

Frida shook her head. 'Tigers need shelter from the rain, just like the rest of us.'

The tiger was Frida's now; and not just this tiger, but the entire species. She was proud of him, and of her arm; the heroics of the night before seemed to give her precedence in all household matters. She refused to eat lunch and went into Ruth's bedroom – she preferred the light in there, she said, for arranging her hair – and closed the door so that Ruth knew not to follow her. When Frida re-emerged, she wore her grey coat and a green scarf over her hair; under the influence of the green, her hair verged on a dark, distinguished red.

'Chilly this arvo,' she said, tilting her head towards the back door, which was open and admitting a stiff wind. 'Let's close this, shall we?'

'The cats are still out,' said Ruth, who was a little cold herself; she was wearing a thin summer dress. She sat with her chair pulled up to the dining table reading *The Term of Her Natural Life*. The letter to Richard lay at her elbow, snug in an envelope, addressed, and awaiting a stamp.

Frida smothered a cough. 'I have a weak chest.' Frida had a chest like the hull of a ship. She stood at the back door and called, without conviction, 'Here, kitty kitty.' Then something approximating a miaow.

'You'll scare them,' said Ruth.

'All this fuss over cats, for God's sake.' Frida began to gather things into her handbag. 'They're not sheep, are they – now sheep are *dumb*.' She swayed through the kitchen, gathering, gathering. She plucked the spare keys from the top of the fridge. 'And I have plans this afternoon. I am going O.U.T.' And on that final, plosive *T*, she pulled the door shut, flung its bolts home, and deadlocked it.

'I want it open,' said Ruth.

'I know you do, but I can't leave you here all alone with the door open and a tiger on the loose, can I?' said Frida. 'What's this? A letter for Prince Charming? Shall I post it, Your Highness? Yes, no? Shall I?'

Frida swept the letter up into her quick brown fingers and tucked it inside her coat, somewhere in the busty vicinity of her heart.

'Give that back and open the door.'

A car horn sounded from the drive.

'That'll be George,' said Frida. She adjusted her green scarf. 'Don't wait up! See you soon, Bonnydoon!' She waltzed to the front door while Ruth called, 'Frida! Frida!' and there was her merry voice greeting George, the door closing, and the sound of the taxi driving away.

Then Ruth was alone in the house. 'Shit,' she said.

The front and back doors were deadlocked, and all the keys were gone: the set in Ruth's purse, the fridge set, and even the last-chance spare key, gummed to the bottom of one of Harry's desk drawers. Ruth went to some trouble to look for that one; bent and stiff-backed in Harry's study she swore again, with greater pleasure this time, as if the word *fuck* could increase in beauty the more care she took to say it. The cats battered the back door in frantic longing.

'Shoosh, chickens,' she crooned, pressed against the door, which only sent them into wilder spasms; they howled like hungry babies. Ruth retreated. She was furious with Frida for locking her in and the cats out, for making fun of her with this tiger nonsense, for taking the letter, for waltzing and teasing and acting as if she owned the place. In her anger, Ruth kicked a pile of detective novels in the lounge room; the skidding of the books lifted one corner of the rug, much, she imagined, as the tiger's tail might. If he were really a tiger. If he were really a tiger, she thought, he would be as long as the rug. He would turn the corner behind the recliner and in doing so bump the lamp; Ruth bumped the lamp, and it fell to the floor. His tail might sweep over the coffee table and send all the television remotes flying; they went flying, and one set of batteries rolled out. Ruth considered the mess she had made. She liked it. If I were a tiger, she thought, I wouldn't be frightened of Phil's room. Of Frida's room. This realisation sent her down the hallway on soft feet.

Ruth pushed open Frida's door. She stood in the hallway and listened for the return of George's taxi, but heard only a little tick, which seemed to be coming from the room itself but was, after all, only the tiny sound of her heart behind her ears. Ruth inhaled the room's new beauty-parlour smell. Frida had turned the top of the chest of drawers into a vanity: it was covered in creams, mousses, hairspray, combs of different widths, and all the other hardware of her glorious hair. Above this cache, on the wall that used to display a poster of Halley's Comet, hung an oval mirror. Ruth had trouble looking into the mirror; she suspected Frida might look back at her out of it, like a fairytale queen. Instead Ruth saw her own pale face and the reversed room behind it. The bed was made. Phillip's children's books were still lined up on the shelf.

Ruth opened the wardrobe and slid Frida's clothes off their hangers. They pooled at her feet. Most of them were white or off-white, the assorted parts of her daily uniform, but there were other intriguing items: a pink blouse, dark purple pants of impressive circumference, and a black dress with gold sequins stitched into the sleeves. Frida in sequins! Ruth smiled and swam among the clothes, pulling at sleeves and skirts and shuffling in the faint eucalyptus odour. Touching the fabrics lifted the hair on her forearms, but she persisted until every item lay either in the bottom of the wardrobe or spilled into the room. She sifted through drawers, too. Frida's underwear seemed to fly from Ruth's fingers. The bras were particularly aerodynamic and made a lovely soft clatter as they floated to the floor. So this, thought Ruth, is what a tiger feels like, bumping and brawling; but I am not a tiger, she reminded herself. I can use tools.

Ruth fetched a broom from the kitchen and used its handle to poke at the underside of Frida's suitcase, which sat on top of the wardrobe like a long-neglected household pet. She shook and battered the case, and it made a maraca sound as it fell; bursting open, it spread a rainbow of pills and capsules over the bedroom. They crunched underfoot, except where they were caught up in Frida's clothes. Ruth recognised most of them as her own pills; she was delighted to see their picturesque array, the prescription ones all blue and sweet pale yellow, and the thick turmeric ones, and then of course the golden vials of fish oil. Those glowing capsules were the most satisfying to step on because when Ruth pressed them they resisted and bounced and then they popped.

She hadn't finished with the broom; she used it to fish under the bed, and with it she caught two boxes. The first looked official: it contained bank statements in orderly manila files. The names on these files were unfamiliar, except for one: Shelley, the name of Frida's dead sister. Shelley's surname wasn't Young, so she must have been married, and the thought of Frida at a wedding – as a bridesmaid – made Ruth feel a little guilty. So she pushed the box under the bed with one foot.

The second box was old, shoe-sized, and made of a dull, thick cardboard. Ruth, bending to pick it up, felt her back seize and burn, as if a wheel under her ribs were turning a long, hot cord up her spine. Nausea welled in her throat, her mouth filled with spit, and she threw up onto Frida's bed: a dryish welt which looked like something the cats might produce and made her laugh, but sheepishly. Before leaving the room with the box under her arm,

Ruth made one last valiant plunge to the floor for a handful of pills. Most of them were the blue ones she took for her back, and she swallowed a couple down, waterless. The rest she pushed deep into the pockets of her dress.

Ruth opened the box out at the dining table. It was full of rocks and bottles of sand; sections of glass and rock gleamed from the greasy dust. Each object was tied with twine and identified by a small shipping label. One rock was marked *Coral, various.* Another: *Brimstone fr. Volcano, 4000 ft.* Another: *Shell of the Cowrie type.* She looked more closely at this last, wiping at it with her fingers, and a patterned shell did emerge. Ruth recognised its glossy freckles. She knew these things, and this box – she looked again at the lid and remembered the image on it, an advertisement for boot polish; she cried out and her hands trembled in the air. This box had belonged to her father.

Now Ruth went under the sink for cloths and cleaners. Her back throbbed and stung, but she ignored it; she pictured the tiny blue pills dropping down her long, dry throat into her waiting stomach. She removed every object from the box, one by one, and knew all of them. Small explosions flared in her brain; she felt them in specific places, and she could visualise them, too, as if watching a map on the evening news that identified the locations of burgeoning bushfires. Her kindling mind, the good pleasure of cleaning, every moment of discovery: all this was thrilling, was so deeply satisfying that Ruth found herself tapping her foot the way she would to music. She set to cleaning every item with a singleness of purpose she recognised as belonging to an earlier part of her life; she felt her attention as something laserlike and constant, which she could turn with great pleasure onto any item in the box and watch it emerge, minutes later, from its own ruin. Each item required specific care. The coral clung to its dust; when Ruth tried to scrub it, it disintegrated in her hands. She breathed on it gently instead, and pinched the fibrous dirt between her fingernails – how long they were, she noticed, and still sturdy, just as they'd been when she was a girl. Shells shone out of their grime, and Ruth listened at each one to hear the irretrievable sea. There it was – and gone – and there. She recognised the distant roar of her own blood.

In the bottom of the box, dust and bits of rock and broken shell all mingled in a filthy glitter. Ruth nudged the wastepaper basket down the hall from Harry's study to the dining room. She loaded it up with dirty cloths and papers and shook the box out over it. Then she replaced the lid, from which a dark, happy shoeshining boy smiled up with oversized teeth. She set the box down next to her chair.

'Now look,' said Ruth, to nobody; to herself. She had forgotten Frida, and even the cats.

Everything was clean. Everything was laid out on the table, orderly and labelled; nothing touched anything else. Small bottles of brown and blue glass looked as if they'd been fished, moments before, from the sea. Inside each one, mysterious substances settled and slept. The shells were now pink and purple again, flesh-coloured, immodest. They nestled into themselves like ears.

Ruth wanted to share all this with someone. It should, she thought, have been Harry; she called Richard's number. It rang four times and then clicked and popped; there was Richard's voice, but with a mechanical buzz to it, as if he were still a smoker. I can't come to the phone right now, he said, and his was an old man's voice, an ending.

'Richard?' she said. 'It's Ruth.'

The line exploded with sound – there was that same young woman's voice saying 'Hello? Ruth?' and Ruth was sure she heard laughter in the background, and one laugh in particular: she rarely heard it, but when she did, it was a golden, bouncing swell, a brass ring, and unmistakable. It was – Ruth was quite sure – Frida. What could Frida be doing at Richard's house? And in fright she hung up the telephone. It rang again, naturally; Ruth lost track of the number of times. She sat in her chair and watched a strange yellow haze pass over her eyes, as if a cloud, in crossing the sun, had been half burnt away by its light. Bright circles formed in this fog, and they pulsed in time with the ringing of the telephone. Ruth watched them even with her eyes closed; they seemed to stick to her eyelids, so she took another pill to make them go away. The phone stopped, finally, and she might have been asleep; her sleep was dusty and angular, punctuated by swimming light. Somewhere in it, she saw the sea running up and over the dune, muddying the carpets and rising and rising, until strange, shelled animals clung to the lower walls, and fronds that were either worms or the homes of worms beckoned from the skirting boards. Then there was nothing but wreckage and ruin. She saw herself and Frida floating on a raft fashioned from the back door. Frida used the broom as a pole and punted them, like a Venetian gondolier, towards the triumphant pennants of the surf club.

This vague sleep broke when Frida returned; Ruth heard her coming through the front door, and she noticed the end of the day's light hanging reflected in the east.

'Ruthie?' Frida called, and she bustled into the dining room in a tremendous mood, unwrapping the green scarf from her hair.

She looked browner than when she had left, and her hair seemed a different shade of flattering bronze.

'What a day!' she sang.

She gave a girlish laugh and claimed to have gained two pounds, and she patted Ruth's arm as she passed by on her way to the kitchen. It was as if she'd been away for three weeks. In her arms she carried a load of pink lilies wrapped in Christmas paper. She dumped them on the countertop before fishing in the fridge for her yoghurt, which she ate straight from the container while leaning against the wall and explaining that George had taken her to a beach far away, 'so I could sun myself like a frog on a log.' On some days Frida was furious with George; on other days he was inviolate. This was one of those saintly days. 'It's so necessary to be with family,' said Frida, her spoon dripping with yoghurt. 'You know I'm crazy about you, Ruthie, but it's not the same thing. And time away gives you a chance to think about what you want from life. Believe me, you'll see some changes.'

'Those are beautiful lilies,' said Ruth. 'Where are they from?'

'Mum's house. What's all this junk?'

'It's my father's. It isn't junk.'

'Are they antiques?' Frida butted the table with one curious hip; a blue bottle began to roll. Ruth caught it with the tips of her fingers. Her head felt a little clearer now, but everything she saw was strangely luminous.

'I suppose they're old. They've survived war and shipwreck, these things. Well, not shipwreck. But they did survive. Even just the sea they survived – the shells.'

'Are they worth anything?'

'Oh, now, Frida – goodness!' Ruth gave a miniature laugh. The lilies burned on the countertop; it was easier not to look at them. 'I doubt any of it's worth anything. Just personal value.'

'But you could take it to someone, couldn't you, and find out? George'll know. He knows about this stuff.'

'I wouldn't sell my father's things.'

Frida prodded a glittering rock. 'This looks valuable. It looks like silver.'

'It's only mica,' said Ruth. 'Look at the label. Your mother grew lilies?'

'And then there's the insurance. Think of that! What if the house burned down – this stuff might be worth millions.'

Frida touched the curve of a shell with her finger and watched it vibrate against the table.

'That's pretty,' said Ruth. 'Shell music.'

Frida touched another. It was a spotted shell, but she wasn't really looking at it; something else had occurred to her. 'Ruthie,' she said, 'where did you find all this?'

'There used to be other shells, too – big ones. What do you call those big ones? Starts with a "c"? Not conches. Cowries.'

'Cowries aren't that big.'

'We had some big ones with island scenes etched in. They must be around somewhere.'

Frida bent to the floor; the action seemed so effortless, so well-oiled. When she stood again, she had the box in her hand; she rubbed its sides with her big thumbs and looked into its empty corners. The expression on her face was one of recognition, as if she, too, remembered the box from childhood.

'That's my father's,' said Ruth. 'It's mine.'

Frida didn't speak. She held the box to her chin to inspect it further; then she turned into the hallway, towards her room, and Ruth began to recall what she would find there.

'You locked me in!' Ruth called. She rose from her chair and hurried to the lilies – it was easy, when she had taken multiple pills, to rise and hurry. The lilies were still damp. Ruth tore the wrapping paper away in order to be closer to them. Each petal was flooded with pink, but the centres paled out to blond, and the stamens, which shook as Ruth held them to her face, were loaded with dusty yellow. Frida bellowed from her room; Ruth fenced herself in with lilies. They smelled both clean and definite. They smelled of a saltless garden.

Frida was quiet coming back down the hallway. Still holding the box, she stepped into the kitchen as if walking out onto a rickety jetty. Her shoulders were drawn back and her chest was full of air, as if she were about to recite the days of the week; but she didn't. She didn't even shout. She looked at Ruth among her flowers and said, 'Those aren't yours.'

Ruth held tighter to the lilies. 'They're from Richard,' she said.

'Poor dear crazy. Give them here.'

'I'm not crazy.'

'Confused, then. As usual, poor Ruthie's just a bit confused.'

'No,' said Ruth, but she recognised the word *confused* as approaching what she was, after her sticky, bright dream.

'All right,' said Frida. 'Let's see. How old are you?'

'Seventy-five.'

'What colour are my eyes?'

'Brown.'

'And what's the capital of Fiji?'

'Suva.'

'No it isn't.'

'It is,' said Ruth. 'I lived there. I should know.'

'You *don't* know,' said Frida. 'You only *think* you do. That's what I'm talking about – confused! Now that's cleared up, maybe you can tell me what you were doing in my room.'

'It's my room. My lilies.'

'Give them to me. I'll put them in some water.'

'No.'

Frida came no closer to Ruth. She held her arm out with the box at the end of it, as if it might be the perfect receptacle for flowers; then she turned and threw it into the wastepaper basket that sat beside Ruth's chair.

Ruth winced. 'I know you were at Richard's house. Why? Why was my box under your bed?'

'What were you doing looking under my bed?'

'You locked me in.'

'I didn't lock anybody in!' Frida cried. She was in the kitchen now, tearing at the wrapping paper, which was wet from the lilies and stuck to her angry fingers. She shook it off into the wastepaper bin. 'I closed the door so you wouldn't go wandering out there with all the traps in the grass. The bloody doors weren't locked.'

But Ruth had tried the doors. She had tried them. 'What do you want?' she asked, because it occurred to her that Frida wanted something from her – was always wanting, wanting, without ever quite admitting it.

'I want you to apologise for trashing my room,' said Frida. 'For wrecking my stuff and for disrespecting my privacy. I want you to give me those lilies, and I want you to admit Suva isn't the capital

174

of Fiji.'

Ruth shook her head.

'All right then,' Frida said, and, her face expressionless, used her forearm to sweep the objects across the dining table. They clattered over the surface, catching and dragging, and the bottles tipped and rolled to the left and right, but they were all carried by Frida's arm to the table's edge, and then they fell into the waste-paper bin. None of the glass shattered; everything fell neatly and quietly, almost as if the objects were taking up their original places, snug in the bin as they had been in the box. It was like a magic trick. Then Frida lifted the bin and held it on her hip like an awkward baby; she opened the door with one quick hand and, still matronly, marched into the garden.

Ruth couldn't understand how the door had opened, but she was safe behind her lilies. She followed and watched as Frida shook the contents of the bin out over the edge of the dune. Some of the shells and coral bounced a little before rolling, and all the grit and dust swarmed up in a grubby cloud before puffing away, abruptly, as if with a specific destination in mind. The box flew from the bin and caught a little in the coastal wind; it subsided among the grasses after a short, desperate flight. Then Frida threw her arms out so that the wastepaper basket swung high and spun onto the beach.

Ruth stood beside Frida at the crest of the dune. The lilies were growing heavier in her arms. Down the slope, the coral and the shells were beginning their primordial crawl back to the sea.

'Those things belong to my family,' Ruth said.

'A little life lesson for you, Ruthie,' said Frida. 'Don't get attached to *things*.'

Ruth began to test out the slope of the dune with one foot. Frida was grinning into the salt of the wind. There was a tremendous wellbeing about her, and she lifted her face to the sky as if feeling the sun for the first time in months. Frida often gave off an impression of post-hibernation. She was a great brown bear, a slumbering hazard, both dozy and vigilant. And Ruth was used to her slow surety of movement; but now she had woken up.

'You're an awful woman,' said Ruth, and Frida gave a gnomic titter. The chalky sand rubbed at Ruth's bare feet. 'A savage woman.' Frida laughed harder, with that same round gong Ruth had heard on the telephone. Ruth pointed down the dune with her lilies. 'I want everything back.'

Frida dusted her hands and emitted the sigh she often did immediately before standing up. 'Two things,' she said. 'First of all, apologise. Second, tell me Suva isn't the capital of Fiji. Then I'll pick it all up for you. Otherwise, you can do it yourself.'

Ruth began to descend. She still clung to the lilies. This was the very worst request to make of her back: to walk down a steep slope with her arms full. She bent into the dune and it fell away beneath her; she kicked up whirlwinds of sand.

Frida watched from above. 'Mind your step,' she said.

Ruth moved forward and the grass collapsed; she felt her feet slide, and then she was lying on the ground with the lilies scattered over and around her. She wriggled them off. She didn't think she was hurt; it didn't even feel like a fall. It was as if the dune had scooped her up and she was caught in a shallow, sandy bowl.

'Oh, Ruthie,' said Frida from above.

'What is it?' asked Ruth from among the grasses, but she knew she had fallen into the tiger trap. It had filled considerably in the hours since its construction; now it cradled Ruth. It was fragrant with lilies. She closed her eyes and opened them again, and the world bumped up against her and tilted away. She was lying on her side. Ants moved among the sand, over and under each grain, and all of this was too close to Ruth's nose. Above her she saw the very edge of the lawn, or what remained of it. It was a frayed rug of green. Ruth was able to roll onto her back, and then the sky appeared, a dark, blank blue. She felt a dizzy sting behind her eyes.

'Any bones broken?' called Frida.

Ruth looked to every bone for information, and each reassured her. But her back was beginning to burn. She felt around for some kind of handhold and found a small mineral lump with string still attached. A flurry of sand from above suggested Frida might be coming down the dune.

'Don't!' Ruth cried.

'Please yourself.' Frida sighed again, and the sound was both resigned and happy. The sand settled. 'You know, this is exactly what I said to Jeff. I said to him, it just isn't safe to have an old girl like your mother living in this kind of environment. She walks in the garden, and what do you know, she slips and falls. I've seen a fall do someone in – never the same again. And that's why I'm here twenty-four hours a day.'

The sea sounded close, and something fluttered in Ruth's ear.

'But does Jeff ever thank me? Does he ever ring me up and say, "Frida, you're the ant's pants"?'

Some sand scattered across Ruth's face. She wasn't sure if the wind was at fault, or Frida. She tried to sit up and found that she couldn't. 'I can't get up,' she said, but not to Frida; to herself.

'Not with that attitude, you can't.'

'I really can't,' said Ruth, still to herself. She would have liked to see one cloud in the sky. That would have been fluffy and merry and in some way comforting. If I see a cloud, she thought, it means I'll get up again. It means I haven't fallen.

'Take me, for instance,' said Frida. 'If I went around all day saying, "I can't, I can't," I'd get nowhere. What you need is some positive thinking. Say to yourself, "I *will* get up." Then do it.'

Ruth moved one foot experimentally.

'Too many people in this country are old before their time,' Frida sighed.

'Frida.' Ruth heard the bleat in her voice. Her body wouldn't move. 'I think I'm paralysed.'

Ruth felt something tickle at her forehead, like a handful of thrown grass; she knocked it away with her right hand.

'Not paralysed,' said Frida. 'See? So negative. You know, this might be good for you. Give you a bit of a challenge, break you out of your can't can't can't and show you your actions have consequences. I'll be inside, Ruthie, tidying your mess. And one day you'll thank me for this.' Frida inhaled loudly, as if she were filling her lungs with the sea, and then she was gone. Sand rose in her wake and settled over other sand. The back door opened and closed again.

Now the cats emerged from wherever they had been hiding. They sniffed at Ruth's cheeks and shoulders. One of them curled against her side. The dune had shifted to accommodate her, and it was pleasant to think – or at least less frightening to think – that eventually this hollow would shape itself around her and be perfectly moulded to her back and bones. Then she would sleep the way she had as a child, when everything was supple and new and it was possible to abandon her body entirely, night after night, without ever knowing how lucky that was. Something whirred in the grasses near her head, some insect, and it occurred to Ruth that Frida's tiger might be nearby. He might come as night fell and find her. Frida might make him come; she might make him a real tiger, with real teeth. This alarmed Ruth into action. She would have to make her way back to the house, even if it took her all night, and then she would escape. She would go to Richard: find his address on the envelope she had saved, take the bus into town, catch the train to Sydney. Ruth felt around with her hands and caught at the grasses; she felt them cut into her palms, little quick slits, as she pulled herself into a half-sitting position. The cat at her side leapt away, indignant. Her hips were a faulty hinge, and she fell to the sand again.

Ruth's back objected to all this. She often imagined her back as an instrument; that way she could decide if the pain was playing in the upper or lower registers. Sometimes it was just a long, low note, and sometimes it was insistent and shrill. Lying in the sand, it was both. It was a whole brassy, windy ensemble. She cried out, but there was no one to hear her. The lifesavers would be sitting in their flagged turrets down at the surf club, scanning the sea, ready to pack up for the day; they didn't know she was drowning. The wind was a little cold. Perhaps, if she lay still enough, it would make her a coverlet of sand.

The cats watched her from the grasses. They seemed to be encouraging her with their dumbstruck eyes. This is what you get, she thought, for living on a beach, not a road; and that was Harry's fault, since Harry had insisted on this isolation and then killed them both with it. Because now she felt she was in danger of dying out on the dune, and that Frida had been trying, all along, to bring her to this point – had sent a tiger, and built traps, and now was trying to kill her. And Ruth was sure, too, that if Harry had stayed in Sydney and walked every day beside the Harbour the way he used to, he would still be alive; he would have been whisked to a state-of-the-art hospital, where the business of saving the lives of stupid old men happened every day. Not that she blamed the girl who picked him up from the gutter. What was her name? Ellen something. Jeffrey had told her this Ellen Something had held Harry's head as he died. What a stupid old isolated head. Now Ruth lay dying in a tiger trap, and no one was there – not even Frida – to cradle any part of her.

She might have cried, but one of the cats had climbed onto her chest and was clawing lovingly at it. She felt the fraying of her thin skin. In shifting to shake the cat off, Ruth managed to lift herself onto her elbows. This presented new possibilities. She saw her feet now, and that thin sickle was the edge of the sea. If she pushed her feet towards the water and kept her elbows propped underneath her, she could manage a slow backward shuffle up the dune. She reversed an experimental inch and her back didn't make any special objection. At first this filled her with wild energy. She thought of the grim joy of mountaineers trapped on glaciers, who realise they can cut off their own crushed arms. An inch later, she lay back in the sand, exhausted, and slid a little way towards the beach. She wasn't overly disheartened, because she had accepted that this would take hours. Part of her welcomed the effort of it; it was so allegorical. The fight for life! Ruth was quick to feel sorry for herself, and quick to congratulate. This was deliberate on her part; a lifelong mechanism which in her opinion had served her well. She lifted her elbows and renewed her backward crawl.

Everything was millimetres away, particularly the sea, but the house was impossibly far. Whenever she paused, she slipped down the dune, and those were precious millimetres lost; but if she didn't rest, her eyes filled with the pain of her back, and her arms seemed to melt away. Then she had to lie back in the sand and stretch her arms out on either side of her, like wings; or she stretched them down over her body, to touch her thighs. She felt lumps in her skirt, fished in her pockets, and found pills. One more can't hurt, she thought, and she swallowed a pill dry, gagging on her own sandy spit. Then she raised herself up and started again. This may have happened more than once. She learned to turn her feet outward to brace herself against the sand, and to hold on to the roots of the grass, which helped slow her slide. Her rests grew longer and the cats lost interest. Ruth felt the way she did on plane rides: empty, suspended, and consumed by the inconvenience of urination. She knew she had kicked free of the tiger trap when there were no longer any lilies around her feet.

Ruth reached the edge of the garden. She was moving faster now; the grass was thicker, and she rarely slid. She rested half on the dune and half on the lawn and wondered if, summoning her strength, she might make one magnificent final burst for the house. This summoning of her strength took some time. A bright star came out – or was it Venus? Harry knew the constellations. He had taught her some way to look at Venus and figure out the direction of the pole. Or was that in the northern hemisphere? The sky was still bluer than the sea, but the lights were coming on in the town across the water, the Milky Way was scattering, and soon Frida's tiger might run along the beach under the stars of that galaxy.

There was no sign of life from the house until the sky grew

darker; then one window was lit, and another, so that half of Ruth's body lay in shadow and the other in a yellow square. Whose hand lit those lamps? Ruth couldn't be sure. Frida's, of course; but it might also have been Harry's, and maybe her own. Until now she had never experienced vertigo while lying down. She thought she heard a male voice inside the house, but it might be the television. The cats were nearby begging for their dinner, but Ruth refused to join their chorus. She would never cry out. She lifted herself again and now was almost walking on her elbows, dragging her feet along; she made it to the house. She used the wall to reach a full sitting position, and she rested with her head against it, by the back door.

It was peaceful in the garden. It was so separate. The evening seemed to be stalling, to only reluctantly be growing dark. Ruth sat against the wall and thought of Frida inside the house, waiting for her arrival, but at the same time she was inside with Frida, sitting in her chair and being tended to. She was both in and out of the house; she was away from Frida, but bound to her; she was hungry. The cats cried out again – what a noise they could make, those tiny things – and finally somebody opened the door and stood above Ruth without speaking; all she could see was the light. Arms attempted to lift her, but she resisted them. She let her body go limp and drag, and eventually the arms gave up. Then the door closed. Someone was moving in the kitchen, feeding the cats and singing and cooking sausages. The fat smell of the sausages cleared Ruth's mind. It came to her that the box hadn't belonged to her father. It was Harry's – it had come from his family, from the Solomon Islands, and it had nothing to do with her. How was it possible to forget a thing like that?

If the box wasn't her father's, and the doors hadn't been locked, then maybe Suva wasn't the capital of Fiji. And what did that matter? There was so little of Fiji left to remember. There was only this feeling, which everyone must have about their childhood, that it was extraordinary in some way. But she had been to a royal ball. Ruth saw the small figure that was the Queen at the ball. It was funny to watch a queen grow old; it made Ruth feel as if she hadn't grown at all. But of course they both had. They had expanded, as they must, into their responsibilities. She wondered if that was the point of a queen: that she should help you mark the passage of time, because you saw every year how her profile on the backs of coins became softer with age, but at the same time she stopped you from noticing time at all, in the sense that she seemed fixed and immovable on her distant throne. How unlikely she appeared from here, on the ground, in the night, on the other side of the world. But there was something to knowing that one day, in 1953, they had been in the same place at the same time. So Ruth felt proprietary when Phillip talked about how unnecessary the Queen was, how anachronistic, and when she protested, citing the Queen's dignity and suffering, Jeffrey was always careful to say, 'We have nothing against her personally, Ma.'

'Yeah,' Phillip would say, 'I'm sure she's the salt of the earth.'

But didn't salt stop the earth from producing greenery? Didn't crops never again grow in fields sown with salt? So who would want to be the salt of the earth? And didn't salt come from the sea? The salt of the earth, then, was sand. And Frida hated sand. Ruth thought she would wake up one morning and find that Frida had swept all of it into the sea. She imagined Frida with a great broom sweeping at the sea, and the obedient waves swallowed everything she threw at them. The beach would lie empty and open: rock and fossil, the immodest bones of dinosaurs, great petrified sea monsters, the ashy ends of ancient fires. After Frida, everything would be clean, white, and extinct. She would soap it all up with eucalyptus, and only then would she be happy. Ruth couldn't tell if she wanted Frida to be happy. This seemed to be something Ruth had once – perhaps quite recently – held a position on. Frida, Frida, Queen of Sheba. And there, with the Queen in attendance, was Richard kissing Ruth – but all the time loving someone else. The thought of this – Richard loving someone else, loving her, or perhaps both, or perhaps it was the same thing – became, then, more exhausting than climbing the dune. It became juniper trees and pirate granddaughters and funerals, when she, Ruth, wasn't even sure how she would stand up again.

There was a noise from behind her, a creaking, and then arms lifted Ruth out of the garden. She was too tired to oppose them. No one said a word, but doors opened and closed, and then she was lying on her bed. She drank water and swallowed some pills; after that, no one fussed. Ruth lay and lay and became hungry and restless, but because no one came to her, she fell asleep. Her back didn't hurt her in the morning, and the sun was inviting in the trees. Ruth felt she was the only one awake in the house: no husbands, no boys, no one else stirring. She rolled up from the bed and found her handbag in Harry's study; her purse was inside it. Ruth knew, without quite understanding why, that she must act quickly and make no sound. The front door did squeal a little as she closed it behind her.

The grasses in the shaded drive were so tall! It must be a good harvest. This was the way Harry walked in the mornings, out into the drive and onto the road, and so Ruth walked to the road and looked down the hill. She was surprised to see people at the bus stop. They crowded around it as if something dramatic were taking place. She made her careful way down the hill. What a spread the sea made from here, finer somehow with the road running alongside it. A particular glassy quality to its surface meant it lacked colour and was only shine; but by the shore it turned green. Ruth remembered explaining to her children that the glitter on the water was the reflection of a thousand thousand suns off each new angle made by the waves; every point of light was the sun, repeated. She must walk this way more often.

The people at the bus stop, it seemed, were not gathered for a disaster, but for the bus. They had come sandily from the beach – the sky in that direction suggested rain. The thought of rain worried Ruth, but she felt strangely placid, at a remove from the particulars of her life, and simultaneously at one with the pleasurable fates of the people around her, as if they were all waiting together at the gates of heaven. The bus arrived. She fumbled with her coins and had to be helped; the driver selected the correct change out of her palm, a bird after worms. A courteous young boy vacated his seat for her. She sat, feeling sentimental towards herself, feeling beloved and assisted, and watched as the displaced boy swayed farther up the bus. The rear windows depicted, like a painting, a heavyset woman descending the hill. Grey clouds fell into the sea. The windows were moving away from the woman. Oh, but she would be left behind! Ruth cried out, although she felt no distress. The man across the aisle cast a sceptical look in her direction, and Ruth smiled. Together they had all crested the next hill by the time Frida reached the bus stop.

13

The bus deposited Ruth on a hillside street where she expected shops and the railway station – and found only houses. Their tiled roofs were deep orange; they flared up against the colour of the sea like a warning against tidal wave or flood. The horizon felt higher than it ought to, so that the sea tilted dizzily down over the houses and Ruth found it necessary to walk with her hand touching their low brick fences. She remembered this street after all. She'd walked here once with Jeffrey, when he was a boy. He dropped a coin and it rolled beneath a parked car; she risked her back to recover it for him. He didn't cry, but stood with his fists tight and an expression of unbearable suspense on his face. When she returned the coin, he thanked her so formally, and with such solemn grace, that he seemed like a foreign child accepting some attention from a tourist. Then he spent it, minutes later, on a tea bun, and was his sticky, happy self again.

A large red dog walked down the middle of the street. It moved its head from side to side, alert, as if it were hunting. Ruth stayed pressed against the fences. She admired the houses, which were neat and unassuming, with white-framed windows sheltered by awnings and fences the same red as the dog. One of these houses might belong to Frida's mother. Ruth's shoulders had begun to ache, as if she'd been lifting heavy objects all night long.

She turned a corner and found herself on the main street of town. The shops nestled together in tidy rows; it felt like Christmas because lights were strung up across the road. Perhaps there were always lights now, to make shopping feel festive. She remembered the merriness of the butcher, who displayed annual signs declaring him the South Coast Sausage King. This was an official title, apparently, won year after year and jealously guarded. A taxi drove down the street and Ruth hid from it in the shade of the butcher's doorway. That meant she blocked the opening door, and she and the door and the person behind it were forced to do a sprightly little dance, and the person, a woman, turned out to know her.

'Mrs Field! Ruth!' cried this woman. She was so very small – 'petite', Ruth's mother would have called her – that she made Ruth think of a little toy prised from an expensive Advent calendar. Ruth tried to arrange her face into an expression of recognition; she must have failed because the woman said, with a hopeful smile,

'It's Ellen?'

'Oh, Ellen!' said Ruth, and in saying the name aloud did remember her as Ellen Gibson. 'But how funny! Do you live here, too?'

'Yes. Yes, of course,' said Ellen. 'I've been meaning to call you. It's so nice to see you again.'

Ruth beamed. Yes, it was *nice* – what a true word that was, how fine and underrated. It meant more than kindness; it meant a fastidious effort to be thoughtful and good. To be nice in this world, thought Ruth, was to be considered – what? Milky and feeble, she thought; fragile. But Ruth valued niceness, and so did Ellen Gibson. This was their bond; this was why Ellen would stop her car to ask after an elderly man of distinguished bearing, breathing strangely on the side of the road.

'And how are you doing these days?' asked Ellen.

'I'm doing very well, my dear. And of course I have Frida to help me.' Ruth recognised Frida, then, as a shield of some kind; she seemed to be wielding her. 'Frida cooks everything and cleans. She's my right arm.'

'I'm so pleased,' said Ellen. 'What brings you into town this morning? Some shopping?'

At this moment, Ruth was unsure what had brought her into town. She had an idea that her business would eventually lead in the direction of the railway station.

'Can I drive you somewhere?' Ellen was asking. 'I'd be happy to take you home. I love driving out that way.'

Ruth wanted to accept because it would please Ellen so much. Wasn't it wonderful to please people? But that was impossible. 'I don't want to go home,' she said.

'All right,' said Ellen. She wore sunglasses pushed up into her hair; that was why light flashed from the top of her head. 'Can I take you somewhere else?'

'I have some shopping.' Ruth looked in her purse for her to-do list. She always brought a to-do list to town with her, and today it was missing – wasn't that just typical? But she was there at the butcher's. 'Sausages,' she said, and the butcher's door sang as she opened it; inside, the shop had a cold, bloody smell. Ellen remained for a moment in the street with a look of surprise on her face, but Ruth refused to let that worry her. The South Coast Sausage King stood behind the counter, chatting and beaming, while his courtiers ordered lamb chops and steak. He knew her name, too; did everybody?

'Mrs Field!' he called.

She felt quite famous. This might have been why he won that prize, year after year; not for his sausages, but for his memory. Ruth used to know the name of the Sausage King. He used to hold a barbecue for his 'favourite customers' in the New Year, when Ruth and her family were always at the coast for the summer; she had been to his house. He barbecued with fierce pride and made people taste everything. He winked at her now, which was his way of saying, 'I don't want to serve this woman, I want to serve you; I can't wait to serve you,' and flattered, Ruth waited her turn. She and Harry used to laugh about the jolly flirtations of the Sausage King. They never offended any husband. She had known this man for nearly forty years.

'Mrs Field,' he said now, turning towards her. He was tall and merry and trim. She remembered there had been some heartbreak over a son who didn't want to be a butcher; or maybe the trouble was that he did. The Sausage King wore a striped apron and seemed to have absolutely no hair on his arms. His hands were big and pink, and youthful from the handling of all that meat.

'We haven't seen you in town for months,' he said, twinkling. 'Tell me where you've been hiding.'

That was another thing she remembered: he always used the royal plural, as if speaking for both himself and his sausages. But what was his name?

'Nowhere, nowhere,' she said, bashful. He always made her blush, and she supposed this was how she knew his attentions were harmless. 'I have someone to shop for me now.'

Frida bought all their meat in styrofoam and plastic from the supermarket, but he didn't know that. Still, Ruth felt the guilt as a new heat on her face.

'It's just a treat to see you,' he said, and turned to the other people in the shop – people younger than Ruth and the Sausage King. 'Mrs Field is one of my oldest and most loyal customers. We've known each other since before you were all born.'

Ruth blushed further. No one in the shop was that young, but she might have been that old.

'And what can I get for you today?' he asked. 'The lamb is a miracle, the spring lamb.'

'Oh, yes, lamb. From New Zealand.'

'Australian lamb, Mrs Field! Always! Now – a roast? Chops?'

'Oh, dear,' said Ruth. The other customers began to stir with polite exasperation. Many of them had been in the shop before the arrival of the steadfast Mrs Field. 'Chops,' she said, because Frida would scold about a roast. Frida, returning home from the supermarket, talked at great length about the expense of groceries in this day and age.

'Chops it is. How many? How many?' sang the Sausage King. His busy pink hands worked over the lamb chops, selecting good specimens and shifting the plastic parsley. 'Five ninety-nine a kilo, five-fifty for you.' The customers shook their heads at the lovable favouritism of the Sausage King.

'Five-fifty,' said Ruth.

'One kilo it is. Anything else I can do for you today?' He wrapped the lamb in waxy white paper. Ruth loved the cool weight of butchers' bundles; they reminded her of babies.

'That's all,' she said, wishing she could be sure it really was.

'No sausages? I tell you what, I'll throw a couple in, on the house.' Now the shop threatened mutiny. The door opened and the bell rang; someone was leaving. The Sausage King swaddled the sausages in white paper. Ruth saw him wink at another woman; he would serve her next. 'And that's five-fifty for Mrs Field.'

Ruth nodded. She opened her purse and there was no money in it, except for the few coins she had left after the bus fare. The only other thing in there was a library card. 'Goodness,' she said. 'I've forgotten my purse.'

The Sausage King looked at the purse in her hands.

'I mean, it's empty. What a duffer!'

He was poised with the smooth white packages. 'Not to worry, not to worry,' he reassured, but he grinned now at the other customers. His grin said, 'Silly old bird.' It said, 'Stupid, stupid, and old, old, old.' Once, when he was still young, he had presented her sons with hats folded out of butcher's paper; they had loved them for a whole afternoon.

'I can't think —' began Ruth, but the woman who had been

winked at stepped up, businesslike, although determinedly kind, and passed six dollars to the Sausage King.

'There now!' he cried, as if a spring-lamb miracle truly had come to pass. How he trusted and loved the world; it was everywhere on his face. He patted the woman's hand. She would be invited to the New Year's barbecue.

'Oh, thank you, thank you so much,' said Ruth, taking possession of her packages and their smooth infant weight. She had some idea of sending Frida to her saviour's house with six dollars, but the woman was ordering now – a complicated order, designed for a family, which called on all the skills of the delighted butcher. Her expression was resolutely against interruption or further gratitude.

'Goodbye, Mrs Field!' the Sausage King called, and Ruth waved from among her parcels and empty purse, and a woman opened the door for her. The bell shook. When she passed into the street, the customers laughed at some joke he made. Ruth hated him and his lusty courtesies. Harry was truly kind, truly chivalrous. None of it was for show. She would tell him that, when she got home, and she would also conceal the embarrassing free meat from Frida, who frequently expressed her contempt for handouts, freeloaders, and anyone who didn't perform honest hard labour for her money. Frida would never hear about the empty purse or the helpful, mortifying woman or the temptation of the lamb roast, and she wouldn't be angry. To believe this filled Ruth with busy purpose. Where to next? The street was lined with conveniences. Next door was the chemist, across the road was the bakery, and farther down was the bank. She wondered why she didn't come to town more often. Where had she parked the car? She was always forgetting that. No – she had caught the bus. And at the end of the street was the railway station, where the trains pulled out for Sydney every three hours. Why should that be such a comforting thought? Her arms still ached.

Two boys waited outside the chemist with that particular alert boredom of boys who have been promised a reward for their patience. They watched every passing car with interest; whenever the street was empty, their shoulders fell; their feet stepped over each other, shifting their bantam weights, like newly foaled giraffes. They had pretty faces, choral and virtuous, as if cast in a Nativity play, and long light hair which they threw out of their eyes with a beautiful backward motion of the head. They were maybe nine and eleven. The older boy was sure of his gestures – the movement of his head, the stepping of his feet – and the younger one copied him, so their resemblance seemed less genetic and more an act of desperate study. Ruth's heart was burdened with love for these boys, who waited outside the chemist and cancelled out the Sausage King. They wore blue-and-grey school uniforms. In the shadow of the striped awning they waited and slouched, and because they had been so patient, she would buy them a milkshake each, or an ice cream if they wanted it. Surely she had enough coins for that.

Ruth hurried to them with her hands outspread; her purse dropped right at their feet, and the oldest boy picked it up for her. He was nearly as tall as she was and handed her the purse with a bashful elegance, almost feminine, which drew his features into a courtly mask.

'Thank you, my darling!' cried Ruth, and embraced him.

'S'all right,' he said, in that gulping growl of boys on the very verge of change, and she released his rigid shoulders.

'You're such good boys for waiting so quietly. How about a milkshake?' Ruth held her hand out to the youngest boy, who hung back behind his brother and looked at her as if she had committed some fascinating faux pas, right there on the street. But Ruth knew the way boys could behave when they reached a certain age; she knew to ignore the discouraging twinge it produced in her throat. She shook her hand at him again, cheerfully. 'What do you say? A milkshake, or do you want ice cream? You've certainly earned it.'

'Mum,' he said, and he seemed startled and perhaps a little afraid, and he looked past her at a woman who was leaving the chemist.

'Hello again!' said the woman, who was Ellen Gibson. 'Have you met my boys? This is Brett, and this is Jamie. Boys, this is Mrs Field.'

The boys nodded their blond heads, and their bodies seemed to dip in brief curtsies. They had the same shy smile. Their names were Brett and Jamie. They seemed to have agreed to conceal some residual awkwardness from their mother.

'You've got your meat, Ruth? Can I take you home now?'

Ruth looked towards the railway station. How would she pay for a train, with only a library card? And also – the meat would spoil.

The boys were already walking; Ellen was walking. So was Ruth. She was being led. The sea retreated, as if it had been winched down to its proper level, and that was a kind of surrender.

'This way. Mine's the red car.' Ellen smiled and nodded, that same curtsey of the head her sons made. 'I'll drop the boys at school first, if that's all right? They're late today, they've been to the dentist.'

The boys, already belted into the back of the car, groaned on cue, as if appalled to have had their dentistry made public. Ruth sensed an injustice; she suspected her seat had been promised to one of them for the ride, and now she'd usurped it.

'Oh, dear,' she said, because she couldn't manage her own seatbelt. Ellen snapped it into place while Ruth held her hands, as if at gunpoint, on either side of her downcast face.

The school wasn't far away; the boys ran towards the entrance and seemed to fall into it. Ruth was amazed they could do anything at all on those long feet. 'They're going to be very tall, aren't they,' she said.

Ellen smiled and nodded. 'Just like their father.' She was proud of them; she watched until they were out of sight.

'Isn't it funny to watch children grow.'

Ellen said, 'It's a privilege.'

Ruth scrutinised this possibility. No, she thought, it's melancholy and strange. Children were so temporary. When Jeffrey was born, Harry stroked his son's nose and said, 'What's amazing is that this is *forever*.' But it wasn't forever; it wasn't even a month. In a few weeks Jeffrey was different, and the blind, bumping, waterlogged Jeffrey was gone; he was rosy and plump; he butted at her face the way the cats did. It came to her that she missed her children, not as they were now, with their own children, but as they had been when they were young. She would never see them again. Jeffrey on the beach when the house was still for holidays; Phillip's failing breath; their small hands. She wanted – very badly – to say 'Fuck.'

'Now let's get you home,' said Ellen.

'Do you know the way?' asked Ruth, because she herself was unsure.

'Yes. But you might have to remind me where to turn in.'

Ruth tried to picture where to turn in and saw only grass – long, light grass with a tiger in it. She smiled vaguely. She was so comfortable in the car, which Ellen handled with such confidence. The town passed, and the sea. The suggestion of rain had vanished now, and the pale sky tended cloudlessly towards white. Ellen wanted to know what Ruth had been up to: if she'd had visitors, if she'd been getting out and enjoying the weather. 'How are your sons?' she asked, and Ruth said, 'They're going to be very tall.'

'How often do you come into town?'

'Not nearly enough. You know how it is. Busy busy busy.'

'Oh, yes,' said Ellen.

'You know how it is. You're a mother.'

'And you have someone looking after you?'

'I'm very well cared for,' said Ruth. The car advanced so easily. 'Not only that, I'm *defended*.'

'Defended? Against what?'

Ruth noted the wonder in Ellen's voice – these small currents of response were important to her now, they were signposts for behaviour, and they alerted her to the possibility that she must rethink her previous comments – so she answered, 'Against the slings and arrows of fortune.'

'Of outrageous fortune,' said Ellen, laughing.

And Ruth was grateful to her, and also to Frida, who had worn herself out with constant care on behalf of the house and the cats and herself, and who had driven out the tiger. But she was aware of a sense of misgiving, as if she had done something to make Frida angry; why was she frightened of Frida? The fear came and went. She remembered, then, something about making a mess in the house yesterday: throwing pills on the floor and flowers on the dune. Of course Frida was angry.

The sea was different when travelled along at speed. The sun shone from every part of the sky and water: bright light arrived from everywhere. Ruth closed her eyes and saw strong pink. She could feel the car climbing the hill and said, 'It's just on the right here.' Then, opening her eyes, it was like arriving at her house for the first time. She saw the grasses and tangled scrub that needed beating back from the drive, and the riot of the ruined garden, and among all this frenzy was the neat house with its scrubbed windows. It radiated a tidy quiet, but there was something unusual about it nonetheless; a faint fog seemed to rise from behind it, dimly grey and almost invisible against the water.

Frida was sitting on the low step across the front door of the house. She looked wearily up at the sound of the car, her face resigned to disaster, and her arms fell across her knees so that her wrists turned out, as if expecting handcuffs. But when she saw the unfamiliar car, she raised herself with a slow concentration that recalled her mythically fatter past.

Ellen brought the car to a stop. She leaned over to open the passenger door, and Ruth found herself wanting it closed again; she wanted it shut against Frida. But it was too late now: Ellen was out of the car, Frida was moving. Ruth swung in the seat and her legs came sticking out into the air like a child's. This seemed to prompt Frida to hastier action. She held out her arms for Ruth to run into, and so Ruth did; she was closer to Frida's body at this moment than she had ever been. It gave out an agitated heat. She recognised this embrace; it was the way she'd hugged Jeffrey the day she came home from the hospital with his baby brother. Perhaps Frida wasn't angry after all. Ellen had averted her eyes and was studying the foggy house.

'Where in God's name have you been?' Frida cried, but Ruth, remembering her manners, drew back and turned to Ellen.

'This is Ellen,' she said. 'Frida, this is *Ellen*.'

'Hello,' said Ellen. 'You're Ruth's nurse?'

'I'm her carer.' Frida released Ruth from her arms.

'Frida, can I ask what's happened here?' Ellen sounded terse and assured. She sounded almost detective-like, until Frida took a terrible step towards her; then the difference in their sizes was frightening.

'What's happened here,' snapped Frida, and then she seemed to reconsider her position and temper her voice, 'is that I've been worried sick about Ruthie vanishing like that. I've been waiting for my brother to help me find her.'

The tone was soft, but also efficient and proud. Ruth waited by the front door, cradling her bundles of meat and her purse, concerned that Ellen and Frida's meeting was going badly. She noticed a bitterness in the air, a smell of old bushfire.

'You didn't know she'd left the house?'

'Not till she was halfway to the bus. Listen, you,' said Frida, addressing Ruth now, 'that was quite a stunt you pulled.' She stepped backwards and drew Ruth into a huddle under her arm. Ellen rattled her keys and looked towards the car.

'You better say thank you to your friend for bringing you home safe,' Frida said, and Ruth, who knew this was unnecessary, smiled at Ellen. Who smiled back. There was an understanding between them.

'How often does this happen?' Ellen asked, looking at Ruth.

'Never before,' said Frida. 'But that's just the way it is with these old dears. They get it in their heads to do something, and off they go.'

Ellen continued to address Ruth. 'If you'd ever like to go into town again, please give me a call. I'd love to take you out to lunch one day. You have my number, don't you?' She looked at Frida. 'She has my number. Ellen Gibson. I'm the one who – helped when –'

Frida nodded in a businesslike way. Of course she knew all the details of Harry's death, but this nod seemed to indicate that she considered her own work – the daily drudgery of care for the widow – much meatier than Ellen's glamourous part in proceedings.

'All right then,' said Ellen, and her body turned towards the car, but she seemed to be waiting for something – some reassurance, possibly, that it was all right to go. Frida didn't move. She gave the impression that she had grown on this spot, from tender root to woody trunk, and would never be persuaded to leave it; nor would she, for that matter, release Ruth.

'Drive safely, won't you,' said Frida, in a tone indicative of her merry indifference to Ellen's wellbeing.

'Goodbye, Ruth,' Ellen said, and although she hesitated again, with one leg in the car and the other foot on the ground, she still sat down and drove away and was swallowed up by the grasses.

With Ellen gone, Frida's bravado vanished. She wept. Could this be true – Frida weeping? Ruth held her – was really held *by* her, but in a clinging way – and she watched Frida the way Harry used to watch a fire he was building: with a feeling that he had no real control over proceedings but should probably be on hand for emergencies.

'I thought I'd lost you,' Frida sniffed. 'I thought you were gone for good. How long have you been planning this?'

Now she mastered herself and held Ruth at arm's length. Her eyes were a damp, foggy red, and her face had puffed into a new and compassionate shape, but she shook Ruth a little at the shoulders and pulled her close into another airless clinch. 'Come on,' she said. 'What were you up to?'

Ruth, smothered, only shook her head.

'Who did you see in town, hey?' Now Frida was walking them into the house. 'Did you plan to meet Ellen? Who else were you chatting to?'

When they reached the front hall, Frida released Ruth against the coat rack before locking the door and leaning against it with small exhalations that still managed to lift her chest to her chins.

'No one,' said Ruth. She stood nestled among the winter coats, which hung all year in the hall and gave off a stale, resentful smell. There was the vaguest odour, too, of Harry – just a fugitive whiff. Ruth thought she might have stood among the coats after he died, searching out that smell. 'Only Ellen. I bumped into her outside the chemist. Wasn't that a lovely piece of luck?'

'Just lovely,' said Frida. 'Just absolutely darling.'

Frida seized Ruth's purse and reviewed it in a businesslike way.

'Oh! And the Sausage King,' said Ruth, proffering the white parcels. She anticipated a scolding for omitting the Sausage King, but Frida only straightened her shoulders as if she needed to reassert her own majesty.

'Now listen,' she said, 'I'm going to get this over with. There's been a small accident while you were out, but don't worry. Hardly any damage done. This way – it's the kitchen.'

Ruth followed her down the hall.

There had been a fire in the kitchen: a small, blackish, crawling kind of fire, apparently, because the kitchen hadn't burned. Instead it seemed to have expired, having first given up on something – some former dignity, some presumed usefulness – before slumping into despair. Dark streaks spread up the wall from the oven as if painted by a brush of smoke, and the smell was intense – the comforting fug of a house fire mingled with something bitter and almost salty. Sooty water puddled the floor.

'Oh,' said Ruth.

'I'm sorry,' said Frida. She didn't seem to be apologising so much as imparting information. 'I went crazy when I couldn't find you – I forgot I had oil on the stove.'

Ruth considered the stubbed kitchen. 'What do I do?'

'What d'you mean?'

'How do I fix it?' Ruth supposed she would have to fix it.

'You *don't* fix it. I fix it. Like I fix everything.'

'That's what you're here for,' said Ruth.

'Yeah, yeah,' said Frida. 'Now take a seat. I can't believe you, running off like that. What am I going to do with you?'

She began to bustle in the kitchen. Ruth went to the dining room and sat in her chair. She felt weighed down by gratitude for Frida, who fixed everything. It was as if something heavy and warm had been placed on her lap. Then a thought came to her, and she said, 'But what were you cooking?'

'What now?' called Frida, as if her head were buried at the bottom of some inconvenient cupboard, among linens, when in fact she was only putting the butcher's parcels in the fridge.

'What were you cooking when the oil caught fire?'

Frida sighed and stalled behind the fridge door. 'Fish fingers,' she said.

'Oh.'

'Why, Sherlock, do you want to see the box? Do you want to check the garbage?'

Ruth laughed. 'I only wondered.'

Frida ran into the dining room, sat at the table, and surprised Ruth – seemed to surprise herself – by beginning to cry again. What a fragile Frida she was today. Ruth felt so sad for her.

'This is too much for me,' Frida said in a voice entirely unaffected by the weeping; but Ruth could see the tears on her face and the despairing lift to her shoulders.

'Oh, no, no,' Ruth said. 'Don't cry, dear. Everything's lovely. Everything's fine.'

Then Frida lowered her head onto the table. Her hairstyle seemed perfectly designed for this manoeuvre because it remained fixed in a rigid bun. Ruth could undertake a detailed inspection of the back of Frida's neck. It was smooth, except for one thick fold that traversed it like a moat. Her skin was paler than Ruth remembered it, which worried her momentarily. She scrutinised Frida's arms, which were pale, too, and sallow; then she remembered that winter was barely over. Everyone paled in the winter. Ruth saw that Frida's hair was currently a nutty brown, a rich yuletide colour, which matched her lighter skin perfectly. How clever she was, and how far-seeing. But fish fingers? In oil? And in the morning?

Frida looked out at Ruth from the cradle of her pastel arms.

'You're too good to me. Last night —'

'Now listen, my dear,' said Ruth, who had an idea that a kind severity was called for in response to such statements. 'There's no need to cry. There are plenty more fish in the deep blue sea.'

Ruth found it easy to say these things from the safety of her chair. It was a little like recovering a language she'd forgotten she knew and still wasn't entirely sure of the sense of.

Frida lifted her head from the humid table; her face was blotted and wet, but she had stopped crying. 'You're a funny old thing.'

Ruth didn't feel funny, but she smiled and smiled.

14

Later that day the telephone rang. The noise startled Ruth, who was dozing in her chair, half aware of Frida cleaning the kitchen. Ruth was pulled from a dream about a trapeze and a public swimming pool; she was being hoisted into the air on the trapeze, and the water glinted below, dangerous in some indefinable, chlorinated way.

Frida answered the phone. 'Yes, Jeff,' she said. 'A little adventure, yes. She's fine, the silly duck. She probably won't remember any of it tomorrow.'

And then: 'Now, Jeff, it's not exactly —'

And finally: 'Sure, sure, here she is.'

Frida presented the phone to Ruth, then returned to scrubbing the kitchen. Ruth held the receiver to her ear.

'Ma? I just had a call from Ellen Gibson.' Jeffrey's voice came at Ruth from around a suspicious corner.

'Lovely Ellen!' cried Ruth.

'I hear you went into town today. What was that for?'

'I felt like it,' said Ruth. She suspected she was in trouble, but couldn't decide how to feel about it. 'I'm allowed, aren't I?'

Jeffrey was quiet for a moment. 'I was thinking I might come out for a visit soon, see how you're getting on. What do you think of that idea?'

'That sounds nice,' said Ruth. She had not yet considered it an idea, nice or otherwise.

'You don't sound so sure.'

'There's a problem.' She was filled with sudden anxiety; but what was the problem?

'There is!' Jeffrey pounced as if he had lured her into a confidential trap.

'I know!' she cried. 'I can't get to the railway station.'

'You don't need to pick me up from the station, Ma. I'll take a cab.'

'Oh, that's marvellous! That's just as well. I've lost your father's car.'

'What do you mean, you've lost Dad's car?'

'It's not lost, of course not. It's sold.'

'You didn't tell me you were selling Dad's car.'

'I'm not selling it,' said Ruth. 'It's sold.'

'When was this?'

'Frida arranged it.'

'She did, did she?' Jeffrey used Harry's lawyerly voice – ruminating, withholding, sure of some hidden possibility that ticked over in his mathematical mind. 'Listen, how about this coming weekend? I'll have to check flights, but if I come on Friday night, how's that?'

'Yes, all right, yes,' said Ruth. Then the proximity of Friday startled her. 'This Friday? So soon?'

Frida stopped scrubbing and looked over her shoulder.

'The sooner the better,' said Jeffrey, and this seemed to decide it. Yes, the sooner the better. 'Friday, then. You don't have any more mysterious visitors coming, do you? No more boyfriends? We'll have a great time. We'll play Scrabble and look for whales. Or is it too late for whales?'

So Jeffrey didn't care about the trip to town; not the way Frida cared. He was her good and generous son, her forgiving son. How kind and clement he was. He was just, as his father had been – he was unyielding, but also compassionate. He was the law. Ruth called Frida over to hang up the phone. There was nothing to be afraid of.

But Frida's face was a cliff under a cloud. 'What's happening on Friday?' she asked, leaning against the wall as if she had been washed up, just like that, on the beach. There was a general look of wreckage about everything surrounding her, but the dark streaks on the kitchen wall did look cosier after their scrubbing; almost old-fashioned.

'Jeffrey's coming,' said Ruth.

'Why? What did you say to him?'

'Nothing,' said Ruth. She felt as if she'd been caught up in a procession of events over which she had no control; but she was calm.

'First Ellen, now Jeff. Those two stickybeaks are in it together.' Frida said *Ellen* with a specific spite. She walked from the table to the window and back again, and when she reached the window for a second time, she tapped it with one calculating hand. 'There are a couple of things we might not mention to good old Jeff,' she said.

'What things?'

Frida was coaxing and deferential. 'Obviously the tiger stuff.'

'I thought you were proud of the tiger.'

Frida failed to look proud. She seemed to have failed, generally, in some important way. She gave an impression of pending collapse that she warded off only by tapping the window.

'If Jeff knew everything I do for you, he'd only worry. He'd put you in a home, and you know what that means: no more house. No more sea views. No more picking and choosing what you want for dinner. No more Frida.'

Ruth sat with this possibility. It seemed quite soothing to her, at that moment.

'And he'll never let you go to Richard – you know that, don't you? No one's going to let you do that. They'll say you're too old and he's too old, and you can't look after each other. They'll say it's not in your best interests.'

'Who'll say that?' asked Ruth, startled, not just by the thought of being stopped, but by hearing Richard's name, which had been important to her last night, or even this morning. She had, hadn't she, wanted to go to him?

'Jeff will,' said Frida.

'Jeffrey can't stop me.'

'But the law can stop you, if Jeff wants it to. The government can stop you.'

'You're the government,' said Ruth.

'Well, I quit.'

'When?'

'Right now,' said Frida. 'But I can help you, Ruthie, if you help me.'

Ruth nodded. She needed time to think; also, she was hungry. Why did her shoulders still hurt?

'So that's decided. Now I'm going to use the phone,' said Frida. 'I'm going to call George.'

'Maybe George can sort out the garden.' Ruth was worried about the state of the garden; Jeffrey wouldn't like it.

'I'm going to call him from my room. In private.'

Ruth nodded again. It felt good to nod, so she continued to do so; yes, she said with her pendulous head, and yes and yes again; she was a clock, she thought; she was generous and wise. Frida left, and Ruth went into the lounge room. She went looking for Richard – for some evidence of him. There might be something to tell her he really had put his hand on her knee and said, 'Please think about it.' But the only unusual thing in the lounge room was a dent in the lampshade, which Ruth attempted to smooth and instead deepened. Lifting her arms towards the light, she noticed funny yellow patches on the skin of her arms.

The cats had followed Frida to Phil's room and were probing at the closed door with their adventurous noses; they gave out little cries, and Ruth called for them to come. At the same time, Frida raised her voice. She must be shouting at George. Ruth supposed he didn't want to come and sort out the garden. A new idea came to her: that George, and not the cats, was responsible for its wreck-age. Possibly George was responsible for everything. He assumed a new shape for her: sinister and godlike. Then Frida must have let fly with her foot or her arm; something crashed. The cats baulked and blinked and turned to Ruth for comfort. She coaxed them onto the lounge, where they stretched and sat in funny bundles.

'I don't think I want an angry man in the house,' she told them, but she wasn't sure exactly which man she meant. Maybe Jeffrey? But why was he angry? Maybe George. She couldn't mean Richard, who wanted her to go to *his* house. Frida's voice rose, indecipherable, from her bedroom.

Ruth sat among the cats. They bumped their heads against her and their claws needled her lap. Every window was open, and the front and back doors, because of the smell of the fire. Still the house was hot, and the smell had only intensified. It was a sharp, unmistakably burnt smell, but it reminded Ruth of the night jun-gle; it had the same colour. The lounge-room clock sounded five times, and with each chime the cats twitched and sank.

Frida appeared in the doorway. She looked undone. Her hair had strayed from its style, her mascara was smudged, and her white beautician's pants were soiled with ash. 'I have some bad news,' she said. 'It's George.'

'What's George?'

'It's really bad.'

'Oh, Frida,' sighed Ruth. She thought she knew. She saw George dead in the road, entombed in his taxi. She saw him prone in the grass, maybe a heart attack. Possibly in the sea – buoyant, with burst lungs. There were so many possibilities. Maybe smoking one day, alone in the dunes, and then – the tiger. Yes, she could see that: the water sprawling below his feet, the smoke near his face, a view of her house from where he sat, and also the town – the rigid flag over the surf club – and the tiger, downwind, stalking unfortunate George. She would say to Frida, 'I'm sure it was all over quickly. I'm sure he felt no pain.' She would say, 'I wish I'd known him better.' But she had no wish to know him better. She preferred him as a dark shape in the front of a taxi.

'I'm so sorry,' she said, but Frida said, 'What for?' so quickly that Ruth knew to be quiet.

'Right then,' continued Frida. 'George has stolen all my money and lost the house and ruined me.' She calmly announced this deadpan disaster.

'No!' cried Ruth. Panic and horror were a handkerchief at her throat. 'But you just spoke to him!' Frida just spoke to George, so he couldn't be dead in the taxi or from the tiger; he couldn't have stolen all her money.

'That's how I know,' said Frida.

'But how?'

'Because he told me, is how,' said Frida, defensive, as if she suspected Ruth of not believing her.

'But how did he steal all your money?' This genuinely puzzled Ruth, who had never considered stealing anyone's money and wondered how to go about it.

'It's to do with Mum's house.'

'The house she died in,' said Ruth.

'Yes, yes,' said Frida, impatient. 'I've been giving him my salary and he hasn't kept up with the mortgage and they're going to take the house.'

'Who are?'

'The bank,' said Frida. 'Unless I can pay them right away. And the worst thing is, I can't just catch up on the mortgage. It's still legally half George's house. So I need to get the mortgage up to date *and* buy half the house from George. Otherwise I'll lose it.'

'That doesn't seem fair,' said Ruth. 'You just keep giving George money? That can't be right.'

'It doesn't matter, because I don't have any money to give.'

'I know what we'll do,' said Ruth, and Frida raised her head with a quick, sharp look. 'We'll talk to Harry. He'll know how to sort all this out.'

'Jesus,' said Frida.

'He's a very good lawyer.'

Frida sank into the catless end of the couch. 'Ruthie,' she said, with unexpected softness, 'Harry's dead.'

'I know that,' snapped Ruth, and she did know it; she had even known it a moment ago when she suggested they consult him. And she was disgusted with him, because nobody could be really, truly dead; nobody could stand it. It was one thing, maybe, to die – and Ruth held his head as Harry died, she remembered that now, she saw the sand on the pavement at the bus stop and Harry's shaking dying head – but it was quite another to go on being dead. That was obstinate; it was unkind.

Frida buried one hand in the yielding fur of the nearest cat. 'I do have an idea,' she said. 'We might be able to help each other.'

The cat twitched under her fingers, stood and yawned, and trotted onto Ruth's lap.

'Richard,' Frida said. 'I can help you with Richard, and you can help me with George.'

'Do I need your help with Richard?'

'You need me on your side if you're going to convince Jeffrey. You need me to say, "In my professional opinion, your mother should go live with Richard."'

'Should I?'

'I went to see his house yesterday. I wanted to see the setup there, whether or not it'd be good for you.'

'And?' A tiredness came over Ruth; it felt like a blanket, suddenly pulled. She thought she might have done the pulling.

'It's a really nice place. All on one level, a huge kitchen, even a spa bath. It's too deep for you right now, he doesn't even use it, but I could put railings in and – bingo!'

'What about the garden?'

'Very pretty. His daughter looks after it. Jacaranda tree, big herb garden, brick patio.'

'Lilies?'

'He picked the last of them for you. And he has this one fat palm tree that looks exactly like a pineapple.'

'Good for the cats.'

'Well, that's one downside. His daughter's allergic to cats. I thought about not mentioning that, by the way, just for the record. But you could lock them up when she visits. Easy fixed. The other thing is that he sleeps with this mask at night, it's for his breathing, and it's loud.'

Ruth closed her eyes at the thought of these loud nights. 'I can't believe you went there without me,' she said from her lidded darkness. She saw the garden: green, with a fence, and other fenced greens at its edges. She saw that ear of Richard's again, horizontal against his head, and his head lying still: his sickbed. And no more sea.

'Now, if I help you with Richard, maybe you can help me with George.'

Ruth opened her eyes. 'Where are the lilies he picked for me?' She thought perhaps she knew where they were; she thought they might be related to the yellow stains on her skin. But she couldn't quite recall.

'They're gone,' said Frida, and Ruth closed her eyes again; she had been waiting for that answer. If the lilies are gone, she said to herself, if they're finished and I never saw them, it means – what? The cat squirmed on her lap and couldn't get comfortable, so she pedalled her knees until it jumped away. There were lumps in her lap – they were the leftover pills from yesterday, still in her pockets. Then she remembered where the lilies were. She remembered falling into the tiger trap. She was wearing the same dress she'd climbed the dune in; she'd slept since then and been to town, with pollen on her arms and dirt in her shoes. Now her gritty grey skin declared itself, and the sand at the roots of her sticky hair. No wonder Ellen had called Jeffrey.

'I'm a wreck,' Ruth said.

'We'll both be, soon enough,' said Frida. 'Unless we act quickly.'

'Why do you want me to go to Richard?'

'I want you to be happy,' said Frida. Ruth suspected her of telling the truth. 'You don't know what it's meant to me, living here with you these last few months. You're like the mother I —'

'No,' said Ruth.

'No?'

'I won't go to Richard.' That was easy enough: the lilies are over, don't go to Richard. Ruth was irritated at herself, actually, for almost falling for it: that version of leaving her house, of ending her life, as if she might scrub out the disappointment of fifty years ago and step, bridal, over Richard's door. 'If he wants me, he can come here. I hope he comes. I'll invite him.'

'But —'

'You can still help me. You can go away,' said Ruth, and that was easy too. 'You leave me alone, and I'll help you. I'll lend you the money for your mother's house. I have plenty of money. I'll pay the bank – tell them that.'

'I can't tell them that,' said Frida. She was very still at her end of the couch, but Ruth could see the tick of her temple.

'Why not?'

'It's too much money.'

'You took care of my house, and now I'll take care of yours. It's like a poem.'

'What are you talking about?'

'It rhymes,' Ruth said, explanatory.

Frida sighed. 'Do you know how much money that would be?' She shook her head. Something was amazing her.

'I have plenty of money,' said Ruth. 'Harry sold the Sydney house. That was a big house.'

'I don't know what to say,' said Frida. She seemed caught up in a kind of sad, disbelieving relief.

'But you have to leave. You can't live here anymore. You should live in your mother's house and leave me alone.'

'I'll go,' said Frida. 'I'm already going. But I want to make you happy, you understand? I don't want to leave you all alone in this horrible house.'

'There's nothing wrong with this house,' said Ruth. 'Only I worry – isn't it silly? I do worry about that tiger.'

'Really? The one thing you're worried about is the tiger?'

Ruth nodded, embarrassed.

'We can't have that,' said Frida. 'You leave the tiger to me.'

'What will you do?' asked Ruth, a little fearful.

'What needs to be done.' Now Frida sat upright. 'How do I know you won't forget all this tomorrow?'

'I might,' admitted Ruth, trying to smooth out the lumps in her skirt. 'So I'll write myself a note. Isn't that what people do?'

This prompted Frida into action. She rolled up from the couch and into the dining room; the first suitable surface she found was Ruth's detective novel, which she opened to the first page and set- tled on Ruth's lap.

'Write it here.' Frida produced a pen from about her person.

Ruth felt as if she were signing a book she'd written. She tested the pen with a little flourish at the top of the page, then wrote, under the title, 'TRUST FRIDA'.

'What's the date?' she asked.

'I don't know,' said Frida. 'Tuesday night.'

So Ruth wrote, in brackets, 'Tuesday night'.

'How do we do this?' she asked, blowing lightly on the book. The pen's ink had blotted on the cheap paper. 'Do we go to the bank?'

'Yes,' said Frida. 'But! But! You can't just go into a bank and say you're buying a house. We need George, we need a solicitor, we need all kinds of things. I *told* him we couldn't rush this.'

Ruth, knowing Frida would find a way around these problems, remained silent and waited for it.

'But,' said Frida. 'But! How about this? You transfer the money to George, I get a written agreement from him – we sort out the details later. The main thing is to get this done before they take the house.'

'When do they take the house?'

'Friday.'

'I'll write a cheque,' said Ruth. 'Bring me my book.' Ruth had always enjoyed writing cheques. They were so businesslike.

'A cheque'll take days to clear,' said Frida.

'Not really, not these days.' Ruth remembered Harry explaining this. 'It's only about three business days, these days.' And she laughed, because having said *days* three times made it feel as if those days had already passed.

Frida zigzagged up and down the lounge room. This was her thinking walk. 'Three days is too long,' she said. 'All right, all right. This is what we're going to do. If it's okay by you.' She tapped at her forehead as if coaxing her brain. 'We'll go into town tomorrow and go to the bank. They know you in the bank, don't they?'

'Some of them might know me. I haven't been to town for a long time.'

'Yeah, not for *ages*.' Frida shook her head. 'And you can buy cheques that clear quickly. There's a name for that – what is it?'

The word dropped into Ruth's head. *'Expedite,'* she said.

'That's it!' Frida raised her jubilant arms. 'Is that how you say it? Say it again.'

Ruth cleared her throat. 'Ex-pe-dite.' In her mind's eye, she saw ˈekspɪˌdaɪt.

'Expedite!' cried Frida. 'And that's what we're going to do. Now what about Jeffrey?'

'What does he have to do with any of this?' Ruth asked, surprised.

'He's coming on Friday.'

'So let him come!' cried Ruth. 'Let them all come! We'll have a party. If Jeffrey's coming, and Richard's coming, I'll invite Ellen.'

'Richard's coming?'

'Yes, of course. I told you about Richard, didn't I – a man I knew in Fiji?'

Frida walked impatiently to the window.

'He's coming for the weekend,' said Ruth. 'He's coming for Christmas.'

Frida stood at the window, and because the lights were on and the curtains were open, Frida stood in the window looking back. Her face was so severe; probably she didn't approve of Richard. She was such a prude, really. She drove those naked children off the beach.

'Are you really frightened of the tiger?' Frida asked.

Ruth only laughed. 'Of course, Phil should come, too, if Jeffrey's coming. I'll call him, shall I?'

'By all means,' said Frida, magnanimous. 'Call Phil, call every-one. Call the Queen, my love. Why the hell not.'

'I saw the Queen,' said Ruth, and they both said together, 'In Fiji.'

'Jesus, Ruthie,' said Frida in the window.

15

That was the night Frida fought the tiger. He came earlier than he had the other nights: Frida was in the bathroom and Ruth was sitting up in bed with the lamp still on. She was thinking about calling Richard, but couldn't be sure of what she wanted to say: something about an invitation to Christmas, and also about hating Sydney because of bad junipers and good pirate plays. She was aware of being very tired and thought she would probably make a fool of herself. So she sank down into the bed and, as she did so, heard the first suggestions of the tiger: the footfalls in the lounge room, the moving lamps and chairs. He had come without

the jungle, although Ruth could feel that it was nearby, outside the windows, in a way that reminded her of Fiji. It was like
night-time in their wide, hot house beside the hospital, where the
moths knocked up against the windows and the gardens dripped
in the dark. The light around her bed stirred like the mosquito
netting she had slept under as a girl. Then the tiger: softly at first,
his usual nosing and breathing, which was all so quiet that Ruth
was inclined to ignore this evidence and assume he was still banished to the beach. The cats, however, stiffened and stared – a bad
sign, a tiger sign – and shortly after this, the tiger began to make
a sharp whine, as if he were hungry. Then he was unmistakably
the tiger.

Frida was still in the bathroom. Ruth's door was ajar, and she
could see light falling across the hall in a way that meant the
lounge-room door was open. The tiger was there, in that light!
What would it mean to actually see him? Would it hurt? The jungle pressed against the windows, not insistent, only present.

Ruth got out of bed. She felt lately as if she were always hero-
ically rising from bed. Tonight her back hadn't had the chance
to freeze in sleep; it still had the day's limited elasticity. The cats
watched her. They were in no hurry to leave the bed. Ruth shook
her head at them to say, 'Quiet!' She crossed the floor and leaned
into the hallway. It was empty. Then Frida was at the end of it, and
running towards her.

'Did you hear it?' called Frida.

'Quick!' cried Ruth, and she pulled Frida into her room. Frida
wore a white towelling dressing gown. She was soft and without
shape. 'Close the door!'

Frida closed the door. 'Did you hear it?'

'Yes,' said Ruth. 'I think – yes, I did.'

They both stilled and listened. He had come into the hallway, Ruth was sure of it. He must have heard Frida, or seen or smelled her, and now he knew with certainty they were there. Now he nosed at the door.

Frida flew against it. 'All right, all right,' she said. 'Think.'

They both thought. There was nothing to think. Ruth's mind was blank of everything but the tiger. Frida pressed against the door. Finally she said, 'I'm going out there.'

'You can't!' cried Ruth. But she was certain Frida would; there was no alternative.

'I can and I will.' Frida's face was resolved above the white fluff of her dressing gown. She pressed one ear against the door, listening, but there was silence in the hallway. Ruth waited for a hungry howl.

'Promise me you won't come out, no matter what you hear,' Frida said. 'And if something happens, promise me you'll call George and tell him about it yourself.'

'Frida!'

'Promise me.'

'How do I call him?'

'Look him up in the phone book. Look up his taxi. Young Livery. Can you do that?'

Ruth nodded.

Frida adjusted her robe, took a deep scuba breath, opened the door, and disappeared into the hallway. The door closed behind her. Then it was definite: Frida was going to fight the tiger.

'Can you see him?' Ruth asked through the door.

'Not yet. I'm going to find a weapon.'

'Get a broom.'

'All right, a broom,' said Frida. 'And maybe a knife.'

Ruth heard Frida run into the kitchen in search of a broom and a knife; then came the sound of the tiger's paws on the floor of the hallway. This sound reminded Ruth of the soft rhythm of a particular trolley on the floor of the clinic; she'd heard it passing up and down while she waited in her father's consulting room. The tiger was following Frida, but without hurrying; he was a cat in long grasses; he was hunting. Pressed against the door, Ruth could hear her busy heart, the hunting tiger, and the hospital trolley; then the sound of Frida finding a broom.

'Frida!' Ruth called. 'He's behind you!'

The broom cupboard was stiff with equipment, mops and brooms and buckets all piled in together, and they fell out on the floor as Frida selected her weapon – Ruth heard all this from her room.

The cats jumped from the bed and clamoured at Ruth's feet. Frida was swearing in the kitchen now, among the mops and buckets, but she stopped when she saw the tiger and cried, 'Aha!' The tiger answered with a crisp, proud puff from his nostrils. Then he sprang onto the table – Ruth heard the table scrape over the floor. Frida was in the knife drawer now. Its metals rang. Frida would carve the tiger! But he was ready to pounce.

The house was hotter than ever before. Ruth pressed her sticky hand against the door, as if checking for fire. The kitchen had burned today! Frida was facing the tiger! Had Ruth really stood in the Sausage King's with an empty purse only this morning? Was there such a thing as a bus, a town, a mortgage? The cats clawed at Ruth's legs. Whose side were they on? They were wild with panic and fear, and Ruth could barely recognise them.

Frida wielded her broom – she was trying to force the tiger out the back door. But he wouldn't run tonight. Frida commanded, 'Out! Out!' The broom battered the shutters and walls, but he stayed put. Ruth had seen the cats hunting birds in the garden; she knew the tiger's whole rusty front would be still and low, and his back paws would be lifting, lifting, beneath his undulant tail. Then – the table moved again, sharp against the floor – he flew at Frida. She lifted her broom, which cracked against something hard. They were both so quiet; Ruth marvelled at it. Every now and then, Frida produced an 'Oof,' but there were no shouts of pain or whimpers from the tiger, only the noise of furniture shifting, and periodically a shatter of glass. Ruth closed her eyes. The tiger was stronger than Frida and determined to fight.

But Frida was fearless. She didn't give up any ground or lose hold of her weapons. She struck! And now the tiger gave out a high squawk. The cats went mad at the door, and Ruth – her eyes still closed – opened it for them, quickly, and closed it again. They ran through the kitchen, through Frida and the tiger, and outside. Their flight was enough to distract him; Frida struck again. Now he ran. All through the hospital the tiger fled, into the house and the hallway and through the clinic, and as he ran, the patients sat up in their beds, even those that couldn't sit, as if the trumpets of the resurrection had sounded and their souls were rising from perpetual sleep. Someone began to ring a bell, which might summon the fire brigade; it might wake the doctor with his canny, flimsy hands and bring him running in expectation of surgery. It might wake the whole town, the whole island; it might bring the sea to a halt, waiting, waiting to see the tiger run by. He ran into Phillip's room and out of it again, and everywhere he ran, Frida followed him with her broom and her knife and her battle cry. Ruth heard, along with the bell, a new sound – the beating together of the compost-bin lids, sailing across the sand. Children fled from the beach. Children in the wards began to cry out, but not in alarm; they called, 'Frida! Frida!' Lights came on in every room. The bell rang. Lights disappeared and came on again in every room. The tiger ran blindly into furniture. His claws skidded over the floors.

'Oh, no, you don't!' called Frida, and Ruth called – everyone called – 'No you don't!' along with her.

The tiger was trapped in the hallway. Ruth pressed against her door; her heart struck again and again. There he was in the hallway, there was his snarl and the fury of his breath. The cats cried out in the garden. Now Frida began to roar; she was magnificent. The tiger answered – his roar was a stone flying over water. Then Frida struck. The speed of her striking arm lifted a wind in the house. The tiger yelped in surprise – a startled, domestic little yelp – and then he was in the jungle again, or of the jungle, and enraged. Ruth felt for a moment on the verge of understanding exactly what the tiger was saying when he roared. He wasn't concerned for his safety, but for his dignity. There was a sense of enormous injustice, not quite conceivable to him. But you must take Frida seriously, thought Ruth. She found herself pitying the tiger. He was fighting to save his territory, but Frida meant to finish him off. Then he roared again, a war cry, and she stopped trembling for him. She was never afraid for Frida.

Something heavy fell against the door; it was unclear which of them it was. But the tiger must have struck because Frida cried out in rage and pain. She fought back. There had been no beginning to Frida and the tiger, and now there would be no end. They both snarled and bared their teeth. Frida called out the strange syllables of a warlike alphabet. Her voice grew louder, but the tiger's slowed. He still roared, but his roar seemed full of static, like the roar of a tiger on television. It came and went. Frida's broom rattled. The bell stopped and all the lights went out. There was no hospital and no house – only Frida and the tiger. Ruth leaned terrified against the door.

Now the jungle started up, sudden and synchronised: insects tucked in trees, and a high peal of hidden birds. The air was a hot, damp gag, barely moving, and carrying something wet whenever it did. Frida had the tiger down near the coat rack now, and she was holding her ground. Probably his ears were flat against his head. His tail moved to and fro. There was the scrape of his claws on the wood of the floor.

'Frida!' cried Ruth, and when she did, there was the sound of falling bodies, more cries, more knocks of the broom on the wall, but it was as if nothing more serious than a scuffle were taking place, a closing-time fracas, until there came at last a screech – the sound of a cat whose tail has been trampled. Frida grunted; she was pushing something hard. She called out, and then her body – or his body, a heavy body – fell. The hallway was quiet. Then light came in under the bedroom door.

'Frida?' said Ruth. Frida groaned. 'Are you hurt? Can I come out? Are you all right?'

'Stay where you are,' said Frida. The words heaved out of her. The light disappeared. 'Open the door,' she said. 'Don't look out here.'

Ruth opened the door. The wet smell of the tiger was everywhere. Frida came in carrying the broom, but not the knife.

'It's finished,' she said, and accepted Ruth into her arms. There was blood on her white robe and on her face; tiger blood.

16

Ruth rose early the next morning. She crept by Frida's bedroom door as high on the tips of her toes as her back would allow. The house was in disarray. Sand lay in banks and eddies all over the floor. Ruth decided to sweep it, but it seemed to be sticky at the bottom, as if soaked in liquid – each clump had the long, damp foot of a mollusc – and sweeping only thickened the bristles of the broom with mud. Her back hurt. Her chair lay shipwrecked on the sandy floor. Ruth kept walking over hard objects that she worried were teeth and tiger claws but turned out to be miscellaneous grit. Frida's broom, or the tiger's tail, had knocked glass to the floor, and the lamp tilted drunkenly in the lounge room. But the tiger's body was gone.

Frida had covered the area by the front door with a tarpaulin, and she had weighed this tarpaulin down with buckets of water. The water smelled rusty, and it was a rust colour when Ruth dipped her finger in it. She couldn't lift the buckets to see under the tarpaulin, and when she opened the front door, she could see only that something large had been dragged to the grass at the edge of the drive.

When Frida emerged, fully dressed – in her white uniform, with her hair pulled so tight into a bun she looked more like a beautician than ever – Ruth was dozing in the recliner, still wearing her nightgown.

'Come on, lazybones,' said Frida. 'The bus is due at quarter past ten.'

'What bus?' Ruth blinked and squinted.

'To take us to town? To the bank?'

'Isn't George going to drive us?'

'I told you, darling heart, George's run off. Now get a move on, or we'll miss it.'

'We're going to the bank?'

Frida flourished a book in front of Ruth's face. The first page had handwriting on it – it said 'TRUST FRIDA.'

'I know, I know,' said Ruth, a little crankily.

'Chop chop!' cried Frida, clapping her hands. She hauled Ruth out of the recliner, marched her into the bedroom, and took charge of dressing her. Ruth sat mute on the end of her bed. Frida's hair was so severe, and her uniform so white, that it would have been impossible to conjure the bloody Frida of the night before except that bruises were beginning to bloom on her forearms.

Frida muttered at Ruth's open wardrobe. 'Something sensible, something sensible. Try this.' She pulled out a neat grey skirt suit.

'It's very formal,' said Ruth.

'Just try it. Can you manage?' Frida advanced on Ruth and began tugging at her nightgown.

'I can manage!' The thought of being naked in front of Frida was terrible: proud, firm Frida of the lacquered hair, who had killed the tiger.

Frida threw up her hands. 'Then hurry,' she said. She turned her back to Ruth, but stayed in the room.

Ruth struggled with the skirt. When had she last worn this suit? Years ago, surely, and it was a little big for her. When she managed to button the skirt, she was so pleased with herself that she mustered the courage to ask, 'Frida, where's the tiger?'

'You don't need to worry about that anymore,' said Frida.

'I only want to know where he is. I thought there could be something – some kind of ceremony. A funeral?'

'I killed him for you, and you want a funeral?' Frida used her most incredulous voice. 'Now get a wriggle on. It's nine fifty-five.'

'I need stockings,' said Ruth. Frida turned, appraising. Ruth hated to wear those thick flesh-coloured stockings she saw on other old women. For formal, suit-wearing occasions, she liked thin black ones. 'They're in the top drawer.'

'You look just fine,' said Frida. 'Get some shoes. Quick, quick! Or we'll miss the bus.'

'We could call a taxi,' said Ruth, despairing, but Frida blocked the way to the chest of drawers and tapped her wrist as if she wore a watch there.

'How many times do I have to tell you,' said Frida, guiding Ruth to the door now, 'George has run off?'

'There are other taxis in the whole wide world.'

In the hallway, Frida had a glass of water and Ruth's pills; Ruth swallowed these expertly. She took her handbag from the coat hook it hung on.

'Watch the buckets,' said Frida. 'Watch your step.'

She hurried Ruth into the front garden and towards the drive, where Ruth dawdled looking for evidence of the tiger. By the time she reached the road, Frida was already partway down the hill, waiting for her.

'What do you want me to do, give you a piggyback?' Frida called. Ruth didn't answer. Frida began walking again. She called out, 'What you need is a wheelchair.'

Ruth wasn't happy at the thought of a wheelchair. She made little tripping steps to catch up. If only Frida wouldn't walk quite so fast; if only this skirt didn't restrict her movement. How typical of me, she thought – of me and of any *old person* – not to want a wheelchair. When really, what could be so bad about being pushed around? Right now she would have liked to be piggybacked down the hill. She half hoped Frida might offer again.

'Wheelchairs,' Ruth said, 'are for people whose legs don't work.'

'And backs!' cried Frida. 'People with bad backs!'

There was no one at the bus stop. It loomed up before them, unaccountably familiar. The day was that wet, pressed sort on which no one would make an effort to come to this part of the beach. In weather like this, the beach was revealed as both danger-ous and dirty. The sea was oppressive, and the sky was bright and colourless and dragged down upon its surface. Frida fretted at the bus stop, as if it might be a trick of some kind; no bus would come, and they would be left waiting forever. She always seemed so angry at the possibility she might be made a fool of. Ruth sat on the bench, which felt harder than any other hard material she had previously encountered. A car slowed and then moved off again. Ruth didn't like having her back to the sea or the road, so she sat in a nervous silence, as if by being completely still she might ward off a possible ambush. Frida was silent, too. In fact they might never have met; they might have come together by chance at this bus stop, and Frida out of courtesy would allow Ruth to board the bus first, and she might even smile at her, and that would be the extent of their dealings. Then another life would take place, riskier, in which they would never know about the other.

'The bus is coming,' said Ruth, although that was perfectly obvious.

Frida boarded first and paid for them both. Ruth recognised the driver. He had the thick, high hair of a young man, but it was completely grey. He smiled at her and said, 'Out and about again, eh?' The smile pleated his forehead up into his verdant hair.

Frida took Ruth's hand. 'Come on now, Ruthie,' she said.

Frida's palm felt like a steak wrapped in baking paper.

The bus was emptier today. The few passengers sat in studied silence, as if the grim weather wouldn't permit sociability of any kind. Frida walked down the aisle with a maritime stride, and she dragged Ruth along with her.

'Isn't this nice,' said Ruth, settling in beside Frida, and a woman of about Ruth's age, two seats down, with her remnant hairs united in a Frau-ish scarf, scowled as if Ruth had spoken in a movie thea-tre. Frida said nothing. Ruth's back snapped with every shake of the bus. With so little room on the seat, she was forced to hold firmly to the rail in front of her at any suggestion of a left turn, for fear of being tipped into the aisle. She adjusted her position until Frida said, in a low voice, 'Stop pressing into me, would you?'

Town seemed different today: more grey, and emptier. It hadn't rained, but the houses and gardens huddled in expectation of bad weather. The bus paused at a stop sign, and looking down the side of a house, Ruth saw a woman taking towels off a clothesline with frequent glances at the untrustworthy sky. The line swung in the gathering wind, and the woman's arms became heavier and heavier with towels. She had no Frida to do her laundry for her. Ruth felt a wild disdain for this anxious woman and her cradled laundry. If only the sky would break open at this very moment so Ruth could witness the unfortunate flurry of woman and towels. But the bus moved on, and no drops flattened against the windowpanes.

'Here's our stop,' said Frida, and she began to stand, so Ruth stood; the bus lurched as it stopped and Ruth nearly fell. Frida caught her and sighed aloud, while other passengers – all but the severe scarfed woman – half lifted from their seats to help.

'You're making a scene,' said Frida, guiding Ruth down the aisle, and then they were on the main street of town with people pushing out of the bus behind them. 'Out of the way, out of the way,' Frida urged, pulling Ruth to one side of the pavement. Ruth held her bag tight against her hip. Her jacket had skewed a little to the right. Frida was walking, and Ruth, adjusting her suit, followed. 'I'll never know,' said Frida over her shoulder, 'how you managed this on your own.'

Men from a construction site crossed the road among the traffic. They had broad, happy faces, and Ruth watched them fearfully because they were courting bad luck. A woman with very red hair stopped and smiled at Ruth, talking; Ruth knew she should recognise her, but didn't.

'We're going to the bank,' said Ruth, indicating Frida, who waited under the Sausage King's awning.

'Don't let me keep you!' cried the woman, and moved on.

'Do you know *everyone?*' snapped Frida, so Ruth kept her head down. When she caught up with Frida under the awning, she turned her face away from the butcher's window. She opened her purse and peered inside: she saw banknotes, and her cards were back in their slots. Perhaps they'd been there yesterday, under the watchful eye of the Sausage King. Frida was fiddling with papers she had drawn from her bag, smoothing them down and looking them over. Her bag hung open, and for some reason that book Ruth had written in was wedged inside.

Ruth was interested to notice that Frida's size diminished when compared to the doors and cars and letterboxes of the world; she was still, however, the most conspicuous thing on the street. What else was there to look at? Her hair shone out in the grey light of the skyless day, and her shoulders were as broad as the construction workers'.

'You ready, Ruthie?' Frida almost held her hand out to Ruth; Ruth almost took it.

'I want to see the tiger,' said Ruth. She knew how sulky she sounded.

'You can't,' said Frida. 'He's in the sea.'

'How did you get him down there?' People stepped around them to enter the butcher shop, and the bell chimed sweetly. Ruth crowded closer to Frida.

'I started out dragging him and then I used the wheelbarrow. I made a mess of him, Ruthie. You didn't want to see that.'

'How much of a mess?'

On closer inspection, Frida looked exhausted. With her hair off her face, she was older and sadder, and the rings under her eyes were more obviously plum-coloured. She had been awake most of the night taking the tiger to the sea.

'I cut open his stomach,' she said. 'Do you really want to know? His guts came spilling out. And then, to kill him, I slit his throat. There was a lot of blood.'

'I'm all right with blood. I practically grew up in a hospital.'

'Didn't we all.' Frida zipped up her bag and set her square shoulders. 'You ready for the bank?'

'But how did you get him right into the sea?' Ruth insisted. 'What if he washes up again?'

'What I did,' said Frida tonelessly, 'is I crammed him into the wheelbarrow good and tight. His tail, his paws, his head on top.'

'Was he heavy?'

'Bloody heavy. Then I pushed the wheelbarrow down to the water, which was tough going, let me tell you. The tide was out. The sun was just thinking about coming up. And I pushed the wheel-barrow out into the ocean as far as I could go, until he started floating.'

'In your dressing gown?'

'I took it off.'

So Ruth saw Frida down in the lightening sea, naked, straining at the wheelbarrow; she saw the water lift the tiger and carry him away. He would be smaller and darker while wet and knife-slit, but still a tiger.

Frida put her hand on Ruth's arm and squeezed it. 'Are we doing this, Ruthie? Should we go save my house?'

'The house she died in,' said Ruth.

The bank was a safe and scrupulous place, although Ruth didn't quite approve of a seaside bank. She had lived by the sea for years, but there was still a holiday air to the sound of the gulls and the palms among the pine trees. A bank in this place should be issuing money for the buying of ice creams and beach towels and surely had no business with the solemnity of mortgages. Harry and Ruth had taken out a mortgage to buy the holiday house. Harry spoke of this mortgage as if it were an aged relative, slowly convalescent but sure to mend. When it was paid, they came out for a weekend – the boys were adults, now – and Harry said, 'I think we should move here permanently when I retire.'

'Oh, no,' said Ruth, without thinking. 'Really? What would we do all day?'

Harry retired, and they moved, and all day they were Ruth and Harry.

'You go first,' said Frida. The automatic doors were opening and closing, a little wildly, with no customers to prompt them, and a few ordinary pavement pieces of paper and plastic were gusting in and out. Frida prodded Ruth in the back. 'Smile,' she said.

Ruth smiled. She would have liked to hold Frida's hand. A woman in a red suit sang, 'Good morning!' and Ruth sang back, 'Good morning!' It was like being in church. What would the woman say next? What would Ruth reply?

'How can we help you today?' the woman asked. She was pretty and young and held a clipboard; Ruth was unsure how a woman like that could help her, although she was receptive to the idea of being helped.

'We're right, thanks,' said Frida, steering Ruth towards the queue, which was made up of more pretty young women, many of them strung with children.

'If you let me know what you're here for, I might be able to speed things up for you,' said the woman, following them with high-heeled steps. Her hair was frosted into a surf of blond, and she wore a name tag: JENNY CONNELL, CUSTOMER SERVICE ASSISTANT.

'Your doors are haunted,' said Ruth.

'Haunted!' Jenny Connell smiled. 'I like that. They always act up on windy days. I'm so sorry.' She wasn't sorry at all, which Ruth appreciated. The doors opened, and the paper and plastic blew in; the doors closed, and the rubbish settled; the doors opened again, and the papers were sucked out. It was tidal.

Frida pressed close at Ruth's back, the way Phillip used to as a boy.

'So what can we help you with today?' asked Jenny, but she was looking at Frida now.

'We're here to save the house,' said Ruth, and Jenny's smile widened, but she continued to look at Frida.

'We're here to transfer some money,' said Frida.

'Wonderful!' cried Jenny, and Ruth was delighted. 'Did you know you could do that from the convenience of your own home using internet banking?'

'It's a lot of money,' said Frida.

Jenny nodded appreciatively. 'Our daily online limit is five thousand dollars,' she said.

'It's more than that,' said Frida.

The woman in front of them in the queue turned to look, and

Frida shuffled on her white-clad feet.

'Much more,' said Ruth.

Jenny continued to nod. 'Then you're in the right place,' she said. 'Our daily transfer limit in the branch is twenty thousand dollars.'

'We have a cheque,' said Frida.

'So it's not a transfer, then.' Jenny seemed relieved. 'We have a cheque deposit station right over there.' She gestured towards a helpful-looking wall.

'I was asked to have Mrs Field come in herself to verify the cheque,' Frida said, without looking at the wall. She repeated dully, 'It's a lot of money.'

The bank doors opened and closed, admitting paper and wind and more customers. Jenny looked at these newcomers anxiously, as if they had tugged on her sleeve. 'Just go ahead and wait in line,' she said, 'and someone will be right with you.'

Frida rolled her eyes.

'We have a cheque?' said Ruth.

Frida exhaled loudly. 'No,' she said.

'Why did you say we did?'

'We need to buy a cheque.'

'I have cheques at home,' said Ruth.

'This is a special cheque. Remember? Expedite. A fast cheque. Don't worry about it, Ruthie. I've got it under control.'

Frida didn't look as if she had it under control. She seemed to be brimming with a scarcely concealed fury. The line in the bank was long, and the wind that came through the doors was cold for November. Children cried and were shushed and continued to cry, but mutedly. Ruth leaned into Frida to manage standing for all this time. The woman in front of them turned again and said, 'There are chairs by the window,' and both Ruth and Frida looked at her, not smiling, as if she had spoken in an unfamiliar language. 'If you want to rest,' she added, but Ruth only leaned farther into Frida and nodded her head one time. The woman jogged a baby on her hip. She turned away with a shrug, but the baby continued to watch Ruth until Ruth made a face at it. It regarded her with a jaded expression before hiding its round head.

Frida adopted a new vigilance when they reached the front of the queue. She clutched her handbag and watched for a teller to become available, and when the signal finally came – a flashing gold number and a cheerful chime – she walked with such brisk purpose that Ruth, who was still leaning against her, stumbled to keep upright. So Frida paused and took her arm, not roughly but without patience. She steered Ruth towards the counter with the pulsing number and presented her to the woman behind it as if she were a piece of evidence.

This woman, also dressed in a red suit, was unlike Jenny Connell. She was older, with broad shoulders, as if she had evolved to move quickly through water, and her hair was girlishly cut. She wore a wedding ring but bit her fingernails. Her name, according to her badge, was Gail, and then something complicated and Greek.

'Good morning,' Gail said from behind a wall of glass. Her voice issued from a small microphone, as if it needed assistance to travel so far.

'This is Mrs Field,' said Frida, and she began to produce items from her handbag: Ruth's bankbook, some documents, and a piece of paper with numbers written on it.

'Good morning,' said Ruth.

'I'm Mrs Field's carer, and I'm here to help her write a cheque.'

'I don't have a cheque,' said Ruth conversationally.

'We need to purchase an expedited cheque,' explained Frida.

Gail looked between Ruth and Frida as each one spoke, and her face was calm and dispassionate.

'That's very fast, isn't it?' asked Ruth. 'An expedited cheque?' She liked the sound of the word *expedited*. It sounded risky and important.

'It's not immediate,' said Gail. 'But it does clear in one business day.'

'One day, Frida!' said Ruth. 'Usually it's three.'

'The fee is eleven dollars,' said Gail.

Frida produced eleven dollars like a magic trick from her handbag.

'Thank you,' said Gail. What a polite woman! She began to consult Ruth's bankbook and then the computer, typing quickly with her bitten fingers, but the rest of her movements were unhurried. Frida gripped her handbag as if she would have liked to vault the counter and manage everything herself.

'Would you like to fill the cheque in right now, Mrs Field?' asked Gail.

'Oh, yes,' said Ruth.

Then the cheque seemed to swim up to the glass as if Gail could only just contain it; it had a life of its own. It flew through the gap between the glass and the counter, and Gail pushed a pen behind it. Now everyone was looking at Ruth.

'Would you like me to help you with that, Ruthie?' asked Frida.

Ruth peered at the cheque. Her name was printed on it already, and a series of numbers she recognised as belonging to her bank account. Her memory for numbers was good.

'This is for George,' said Ruth.

'For George Young,' said Frida. 'That goes right on this line.' She put her finger on the cheque.

'Young Livery,' said Ruth.

'George Young. You write it just here.' Frida looked at Gail again. 'I'm her carer.'

Gail nodded. 'I believe we have you right here on the account. Technically you could write the cheque yourself.'

'Not for this amount of money.' Frida sounded aggrieved. 'I was told Mrs Field would need to authorise that herself.'

Ruth wrote *George Young* on the line. She wondered why Frida's name was on her account.

'Excuse me for one moment,' said Gail. A telephone was ringing – had been ringing for some time, Ruth now realised – and Gail went to answer it. She was taller than Ruth expected.

'Concentrate,' hissed Frida. 'Here.' She took the pen from Ruth, paused for a moment, then wrote *seven hundred thousand dollars* in an elegant cursive.

'That's beautiful!' said Ruth.

When Frida wrote the amount in numeral form, however, all those o's crammed into one box reminded Ruth of schoolgirl writing, floaty and skewiff.

'Now sign,' Frida said. She gave Ruth the pen, and when Ruth hesitated, still looking at the crooked zeros on the crowded cheque, Frida flicked open her bag and produced the book.

'Look! Look!' she said, holding it open to the title page; there was handwriting there, but it was shaking too much for Ruth to read. Why was Frida making such a fuss?

Gail returned to her place behind the glass. Other golden numbers were flashing over other counters, and the line grew longer, and Jenny Connell greeted each gusty new arrival.

'Banks are so friendly these days,' said Ruth, and she smiled at Gail, who failed to smile back.

'We're holding people up,' said Frida, sliding the book away.

Ruth signed the cheque. Something seemed to deflate in Frida; she shrank a little, as if she'd been standing on the tips of her toes and holding her breath. Ruth passed the cheque under the glass. She waited to see Gail respond to the amount; she was proud to think she could sign a cheque for so much. But Gail made no acknowledgment of Ruth's generosity. What kind of bank was this, then? Did millionaires wander in every day, passing enormous cheques into the care of indifferent Gail?

'Do you have some form of identification, Mrs Field?' asked Gail, and Frida gave an impatient whinny.

'Let me see.' Ruth began to dig in her purse. 'What kind of identification?'

'A driver's licence, for example.'

Ruth remembered keeping her driver's licence in the glove box of Harry's car. She heard the car, once again, make its final journey down the drive.

'Or a passport,' said Gail.

'A cheque is a cheque,' said Frida. She leaned towards the hole in the glass, and her breath smudged its outer edges.

'My passport is at home,' said Ruth.

'She's clearly who she says she is,' said Frida. 'You have her bankbook.'

240

'We need photo identification for any large withdrawal,' said Gail, immaculate behind her Frida-proof glass.

'We'll come back tomorrow,' said Ruth. 'I know exactly where my passport is. It's in the top drawer of Harry's desk.'

'We don't have time,' said Frida.

'This afternoon!' said Ruth. 'We'll take the bus.'

'What about your Senior's Card, Mrs Field?' Gail seemed to have withheld this possibility and now to enjoy suggesting it.

Frida took the purse from Ruth and began to shuffle cards.

'They really get stuck in there,' said Ruth, and she looked to Gail for commiseration, but Gail was watching Frida's hands. The wind came in and around the edges of Ruth's suit. She remembered that she wasn't wearing stockings and was embarrassed. Frida passed Ruth's Senior's Card under the glass, and Gail checked it and nodded and typed. Jenny Connell greeted a new customer. 'Good afternoon!' she sang. Ruth pressed her knees together. She looked at the clock and saw that it was right on twelve.

17

Frida hailed a taxi to drive them home and paid for it herself. The taxidriver knew her; he was boisterous and nostalgic, describing George at work and play, so Ruth assumed he must once have been part of the ill-fated Young Livery. Frida stayed tight-lipped. No doubt she was maintaining her dignity by protecting George, but Ruth wanted to tell this driver every bad thing she knew.

Ruth was surprised by the state of the house. It was littered and muddy and smelled of salty dirt, as if the tide had washed through it. This was the tiger's doing, she remembered; it made her tired. She wanted to rest her back in bed. Frida was courteous: she removed Ruth's shoes, and then her jacket. She offered to bring water or tea.

'I'll just stay on top of the covers,' said Ruth. 'I'll just stay dressed. I need to be ready.'

'Ready for what?'

'For Richard. Didn't I tell you I invited him for Christmas?'

Frida lifted Ruth's legs to help her onto the bed.

'My feet are cold,' Ruth said.

Frida put the jacket over them. She placed one hand over the jacket and said, 'You sing out if you need anything.' Then she left, closing the door behind her.

Ruth didn't sleep. Her bedroom was bright and there were no shadows. Frida was busy in the hallway clearing the buckets and the tarpaulin, and she hummed a little as she worked. At one point the telephone rang and Frida answered it. Ruth heard talking for a minute or two, considered picking up the receiver next to her bed, and decided it would require too much effort. The talking stopped. The house grew so quiet it became possible to hear someone whistling to his dog on the beach; Frida went outside as if summoned by this whistle, but returned almost immediately. The waves were high and loud in the wind. Ruth felt childishly convalescent. She lay on her bed all afternoon, and when she sat up, only two hours had passed.

'Frida!' she called. She coaxed her back with the breathing exercises Frida had taught her, and when she stood, it rewarded her by not hurting.

'Frida!' she called. The hallway was clear. Frida had mopped the area by the front door, and it shone a rich woody red. She wasn't in her bedroom, the lounge, or the bathroom, but all these places had been cleared of the worst of their tiger mess. Some small piles of broken glass remained in the hallway, swept together into a little archipelago that looked vaguely like Fiji.

Frida was in the kitchen washing vegetables in the sink. When she saw Ruth, she dried her hands and said gently, 'Afternoon, Sleeping Beauty.' Then she stepped forward and kissed the top of Ruth's head.

'What was that for?' asked Ruth.

'Let's get you ready.'

'Ready for what?'

'For your visitors.' Frida took Ruth's shoulders and steered her into the bathroom. 'Richard for Christmas, and Jeff on Friday. We'll do your hair.'

'Wash it again?'

'Better than that. Into the shower.' Frida tugged at Ruth's skirt until it came loose from her hips. Ruth stepped out of it. She raised her arms, and Frida lifted the shirt over her head without unfastening a single button. Ruth removed her bra herself; she was proud of that little operation.

'Don't turn the shower on,' said Frida, heading into the hallway.

Ruth stepped into the shower with the aid of the railings. She had failed to remove her underpants, but didn't let that small slip upset her. She sat on the shower stool and waited for Frida, who returned with a comb and a vigorously shaken bottle. Frida was humming. She wrapped a towel around Ruth's shoulders, instructed her to close her eyes, and then Ruth felt a line of cool liquid on her scalp.

'What is it?'

'Sh,' said Frida. 'Close your eyes.'

A sharp, bitter smell came next, pressing against Ruth's eyelids. Frida combed and smoothed and soaked Ruth's hair in this awful smell, but its pungency felt powerful, like some kind of protection. Ruth recognised it as the scent of Frida's hair when she had just dyed it.

Opening her eyes, Ruth saw deep brown stains on her skin where the dye had splashed and fallen. 'It's so dark!'

'Don't worry,' said Frida. 'I've done a lovely ash blond, very subtle. You'll be so pretty when Richard comes. Can you sit like this for a while?'

Ruth thought she could. From her perch in the shower, she heard Frida moving through the house; she heard her in Phillip's bedroom, shifting things around. She was packing, then. She was leaving. And I told her to go, Ruth thought, and with that thought she became frightened of what she had done. She was in a bell, swinging outwards; she could feel the dome of the bell above her, and also the darkness under her feet where there was nobody, nobody; the fear struck and struck. It echoed, so that every time it came – it came in pulses – it left some of itself behind, and all of that leftover fear gathered under the dome with her. The tiger had never terrified her so much; not even the man on the telephone who told her Harry was dead. She remembered his saying, 'Come to the hospital to see your dead husband,' but of course he couldn't have said that. She swung out over the darkness, holding on to something – was it Richard? It might have been Richard – and didn't drop, but the fear only grew, and then Frida was behind her.

'Stop crying,' Frida said, so Ruth knew she was crying. The shower stall amplified the sound. 'What's wrong?'

'I'm so frightened,' said Ruth. She held out her hands as if she expected to see something in her palms. 'Look how I'm shaking.' But she wasn't shaking.

'What are you scared of? I killed the tiger. The tiger's dead.'

'Long live the tiger.'

'No, you ninny,' said Frida. 'Death to tigers, remember?'

'Death to tigers,' said Ruth to Frida the tiger killer, and then the fear – which had stilled for a moment – came back again, and now she understood why: it was because Frida was leaving. All the safety she had ever relied on flew away from her, out from under her feet, away over the garden and the sea; that was how it felt.

Frida had turned on the shower, and soft water ran in dark brown lines over Ruth's pale skin.

'Close your eyes,' ordered Frida. 'Close your mouth.' But she said it gently.

Ruth closed her eyes and mouth, but a terrible noise was still coming from somewhere; possibly her own throat.

'I was going to blow-dry your hair, too,' scolded sad, sweet Frida. 'But all you're good for is bed.'

The water ran clear and Ruth was no longer in the shower. She was in the bedroom, and Frida was dressing her in a nightgown. Ruth called out that her face was hot, so Frida left and returned with a wet cloth to wipe it.

'I don't know what all this fuss is for,' said Frida, which Ruth considered cruel, and when she cried harder – her chest rose and sucked and fell – Frida swatted at her face, without touching her. 'Oh, shut up, Ruthie. You've taken your pills. You'll be all right. You want me to go, and Jeffrey's coming on Friday.' Frida settled Ruth into bed, looked once about the room, and left it, closing the door behind her. Ruth's cries became deep breaths. She was aware of falling asleep because the childhood feeling of doing so with tears on her face was familiar, but she didn't believe it would ever happen.

Ruth woke in the night, hungry. When she looked at her clock, it was only eleven. She called out for Frida, but there was no response, and because her stomach was making eager sounds she sat up and stood up and was out of bed. Her back was calm. It hadn't felt so soft in months. She saw herself in her dressing-room mirror and gave a small wave – in the dark, she was a blur of greyish white. Her hair felt damp at the back but otherwise dry. She wasn't afraid to walk into the hallway. The house was cool and quiet. Frida had left a plate of grilled lamb chops in the fridge, and the fruit bowl was filled with dimpled apples that reminded Ruth of the green-skinned mandarins she had eaten as a child. She stood at the kitchen counter eating the cold, greasy chops with her fingers and looking across the bay through a gap in the shutters. There were no lights in the town; there was not a lamp on for miles. No ships out at sea, either, and no moon. The foil that covered the lamb was the brightest thing in the world, and the loudest. The cats didn't come into the kitchen, not even with the smell of meat. Ruth felt as she had, younger, when her feet were more steadily planted on the floor, and her children and husband slept; that feeling was like an address she'd returned to, wondering why she'd been away so long. Even the taste of food was younger. The back door was closed, the house was cool, and the tiger was dead. Her head felt rinsed of everything.

'What a tantrum,' she said, scolding herself.

Ruth knew Frida's bedroom would be empty, but she looked

all the same, just to confirm her own instincts. She was surprised, nevertheless, to see it arranged as it had been before Frida moved in: as if Phillip, seventeen, had just walked out and left it for some nobler destiny. Frida had changed the sheets and swept up the crushed pills. She'd removed her mirror and all her grooming equipment, and Halley's Comet had returned to the sky of the mirrorless wall.

Ruth looked through the rest of the house for signs of Frida, but she could find none beyond those that were her enduring legacy: the twilight gleam of the floors, for example, and the new order of the books on the shelf above the television. Otherwise she might never have come. The clocks ticked louder. The furniture was lifeless without the tiger or the birds or Frida, and so it reverted to its previous function, which was to provide comfortable familiarity. The lace was lit grey at the windows, and Ruth crossed to them and looked out at the front garden. An unexpected shape occupied the front step: it was Frida. She sat completely still, but intent. She was stone that had been carved into life. She had her suitcase, and she was waiting for someone. It must be George; whom else did she ever wait for? But George had stolen her money and the house her mother died in. Why wait for George?

Ruth was calm. She felt no desire to cry out, to rap the window, or to open the front door. She knew Frida was leaving her, and not because she had ordered it; after all, she had ordered Frida to leave before, with no results. Frida only ever did what she wanted. Ruth knew that, just as she knew that Frida was not honest and had fooled her in some important way. Ruth went to her bedroom, where she didn't bother to check for her shape in the mirror. There was no one in the mirror: not Frida, not Harry, not even Richard. The cats followed on their springy feet, and they slept the rest of the night the way she did: motionless, undreaming, and without making any sound. In the morning, when she woke, Ruth returned to the lounge room and looked out the window. Frida was still sitting on the doorstep.

18

That morning was spare and bright. The sun had risen clear, the whole sea was visible and without shine, and there was no wind in the grass. It was springtime still; only November. Ruth knocked at the window, moved the lace curtain, and continued knocking until Frida turned to face her. Frida looked very young, sitting on the doorstep and staring up at Ruth, as if staying out all night had wiped her face clear of everything she had collected on it, and now she was only tired and childish. She was smooth, like delivered milk. Then she turned away, and although Ruth knocked again and called, 'Frida!' through the glass, loudly, with her hands cupped at her round mouth as if that might help the sound travel, Frida remained on the step for another twenty minutes; then she came in.

'I just need to make a phone call,' she said heavily, and she walked heavily to the kitchen where she eyed the phone as if it were a disguised enemy. She said, 'Aren't I allowed one call, Officer?' – and then she laughed.

Ruth stayed in the lounge room and looked out at the doorstep again. Frida's suitcase still sat in the sandy grass. It could convincingly have grown from a stalk into a grey-white fruit.

'Your suitcase, Frida!' called Ruth, but Frida didn't respond. She was pacing in the kitchen, cradling the phone, and she wrapped the cord around and around her arm until she could no longer pace and had wound herself to the wall. She was waiting and listening. Then she hung up and tried another number, then another. Only once did a voice respond at the other end of the line, but even at this distance – Ruth hovered at the end of the dining table, leaning on it for support – the voice was obviously recorded. Ruth went into the kitchen. Frida took a deep breath, replaced the receiver, and pressed her head gently against the wall.

Then she turned and looked at Ruth. 'George is gone,' she said.

'I know,' said Ruth.

'No, I mean, this time he really is. This time it's real. And he's taken all my money. Which means he's taken your money, too, my darling. He's taken everything.'

How could this mean anything? It meant very little.

'He's done it now,' said Frida. She leaned against the windowsill. She was so amazed that her face looked slightly happy.

'He's actually gone and done it.'

It began to mean something. Frida was no longer in control; Frida was frightened. She had fought the tiger, but now she was leaning, pale in the face, against the windowsill because she couldn't trust her legs to hold her.

How could he have taken everything? Everything was still here: the house, the cats, the sea, Ruth, Frida.

'He's taken us both for a bloody ride,' said Frida, with that note of wonder in her voice. 'A bloody joyride.' Now her voice rose. 'That bastard has ruined everything, and I have worked *so hard*. Look at this!' She flung one arm out. 'I've washed these floors a thousand times or more, I've cooked and cleaned, I've *lived here* because he said we could save on rent, we could get more done, he said, we could worm our way in – I've lived and breathed this house and you, Ruthie, you! For months! All he did was say, "You've earned it, just you wait, you deserve it," and drive around in that bloody taxi, and now he's taken everything.'

Frida looked at Ruth as if she might be in a position to right things; as if she might be in a position, at least, to acknowledge Frida's misfortune. Ruth gave her a small smile. She wanted to say it would be all right, but she seemed to be having trouble breathing; some part of her, she thought, was furious, but which part? She was supposed to be angry at George, and so she was.

'I told him we needed to wait for a man!' raged Frida. She stood now. 'There's no use with a woman. I *told* him how much harder it would be. People always fuss over a woman. A woman with sons! Sons always fuss. But oh no, not a minute to lose, this is the one, Frida, this is it. What I should have done' – she spun to look at the telephone, as if it connected her to George in some mystical way – 'what I should have done is made *him* come along and do it all. *I* could be the one running off into the sunset, and then where would he be?'

'Oh, Frida, I couldn't have had a man in the house,' said Ruth. 'What would people think?'

'Exactly!' cried Frida. 'The two of you would be married by now, my love. Oh, yes, you would. Don't look at me like that, so innocent! And George would have driven Richard off with a stick.'

'I don't even know George,' objected Ruth.

'But *I* do,' said Frida. 'Jesus, do I know George. He'd screw a goldfish if he thought it had any money.' She stood at the window and beat it with one flat hand, so that the glass and the sea all shook, and she stamped one foot as if it were chained to the table. There was a quiet minute in which Ruth tried to determine whether Frida was weeping. Then Frida turned suddenly and cried, 'What now, what now?' and there were no tears, but her face was so fierce and so abandoned; suddenly she doubled over as if in pain. Her buried head said, softer, 'What do I do now?'

'Stand up,' said Ruth. 'I can't bend.' She tried, anyway, to bend, and Frida held out one hand to stop her.

'No,' Frida said, and righted herself, but as she did so she gathered Ruth in her arms and lifted her a little way off the floor. Frida's face was softly creased. Her body vibrated. 'He's left me, Ruthie,' she said. 'I've got nothing. What do I do?'

'Put me down,' said Ruth, although she wasn't sure if that was what she wanted, and Frida set her back on her feet.

'I had this dream that the sea came right up to meet us, up here on our hill.' Frida was looking out the window at the water, and the wondering expression had returned to her reddening face.

'And there were all these boats on the waves – old-time boats, you know, like they have on TV, some with sails, some with clouds of steam and huge chimneys. They were heading straight for us up on the hill, and the people in all of them were waving like crazy. I couldn't tell if they were waving hello or telling us to get out of the way.'

'What did you do?' asked Ruth. It seemed like a comforting vision; it was like the boats on the water at Suva, and in one of the boats would be the Queen. The Queen had sailed away in a boat with Richard, all the way to Sydney.

'I woke up,' said Frida.

'I suppose that's best,' said Ruth, disappointed.

Now Frida walked to the back door. She wore her sandshoes and coat, but under the coat, Ruth noticed, were brown trousers. Ruth had never seen Frida in brown. She must have changed clothes in the night.

'What should we do, Ruthie?' Frida asked in a considering voice. 'Because this is the thing – we can do anything. You know that? Should we go out in the garden? Should we go down to the beach? No, not yet. There's things to do first. What things? What things?' Frida was talking to herself. She backed into the kitchen. 'What's today?' she asked herself. 'Thursday? Thursday! Do you understand, Ruthie, that George has left me and stolen all our money?' And she went out of the kitchen and down the hallway towards the front door.

So George had taken everybody's money. Ruth clapped her hands once, twice. It was what she did when the cats were brawling, or her children misbehaved. The sharp sound appeased her. Her back didn't hurt; it was perfect. But still: all our money! She remembered her empty purse in the butcher's, and the patient, pompous look on the Sausage King's face, and she wondered exactly when George had done it. They'd been so worried about the tiger, and all along the real danger was George. Ruth felt most sorry for Harry, because he was proud and careful and wouldn't, for example, have let her keep the door open at night. It was an embarrassment for Harry and would hurt him if he was here. Where was he? All our money!

Frida came back with her suitcase. 'I want you to know that if it came to choosing – you or George – I'd always choose you. I want you to know that.' Frida was very serious. She had her suitcase on the dining table, unlocked, and was removing things from it; things made of glass and silver and gold, which Ruth thought she recognised. 'If I'd known how everything would work out, is what I'm saying,' said Frida. 'If I'd known what a bastard he was.'

Ruth peered at the objects on the table.

'Look at me,' said Frida, and Ruth looked, and then back at the table, and then at Frida again, because Frida took her chin and made her. 'Tell me you know I would choose you.' What was clear on Frida's face was neither love nor hate but conviction.

'What's all this?' asked Ruth, pulling her head away.

'Presents.'

'For me?'

'They *were* for me,' said Frida. 'But you can have them now. May as well.'

One of them looked like Ruth's mother's engagement ring. Ruth stretched her hand out and Frida passed her the ring. It was gold with a nest of diamonds; it was her mother's ring.

'It's beautiful, isn't it,' said Frida, who had never said the word beautiful in Ruth's hearing, and so Ruth was filled with pride. She put the ring on her finger, where it spun above her other well-fitting rings. Frida gave a small humph and said, 'Too big.' Then she took Ruth's hand, tapped Ruth's own engagement and wedding rings, and said, 'I told him I wasn't going to take those. They're yours forever.'

Ruth made a fist with her hand. 'They *are* mine. Harry gave them to me.'

'That's what I told him. Now there's something I need to show you.'

'Can you spare the time?' asked Ruth.

'It's only Thursday.'

Frida went to look for something in the study; when she returned, she held a letter on thin blue paper and shook it in the air like a thin blue flag. 'You may as well see this now,' she said. 'What difference does it make?' She passed the paper to Ruth with delicate fingers.

The letter was from Richard.

'This is the latest one,' said Frida. 'There are others. He wrote nearly every day after he left. I'll get them all for you if you want.'

'Oh.' Ruth felt squeezed inside, a great clenching, and then release. She looked at the letter, which began, 'My dearest Ruth' – but couldn't bring herself to read any more.

'You trusted me, didn't you,' said Frida. It wasn't a question.

'There are no guarantees,' said Ruth. She considered it likely that she had never trusted Frida. But then she didn't trust herself.

'You said it.' Frida was writing something on a piece of paper and taping it to the telephone. 'This is Jeff's number, right here on the phone.'

'You press star and then one to call Jeff,' said Ruth.

'Forget that. I wiped that weeks ago. You need to call this number – see it on the phone? You remember how to work the phone? That's something else – sometimes I turned the ringer down low, so you wouldn't hear it.'

'Why did you do that?'

'To stop you from talking to people. I couldn't stop Jeff, though. A guy like Jeff fusses. Do you love me, Ruthie?'

'Yes,' said Ruth, without thinking, which meant she did love.

'I knew it,' said Frida. She lifted Ruth into her arms, like a baby.

Ruth still held the letter. 'Where are we going?'

'Just outside.'

'Do you know what you're going to do?'

Frida shook her head. 'I have no idea what I'm going to do.'

Ruth didn't believe her. As they passed out of the house, Ruth saw herself reflected in the dining-room windows: high in Frida's arms, with different hair.

Frida carried Ruth to a shady part of the garden and set her down to stand on the uneven grass. Her back was partially propped by the bending limb of the frangipani tree.

'I'll be right back,' Frida said.

Ruth watched her walk to the house. Something about her was different, but what? Her hair was still dark and straight, she was still tall and wide; she was still Frida. Because Ruth held Richard's letter, she looked at it again: 'My dearest Ruth, Frida tells me you're beginning to feel better, which is such good news, it calls for a celebration.' And lower on the page: 'Will it embarrass you to hear you are the best of the lovely things?' She remembered his handwriting; once, she used to hoard every example of it she could find. She liked the long, adult forward tilt of his 't's and 'h's and 'l's. He had kissed her at the ball and then in the bedroom. Would he be a good husband? Had he been a good husband? Or was that someone else? Harry was the husband – but he was missing.

'Harry?' she said into the wind. Where was he? Here in the garden, maybe. She listened for sounds of him. 'Harry? Darling?'

The garden was empty. There were no cats and no plants; it was bare and scrubbed. The trees were leafless, as if someone had plucked every branch clean. There was also no sun. Only the dune, greyish, and the sky, greyish, and at some distance the white-and-black sea.

'Here I am!' cried Frida. She had come outside carrying Ruth's chair; she found level ground for it near the frangipani tree. Then she came to Ruth and held her shoulders, something like the way she had when Ruth arrived home with Ellen from town.

'Here *I* am,' said Ruth. She looked about, still, for Harry. He was probably kneeling in some garden bed, possibly among the hydrangeas. Hydrangea flowers don't fall off. They go brown, don't they, and they stay; but really they should fall. In the past, Harry must have cut them. Maybe she could help him. There must be some worm that wanted to come and eat the flower heads. Ruth stamped her feet to call the worms up out of the ground. The sound of her feet travelled through the dune, and other sounds joined it: the shooting of new roots, maybe, and busy crabs and insects burrowing in the sand. Frida held her tighter, to keep her still.

'Now, what's this?' said Frida, and she began to sing a low lullaby; Ruth recognised the tune, but not the words, which didn't seem quite English. Then she recognised them, without understanding. It was a Fijian song. She and Frida rocked on the dune, the words fell over and around them, and the lullaby inhabited some interior place of Ruth's, where it greeted other things – the shape of her mother's mouth and a dog she saw killed on the street in Suva. There was a reunion there, in that place. Ruth attended to it, and to the subtle movement of Frida's big body, and to the feel of the air on her arms as they moved. The nurses sang sometimes as they worked in the clinic. New mothers sang to their babies. Her mother and father sang hymns. Her father read to them in the evening while the houseboy sang in the kitchen: 'Consider the lilies of the field,' read her father, and Ruth considered them. 'How they grow; they toil not, neither do they spin.' I neither toil nor spin, thought Ruth. She leaned into Frida's belly and felt herself arrayed in glory.

What could this song be for? To send babies to sleep. Phillip slept fitfully in his crib. Isn't *pleurisy* a lovely word? Beside his crib: *The Cat in the Hat*; *I Am a Bunny*; *Go, Dog, Go!* Ruth rested and sang. It was humid in the hollow of Frida's arm, and Ruth's hair clung to her cheek. She remembered then that Harry was dead. I remember that I remember that, she thought. Thank God that fact was sticky enough; she wanted to honour it. Every future minute announced itself, broad and without Harry. And then her life, her whole past, crowded up against this minute – entirely filled this minute; it was over so quickly. It all insisted so busily on something Ruth could not identify, something that had to do with happiness. How disappointing it was not to have been happy, thought Ruth, at every moment you expected to be. Now, here, she might be happy, but it was unlikely.

Frida bent her knees to the ground and took Ruth with her. She still sang, but there were no longer any words; Frida was only a tune, and warm breath, taking Ruth towards the ground. The grass was smooth and rough, and Frida laid her out on it. Frida kissed Ruth's forehead; she lifted her free hand to keep the sun from Ruth's eyes. She still sang, but she paused to say, 'This won't do,' and she moved Ruth a little farther into what shade there was under the thick grey lace of the frangipani, with no flowers on it yet, so early in November. A gull sat at the top of the tree, not watching, not sleeping, not anything but a gull.

'How's that?' asked Frida, and she lifted Ruth's head and laid it on something soft.

'My back doesn't hurt,' said Ruth, as if delivering a weather report. 'It's very fine.'

'That's the way,' said Frida. She stood over Ruth and was no longer wearing her coat. She held a glass of water, which she gave to Ruth, and a blue pill, and another, and then – hesitating a moment – another. Frida helped Ruth swallow each one. 'Now you'll be comfy. You just rest there for a little while, and when you're ready, I want you to call Jeff and tell him right away about George. All right? You promise me?'

'I promise,' said Ruth. The ground was more elastic than she remembered.

'What will you tell him about George?'

'Young Livery.'

'That's right, that's his taxi,' said Frida, patient. 'But what has he done? What bad thing has George done?'

'George has run off with everyone's money.'

'Good. Tell Jeff I've left papers on the table for him to give to the police. All right?'

'Frida,' said Ruth, smiling, 'I can't call Jeff from out here.'

'I know. You'll need to get yourself inside – just like that day when you were out here on your own and you got in all by yourself. But this time your back won't hurt you, because of the pills, and also I put your chair out here to help you get up. You just hold on to your chair, and it'll be easy. I'm going in a minute, and then, when you're ready, you start heading for the phone. Call Jeff as soon as you can. All you need to do is give me some time. Got it?'

'What do you need time for?'

'I don't know yet.'

Ruth still smiled. Frida was kneeling beside her now, wearing a pink T-shirt. Pink! Her whole face was lit with the colour.

'The back door is open,' said Frida, stroking Ruth's face, 'and the cats are in your bedroom with food and water. You just go in there when you want to find them. Nothing to worry about, all right?'

'All right,' Ruth said. Frida stayed still, looking at her. 'All right,' Ruth said again, and she squeezed Frida's hand, which she noticed was holding hers. The squeezing produced little effect – Ruth couldn't feel her hand tightening, and she didn't know if Frida squeezed back. Harry always squeezed back. One, two, three squeezes meant 'I love you.' In her other hand, Ruth held Richard's letter.

'I'm going now,' said Frida, but she still didn't move. She had a terrible look on her face, calm but terrible; it was resolved, and patient. The sand and grass would ruin her pretty trousers.

'You should wear pink more often,' said Ruth, and Frida let

go of Ruth's hand and stood. Now her face was gone completely. She stood there for a moment – Ruth could see her legs, and her trousers were a little crushed from the kneeling, but not stained; she had a rim of hair at her ankle, and a small mole. Frida turned and walked into the house. The gull still sat in the frangipani.

19

The empty garden was quiet. There was a lull in everything: the wind, the sound of the sea, and even the light, as if a thin cloud were passing over the sun. Ruth settled her head into the pillow Frida had given her and rested for some time, in order to gather the strength she would require to reach the telephone. She thought of Harry as she lay there in the garden because she knew he was dead, and she knew she had forgotten he was dead. That seemed the same as forgetting he had lived. Mainly she thought of how his face looked beside hers in bed. Ruth thought of Harry and squeezed her own hand. She rubbed her feet together the way happy babies do, but she couldn't feel them. It was as if a soft coat had risen over her legs – something soft and heavy, also warm, but not a fabric. It took her some time to decide what this blanket might be, and eventually it occurred to her – since she couldn't seem to lift her head from where it lay on the pillow – that Frida might have covered her feet with the skin of the tiger. Then she saw herself under the tree under the tiger skin, and what would Harry say? He would say, George, George, George. Young George stole everyone's livery money. Ruth couldn't tell if she had stopped rubbing her feet. She thought Frida should have brought the telephone out here if she wanted her to call George so badly. She thought Frida should have done many things differently. Something was cutting into her hand as she squeezed it, and after she had squeezed some more, she realised it was her mother's engagement ring.

Soon she would have to get to the house to find the telephone. It would be wound in white cord. Ruth couldn't feel her feet, but she thought she could feel her elbows. She tried to lift herself on them the way she had the day she was caught in the tiger trap. They wouldn't lift; nothing would. When she'd lain in the tiger trap, there was only the wide sky, but here there was the green slant of the sun in the frangipani. Ruth knew the size of that sun, and all its properties: it was moving now down the length of her spine, burning some things away and dulling others. Its heat rolled, but subtly. She imagined her spine as a rough shaft, crusted and frayed, like underwater wood. She needed to find this shaft of wood where it splintered underwater; she seized hold of it with her hands; she tugged and the wood came free. Then Ruth came out of the sea. She tasted the salt on her lips to check that it was the sea; she had no memory of getting there. Also she was holding this piece of clammy wood, which was easy enough to throw out over the sand, so that it flew above the dunes and up and into the long-distance wind. The wind made a high piping sound before leaving pinkish traces behind. The sky reddened a little – the tiniest drop of blood stirred in water – which was the strangest weather. A storm might be coming, or leaving; this might be the centre of it. It rattled the windowpanes like a herald, as if to say, 'Prepare! Prepare!' Someone must take the chair into the house before it was ruined. No one could move the gull away from the frangipani, but it might fly off with the first piece of rain. The whales would sound deeper, where there was no storm, and the boy might speed out across the water in his boat to look for them. Then Harry, that necessary man, would call out from the shoreline, 'Prepare! Prepare!' He was too busy to take the chair in from the garden, so it would have to be bound with white cord and pulled, the way the wood was pulled from under the sea. Harry ran along the shore, calling out, and the boat was a narrow yellow spill on the bay. The waves rose up and sent spray out over the dunes. The spray fell across the frangipani tree, but the gull stayed; it only turned one curious eye. The cord was too heavy to lift from the floor, so the chair shook, but couldn't be moved. The sun was gone now; it was no longer the sun. There was no name for it because it wouldn't come again. A papery blue shape fell from somewhere and gusted up into the tree. It wasn't terribly important. The chair would have to stay outside, and so would the man calling below the dunes. The windows could rattle and rattle, and no one and nothing would be inside.

Then the rub of the storm over the trees. There was no rain, only sound. First the birds, objecting, as if morning had come in the middle of the night, and then every insect. A bell rang to call a doctor out of sleep. 'Not in this weather,' said a woman, a mother, but the father went out into the sound nevertheless. He went down to the beach, where people stood with binoculars. He waded there among the people and it was as if a god had come among them; an old, pastoral god, driving sheep. The mother's ring spanned her finger. She had lost her husband, too, and was inconsolable; she said, 'There's no marriage in heaven.' Now the volume of the jungle increased, but it wasn't quite right: there were monkeys and macaws, all the wrong objects, great opening lilies that sent out a smell of rain. Nothing is so loud as the sound of insects. And on the faint sea: a yellow shape that wasn't a boat. It was long and walking out of the water. It paused to inspect items on the beach; it turned every now and then when it heard someone crying out, but at a distance. It stayed in the rough edge of the waves, and it came closer and was recognisable. The tiger was there in the water. His throat wasn't cut, and he wore his own seared skin. Tigers can be patient; they know how to wait.

He was also fast; he was coming. He seemed to know there was nothing to stop him. Now he was out of the water and on the sand; now at the bottom of the dune where the end of the trap lay. His breath came in evenly over the sound of the birds, his ears lay back against his head, and his claws in the sand made a sound of rolling rock. He was the colour of the gone sun. And he sang! He sang a low hymn as he ran, which came out with his breath over his irregular tongue. He came singing up the dune, and all the birds flew screaming behind him, except the one gull in the frangipani tree. That tree swam in and out of the green light. It was bound around with a long white cord that couldn't be lifted from the ground, and a sound intermittently rang out from it. Could it really be so loud under this tree, after all that quiet? Here he was at the beginning of the grass. His heavy head was so familiar, and he still sang in a low, familiar voice. What a large gold space he filled at the edge of the garden. His face flared out from itself, and every black line was only a moving away, so he seemed to be retreating even when he stood his ground. And he was totally unharmed; someone had lied about this tiger. A woman as large as he was, and real as he was, had lied. When he came forward over the lawn, the hydrangeas shook and the dune grass blew back from the greener grass. He stopped at the chair and reached forward – all that length of him, reaching forward – and sharpened his claws on its wooden leg. Then he leant back on his hind legs, and paused, and leapt onto the chair. It tipped to the left. He wasn't singing after all, but his breath was melodic, and he sat up tall with his paws together, like a circus tiger. He began to groom his symmetrical sides.

'Now,' said Ruth. Ruth was her name. It had been promised to her and had remained faithful. 'Now!' she called out, but the tiger didn't move. She noticed she was in the process of standing only because she was no longer on the ground. Weren't those oil tankers high in the water? Her wooden spine was burned away, and she could stand. There wasn't even any need to hold on to the white cord, which was just as well, because where would it lead her? Standing, as she was now, she was as tall as the tiger. He didn't watch her, only licked and smoothed. Ruth held her hands out to him. She crossed the fine, dusty lawn, and every step seemed to sweep it away. All the grass flew down the dune, and only the barest, brownest white showed through.

'Now,' she said to the tiger, but he only swung his lazy head to his other flank and licked it down. He defined his stripes. He fastened them with his tongue.

So Ruth stepped closer. 'Kit, kit, kit!' she said. She reached out with her arms and gripped the rough, warm fur on his shoulders. Now the bird in the tree began to sing out for the first time. It sang, 'Prepare! Prepare!' But there was no reason to be afraid of this calm tiger. He smelled like dirty water. She leaned her head into his soft chest, where his great heart ticked.

20

The cats found a home with Ellen Gibson. She learned of their plight because her sister was a receptionist at the veterinary surgery Jeffrey called to ask for details about the nearest cat shelter. He was apologetic on the phone, Ellen's sister reported, but there were dogs and international flights and allergies to consider, and his tone was both guilty and defensive. Ellen knew that when Jeffrey called the surgery he had just come from the bank – various people had seen him there and witnessed his rage with the manager and with Gail Talitsikas, and they all talked about him in those fresh, suspenseful days, so that everywhere Ellen went she heard new details: that Frida's surname was not Young, for example, and that the government hadn't sent her.

Ellen drove in her red car to the top of the hill, parked it on the coastal road, and made her way to the house on foot. Her intention had been to arrive without fuss or air of judgment, but she was forced to battle with the scrub that had overtaken the drive. Low, stunted trees caught at her legs and in her hair, and the dune grasses shook off a seedy substance that made her sneeze. Jeffrey was waiting for her when she emerged by the house.

'It's like a fairy-tale castle, isn't it,' he said. He wore old clothes that might have been his father's, and gardening kneepads.

'A little.' Ellen sneezed again and gave a small laugh; she felt both intrusive and self-righteous.

'It's much better in a car,' said Jeffrey. 'You just nose your way through and push everything out of the way.'

Ellen thought Jeffrey should be ashamed of having, among other things, allowed his mother's property to reach this state; but she also remembered the condition of the drive only a week before, when it hadn't struck her as nearly this impassable. It was as if the garden had deliberately grown up to hide the house. She gave Jeffrey an awkward hug, and he patted her shoulder as if to say, 'There, there.'

'You seem to be the guardian angel of our family,' he said.

The angel of death, thought Ellen. She had thought about this. She was a bad omen; a bird circling overhead asking, 'Are you all right?' – when no one was ever all right.

'I'm so sorry about – everything,' said Ellen; but that sounded like an apology and there was nothing, really, to apologise for. The part of Ellen that considered it Jeffrey's place to cancel her apology and make one of his own was hushed by another, more sympathetic part. He was leaner than he'd been at his father's funeral, as if that death had surprised him into cardiovascular diligence. But he also stood with one fist balled into the small of his back, stretching it out, as if he'd inherited Ruth's back and was only just feeling it now. Maybe a family's troubles, thought Ellen, are always with them, and they just pass among the members with every death. Of course – silly – that's genetics, isn't it.

'We're very grateful to you.'

'Oh, there's no need. I wish I could have done more.' She wished, actually, that she could have done less.

'We all wish we could have done more,' said Jeffrey, which was intolerable; for a minute Ellen let her full disgust at Jeffrey rise up from some bottomless place. If Ruth had been *my* mother, she thought, as she had thought so many times before; but she gave her head a compassionate tilt. It was difficult to think what to say. Jeffrey had a strange convalescent look, like a man recovering from a dreamlike illness, and all his movements had a submarine quality: he stepped over to a wheelbarrow that lay by the side of the house and half lifted it, then let it drop again. So he was suffering, which Ellen realised she required from him, and then she was afraid she would cry.

Phillip erupted from the house.

'Ellen!' he called. He looked like his mother – light-haired, dairy-fed, round of cheek – and he had her expansive smile. He was the baby of the family and had never quite abandoned the undignified safety of that position. His duty to be sweetly jovial was, under the circumstances, a great burden; he enfolded Ellen and held her for some time. He smelled of fresh laundry. When he released her, he was smiling – but sadly, lovably. He took her hand. Phillip was much easier to forgive than his brother.

'I feel like you're part of the family,' he said as Jeffrey walked away from them around the side of the house. 'Like you're a sister.' Ellen preferred this to being an angel. She squeezed his hand in hers.

'I can't imagine —' she began, but she could imagine, so she stopped.

They went inside to find the cats.

The house was tidy, but important objects were missing – the lounge, for example, and then, in the kitchen, the oven. The wall behind it was stained a deep, frazzled brown, as if there had been a fire. There were no longer any paintings or photographs on the walls, and the lounge room was full of funeral flowers. Ellen had sent hers ahead to the funeral parlour and now regretted it. Ruth's favourite chair stood where the lounge should have been; it looked battered and bleached, as if it had sat outside for many days in strong temperatures. The dining table was covered in papers; Phillip swept his arm over them and said, 'Everything the police didn't want. You'll have a cup of tea, won't you?'

Through the windows, Ellen could see Jeffrey in the garden. He seemed to be pulling weeds out of the dune grass with some difficulty; or perhaps he was pulling up the grass itself. The sea behind him was a drenched green.

'Are you selling the house?'

'Absolutely.' Then, as if to temper the finality of this, Phillip said, 'Yes.' He called for the cats by name but without conviction, and they didn't come.

He was obviously adrift in the kitchen. He opened cupboards and closed them again, looking for cups and tea and sugar in a slow slapstick. Ellen sat in one of the dining chairs and made an effort not to look at the papers on the table. When the water began to rattle in the kettle, she said, 'I hear they found Frida's brother. That's good news.'

'He was her boyfriend,' said Phillip, fussing with milk.

'Oh. For some reason I thought brother. I suppose that makes more sense.'

'More sense of what?'

'Of why she would just – give up. She didn't strike me as the type.'

Then Ellen felt nervous at having raised the topic of Frida; at having said her name like a bad spell in this emptying house.

But Phillip didn't seem to mind. 'You met her, didn't you?'

'Once,' said Ellen. She remembered the way Ruth and Frida had run together like lovers, and how embarrassed she'd been by that intimacy, and, later, how unsettled. A great deal of time seemed to have passed since the day she saw Ruth in town.

Phillip brought mugs to the table and cleared space among the papers with his elbow. He looked out at his brother in the garden. 'I just got here yesterday,' he said. Then he went to the door and called out, 'Jeff! Tea?' Jeffrey stood up from the grass with his arm pressed against his forehead and shook his whole torso to say no. He seemed to be holding a bundle of barbed wire.

Phillip turned to Ellen and said, 'I took the first flight out of Hong Kong. Jeff's been here since Friday.'

'I wish I'd known. I could have brought food out.'

Now Phillip sat. 'You know what we found among all this?' he said, indicating the papers. 'Letters from a man she knew in Fiji. Love letters, all recent, most of them unopened. Did you know she lived in Fiji? We wondered if that's why she dyed her hair. So Jeff called and told him, and he'll be at the funeral. You're coming, yes? Richard, his name is. He came out here to see her, and of course he met Frida. Everyone met her but us.' He blew on his tea. 'What was she like?'

'It was so brief,' said Ellen. 'She was very tall.'

'Her mother contacted us through the police. She's English, apparently. The father was from New Zealand – half Maori. He's been dead for years, and there was a sister, too, also dead, cancer. But this mother – she's really something. She wants to come to the funeral.'

'Goodness,' said Ellen. 'Is she local?'

'She lives in Perth, but she flew out. So that's something else we have to decide.'

'I only talked to Frida for a few minutes,' said Ellen. 'But I got the impression she really loved your mum.'

Phillip remained quiet for a moment. Then he said, 'She was a cleaner, you know, at that nursing home. Seawind? Seacrest?'

'Seacrest Court.'

'We assume that's how she got Mum's details. Jeff rang them earlier this year when Mum seemed a bit wobbly, calling in the middle of the night with bad dreams, that kind of thing. The police think Frida and George were waiting for some opportunity or other, and there she was.'

Phillip seemed so serene as he said all this, but Ellen suspected he wasn't the kind of man to have complicated regrets. He was filled, instead, with a dulling, puzzling grief, which occupied everything. He rubbed one finger over the edge of his mug of tea, and outside his brother pulled weeds. Jeffrey had found Ruth lying under a tree in the garden, everyone knew, but Ellen didn't think this accounted for his industry; he was probably just getting the house ready to sell. Some people in town disapproved of this haste, and others supported it.

Because the town, of course, was electric with all this news, with these events and fears and speculations. Some were sure they had seen George Young's taxi parked at the end of the Field drive late at night or early in the morning; others had seen Frida arguing over cheques in the supermarket. Everyone called their aging parents or dropped in on them at nursing homes. For the couple of days after Ruth was found, when no one knew where Frida and George might be, Ellen, like everyone else, double-checked the locks on her doors and windows, as if anything might come creeping through in the night. And then on Sunday afternoon a fisherman discovered Frida's body where it had been swept among the lighthouse rocks, and there was some disappointment in town; they wanted her brought to justice. She was too heavy for one man to lift out of the water, and by the time the requisite emergency services arrived, a crowd had gathered to watch. For two days, everyone had wanted this woman, and now she was hoisted from the sea. Then the danger seemed to have passed, but the flag stayed at half-mast on the surf club.

Now the cats came in from the garden, but they lingered at the door, unwilling, so Ellen leaned down and made kissing noises; then they approached with caution.

'You really are a lifesaver,' Phillip said, and that was awkward because – in the case of the cats, at least – it may have been true.

The cats wore imbecile expressions; they jumped superstitiously at their own tails, trimmed their tidy claws, and sniffed at

Ellen's offered fingers with mild curiosity. Phillip told her they weren't eating a thing.

'In the spirit of full disclosure,' he said, 'the tabby, the boy, throws up at least once a day.'

The tweedy boy cat looked vacantly at Ellen. He allowed himself to be handled into a carrier she had bought specially, and the tortoiseshell girl was similarly docile. They were fragile bundles beneath their important fur. They made no noise as they were carried from the house and settled into the backseat, but they howled as the car descended the hill, with plaintive, inconsolable cries. As she drove past the bus stop, Ellen saw a cloud of seagulls rise in a body from the sea. They lunged for the sky, then fell back.

Acknowledgments

I would like to thank my family, Lyn, Ian, Katrina, Evan and Bonita McFarlane; I think also of my grandmothers, Hilda May Davis and Winifred Elsie Mary McFarlane. I'd also like to thank my teachers, especially Elizabeth McCracken, Steve Harrigan, Alan Gurganus, and Margot Livesey. I'm grateful to Stephanie Cabot, Chris Parris-Lamb, Anna Worrall, Rebecca Gardner, Will Roberts, and everyone at the Gernert Company; also to my editors, Ben Ball, Meredith Rose, Mitzi Angel, and Carole Welch. This book was written with the generous assistance of the Australia Council for the Arts, the Fine Arts Work Center in Provincetown, St John's College Cambridge, Phillips Exeter Academy, and the Michener Center for Writers – in association with these wonderful places, I'd like to thank Salvatore Scibona, Roger Skillings, Charles Pratt, Marla Akin, Debbie Dewees, Michael Adams, and Jim Magnuson. Finally, I must thank my friends, especially Mimi Chubb, Kate Finlinson, Virginia Reeves, and, most of all, Emma Jones.